BOOK TWO
OF THE EDDIE WALSH STORIES

WHAT AM I?

A NOVEL

BOOK TWO
OF THE EDDIE WALSH STORIES

WHAT AM I?

A NOVEL

J. J. ZERR

PRIMIX
PUBLISHING
THE WRITE CHOICE

Primix Publishing
East Brunswick Office Evolution
1 Tower Center Boulevard, Ste 1510
East Brunswick, NJ 08816
www.primixpublishing.com
Phone: 1-800-538-5788

© 2024 J. J. Zerr. All rights reserved.

No part of this book may be reproduced, stored in a retrieval system, or transmitted by any means without the written permission of the author.

Published by Primix Publishing: 11/06/2024

ISBN: 979-8-89194-263-9(sc)
ISBN: 979-8-89194-264-6(hc)
ISBN: 979-8-89194-265-3(e)

Library of Congress Control Number: 2024913587

Any people depicted in stock imagery provided by iStock are models, and such images are being used for illustrative purposes only.

Certain stock imagery © iStock.

Because of the dynamic nature of the Internet, any web addresses or links contained in this book may have changed since publication and may no longer be valid. The views expressed in this work are solely those of the author and do not necessarily reflect the views of the publisher, and the publisher hereby disclaims any responsibility for them.

For the J-girls.

CONTENTS

Prelude ix

Chapter One 1
Chapter Two 8
Chapter Three 18
Chapter Four 27
Chapter Five 37
Chapter Six 47
Chapter Seven 55
Chapter Eight 63
Chapter Nine 72
Chapter Ten 81
Chapter Eleven 90
Chapter Twelve 98
Chapter Thirteen 107
Chapter Fourteen 115
Chapter Fifteen 123
Chapter Sixteen 127
Chapter Seventeen 137
Chapter Eighteen 145
Chapter Nineteen 152
Chapter Twenty 162

Chapter Twenty One 171
Chapter Twenty Two 180
Chapter Twenty Three. 189
Chapter Twenty Four 198
Chapter Twenty Five 207
Chapter Twenty Six. 216

Acronyms 223
Cast of Characters 225

PRELUDE

Note: I am coming back to the first part of this story after having just finished the first draft. So, now, we are into editing. Ugh. This is what I believe. Writing is harder than work. Editing is harder than writing. Even though it's hard work, I am quite fond of writing. Editing is necessary.

I felt it important to start my editing journey with this note because this piece of work transformed me. If you follow me down the path of this tale, you will see what I'm talking about. Creating this story was like sifting through a dumpster filled with episodes from my life, along with tons of junk that got tossed in there, too. Writing this, I dredged and sifted the dumpster contents to pull out the good stuff. I did not think that is what I'd be doing when I started on this project.

I, Eddie Walsh, thought I knew what I was: a goober eighty-two-year-old coasting comfortably—rather than the other way to go through life, like zorching down an ice-covered chute in an Olympics toboggan race—toward the big **D**.

Now **D** is how I think about it. Talking about it, well, then it comes out—if it absolutely **has** to come out—as a whisper: death.

As I was saying, I was coasting along comfortably when my daughter, Number Five Kid—I want to point out here that I remember my kids' names, however; we have six—and all their names start with the letter J—and although I readily remember how we baptized the oldest and the youngest, the ones in the middle, I always have to start with Number Two and work down to the bigger number to get the labels right. So, Number Five bought a subscription to this outfit that sends me prompts twice a month to answer some question such as: If your house caught on fire, what would you save; or, do you consider yourself an optimist or pessimist?

That second question was easy to answer.

My answer: "Before you asked the dad-burned question, I was optimistic as all get out. Now, for some reason, since you asked the question, I am Mr. Pessimist personified."

And if the house caught on fire?

I didn't have to think about that. First, I'd make sure The One and Only was safe. Then, I'd put on pants. Then, I'd grab my wallet—with pants on, I had a place to put the wallet, see? Next, I'd put on tennis shoes and thank God for the ones that go on and off like slippers. Then, I'd grab the wedding and photo albums from the bookcase in the room by the front door. Once I had the albums safe, I'd take stock of the situation. If it were kinda', halfway close to, sort of safe to do so, I'd go back in the house and grab the top drawer of The Squeeze's jewelry chest—that's where she keeps the best pieces—and I'd throw in a couple pairs of clean underwear for the two of us and get the heck out of the burning house.

And I'd thank God that at least I hadn't had to worry about my hair catching fire.

Where was I?

Oh yeah. Coasting comfortably. Right.

Then, the latest question hit my inbox: **Did You Ever Volunteer for Something Nobody Else Wanted To do?**

Well, yes, I did.

The opportunity to volunteer appeared before me in 1965. I graduated from Purdue and reported to Officer Candidate School

(OCS) in Newport, RI. All of us OCS goobers were assigned to a particular company. In Company C, there were a bunch of civilian guys fresh out of college. Also included were a fair number of enlisted men, including me. So, I wrote the answer to the question. It filled about half a page double-spaced.

Then—sigh—I started editing the piece, and it hit me. On a scale of one to ten measuring not-at-all-interesting to interesting-as-all-get-out, the half page rated maybe a six. I recalled the path I'd taken to get to that opportunity to volunteer, and I thought that story might rate an 8.5—As objectively as I can measure a story about myself. Also, I confess to you, my daughters, brothers, and sisters, that none of the previous Questions-of-the-Month questions inspired me to go all motor mouth on you, but this one's got me, figuratively speaking, literarily speaking, babbling like a brook.

Then I thought, *Why don't you call the first part above a prelude? Then, write this backstory stuff and end the piece with the answer to the volunteer question.*

"*Stop staring at the computer screen and do it.*"

That sounded like Pop barking at me, so I started doing it.

CHAPTER ONE

In 2023, I, Eddie Walsh, turned eighty-two. Thirty-six of those years, I spent in the US Navy. And the US Navy was the first to ask me to volunteer for something. So, let me tell you about the path I had to follow to get to that opportunity to volunteer.

When I was a senior in high school, My One and Only Squeeze and I were going steady. My ambition was to go to college, get a degree in Electrical Engineering, marry The Squeeze, have four children, and live happily ever after in a house with a white picket fence around it.

I was sure The Squeeze's father expected her to marry a college graduate. Her mother expected her to marry a doctor. The Squeeze was going to nurse's training after high school. Why else would a girl want to be a nurse?

I told Pop I wanted to go to college.

"You ain't got the money for it, and I don't neither. And you ain't gonna borrow it. You fed long enough at the family trough. When you're done with high school, you find a job, or I'll find you one."

That was more words than I ever heard Pop string together at one time. The surprise of that set me on my heels for a bit. Then, *fed long enough at the family trough,* it started to rankle. Like I was a pig on grandpa's farm with nothing to do all day but oink, eat, and poop.

Note: At this point, it occurred I had to start the story

1

earlier. I thought about rewriting this, starting from the earlier time. It's just that The One and Only Squeeze is so important to the story, beginning with her seems more proper than not doing a flashback right off the bat. So, I decided I'd leave The Squeeze starting Chapter 1, and now we're flashing back.

Back when I was in third grade, Mom went into the hospital, where she lost a baby, and I started doing girl work around the house. I stood on a stool at the sink and washed dishes. I swept and mopped the kitchen floor. Once I started doing those kinds of jobs, there didn't seem to be a way out of them. I was the oldest, so it was up to me to pitch in, I guess. I even changed my youngest brother's diapers. When they were dirty even. *Fed at the family trough, phooey!* I'd earned my keep. Doing girl work.

But never once, not even then, did I ever consider talking back to the man. Also, never once did I say "Yes, Sir" or "No, Sir" to him. That would imply I had some choice in the matter. Which I did not think I had.

I wound up doing girl work until seventh grade let out for the summer on a Friday. Two things happened then. I wound up getting out of doing girl work for Mom and learned how to do man work.

The first Saturday morning of summer. I'm asleep and dreaming Mom would not make me do girl work the first day of summer vacation. Instead, I'd spend it swimming and fishing all day when I got up at noon. Okay, all afternoon.

"Git up."

Neither dreams nor sleep had a chance against Pop's voice.

And he didn't like to say a thing twice. He was looking down at me, just itching to say it again. I threw the covers back and pulled my pants on lying down. Then I got up for socks, shoes, and a tee shirt. Ran fingers through my hair. Trip to the outhouse. Wash hands.

Mom had breakfast ready. We ate. Pop threw my bike in the trunk of the car and drove me to Heiny Horstwessel's farm next to our parish picnic grounds. As Pop stopped the car, Heiny came out of the house.

"You're working for Mr. Horstwessel," Pop said, unloaded my bike, slammed the trunk lid, got in the car, and drove away.

"You git here by seven. Ever mornin'. Hear?"

I heard. As soon as I arrived each morning, I was to go to the milk barn and clean up where the cows had stood while being milked.

On my first morning in that enclosed, little to no air circulation place, the smell of cow poop crawled up my nose like worms of stench. I was about to unload when Heiny said, "You puke, you clean that up, too."

When I think about him now, I imagine him as a chief petty officer: *Chief Heiny!*

Well, I managed to mind muscle my partially digested breakfast into staying where the heck it was. Which was good because six days a week, I started my day with cow poop. I came to find out cows have four stomachs. No wonder they poop so much.

Cow poop only started my days. The rest of every day, except Sunday, was filled with whatever work the farm needed doing. And farms did then, and still do, need a lot of work to be done every day. Besides cows, there were chickens and pigs to tend. There was manure to spread, fields to plow, disk and harrow, plant and cultivate, and harvest. Heiny grew corn, wheat, and oats. We had timber to clear and stumps to blow.

Dynamiting stumps, now there was a thing that was a special but rare treat.

I grew to like working for Heiny. He explained a job to me and then left me to do it. Except dynamiting stumps. He never left me alone with that job. When Pop finished off the house we lived in, I always asked him if I could help nail flooring in place, hang sheet rock, sand, or paint.

"You want to help?" he'd say.

"Yeah, Pop. Yeah."

"Then don't help."

Mom said I shouldn't feel bad. Pop worked long hours in the grain elevator in town, and only had a few hours each evening to put to finishing the house. He didn't have time to fix the messes I'd make. I couldn't help it. I did feel bad when he wouldn't let me help.

3

So, I liked that about Heiny.

There was one thing I didn't like. I worked for him for two weeks, putting in ten hours per day, minimum, and he never said anything about paying me. So, I asked him.

"Your Pop said I didn't have to pay you."

That day, we baled hay, and I got home later than usual. Pop was reading the paper in the living room. I interrupted him and asked if what Heiny said was true.

He folded the paper in front of him and looked up at me. "A boy needs to learn how to work. He don't need no practice learning how to get paid."

The paper opened in front of him again.

Pop was reading about the St. Louis Cardinals baseball team. What he radiated at me, though, was: *We're done talking, so why are you still standing here?*

The following Saturday, Heiny paid me twelve dollars. "You work hard," he said. "Not right I should let you work for nothing."

> Heiny paying me prevented this from becoming my first volunteer job, even though it was Pop who volunteered me.

Pop's work ethic:

> When you get a job, work harder than your boss expects you to.
> Don't dawdle.
> Get it done right the first time.

And somehow, it became mine.

And it had a major bearing on my getting to that opportunity the Navy put in front of me to volunteer for something nobody else wanted to do.

Pop was wrong about one thing though. A boy, I, did need to learn how to get paid.

WHAT AM I?

Time Break Goes Here

Note: I was going to use five asterisks (*****) as a symbol for a time break, but I discovered something later in this document. If I laid down that string of asterisks, and if I hit enter without my cursor having visited the next line, Word laid down a string of dashes across the page. And those stinking dashes, once on the page, refused to vacate the premises. I wound up cutting and pasting and plain rewriting much of the document, which I would not have labeled "the dad-burned document" before the aforementioned asterisk to indelible dash thingee. To avoid the temptation to call this piece of work dad burned again, I've decided to insert "Time Break Goes Here" when a time break needs to be signaled. So, I came back to this point and inserted my solution to that dad-burned problem.

During the work week, Mrs. Horstwessel fed me lunch, but she never gave me supper. Mom always saved something for me. Two weeks after Heiny started paying me, I got home from work one evening about seven. Hungry as usual. Hungry enough to eat my work boots even though they had dried cow poop crusted on them in a few places.

I entered the house through the side door and parked my footwear next to Pop's. His were a couple of sizes bigger. I always thought my boots would one day overtake his, be bigger, and I'd have height on him, too. In my grade school class, I was the tallest boy. There were six of us, and I was five feet, six and a half inches, at least a half-inch taller than the others. Also, we had four girls with us eighth graders that fall. One of them was taller than me, though. Clarissa was five feet, ten inches. If the nuns allowed girls to play tackle football with us boys, nobody would have been able to knock her down.

As it turned out, my shoes did come close to matching the size of Pop's, but I never tacked on so much as a sixteenth of an inch of height. *Sigh!*

Anyway, as I was saying, I got home and wanted supper, but when I walked sock-footed into the kitchen, Mom said Pop wanted to talk to me.

As far as I could remember, Pop never wanted to talk to me. When I needed "talking to," Mom did the talking. Except, of course, he did tell me to "Git up," "You're working for Mr. Horstwessel," and "A boy don't need no practice getting paid."

When I needed a spanking, Mom did that, too.

"Can I eat supper first?"

Mom shook her head. The look on her face told me that was the dumbest question I'd ever asked her.

Sigh!

Pop was in the living room reading the paper. He lowered it.

"Mr. Horstwessel came to the elevator today." Pop's eyes gored me. "Heiny said you are a hard worker and a big help to him. He said he decided to pay you two dollars a day."

He stopped talking as if he thought it was my turn to conversate. I had nothing to say. He hadn't asked a question. His report of what Heiny had said was the truth. I shifted my weight from one foot to the other.

"Where's the twenty-four dollars you got paid for the last two weeks?"

I hadn't expected that question, though I should have. "I spent it."

"All of it?"

A big lump formed in my throat. I nodded.

"Come Saturday, you bring me your pay." He raised his paper again. Through it, he said, "All of it."

I'd expected him to ask me what I spent it on. Candy, milkshakes, comic books. Candy for some of my friends, too. Sharing my good fortune with my buddies made me a good guy. That's what I thought. The rich kid in town, Oliver Geld, always had money for candy, but he never bought any for us, and he only played with us when he wasn't snarfing Hershey bars.

But here's the thing. Oliver had more money than he needed and spent it with a miserly rein on his pocket.

My normal state, on the other hand, was flat broke, and If I got some money, I hurried to return myself to pauperdom.

Money, I decided, should be for what I needed. Working sixty hours a week and blowing my entire earnings on stuff that only produced pimples, well, I didn't need pimples.

What I needed was a ten-speed bike.

The next Saturday, I gave Pop the twelve dollars I made. He gave me one back.

"Pop, could you maybe give me half of it back? I'd like to save up for a ten-speed."

"Shoulda thought about that ten-speed before you blew your first two weeks' pay."

He went back to reading his paper.

After school started, I worked for Heiny on Saturdays, and in the fall, I helped him in the evenings when there was baled hay to get into the loft. Pop let me keep all the money I earned from those jobs, and almost every penny of it went into a mason jar. With Christmas and birthday cash, I was able to buy a new ten-speed a month into the next summer.

That summer, Pop again took eleven of my twelve dollars each week, and I continued to put the leftover dollar in the Mason jar. With the ten-speed in hand, there was not one more thing I needed—**Then**.

Pop's work and spending ethics, I didn't appreciate them while I was growing up. Later on, though, I considered them invaluable. And there was how Pop looked on education. At some point, Mom probably told me, Pop had only gone through grades one through four. Then his father put him to work on the family farm. Pop wanted his kids to have a better education than he had. I know Mom told me that last part.

CHAPTER TWO

Now, I'll tell you how I got into the US Navy.
Back in my junior year of high school, when I told Pop I wanted to go to college, and he told me no and laid the "Fed long enough at the family trough," on me. The next day, I talked to one of my male lay teachers at my Catholic high school, about wanting to go to college but not having the money for it.

> Note: My intention was to tell the story of how I got to the volunteer thing in a straight line. Like I was pedaling my ten-speed along a bike path, see? The problem is, as the story unrolls, I keep coming across these bunny trails cutting off from the main path. And those side bunny trails just seem to want to be followed.
> So here I'm going to put in a bit about how much growing up I had to do in high school. As a freshman, all our teachers were nuns, as they'd been in grade school in the little town where I grew up. After that first year, I came back to be a sophomore in a new and much bigger building. And we had lay people teachers, which surprised the heck out of me. And some of those lay people were men! That last bit would have blown my socks off, but I had my tennis shoes laced up tight.

And that year, when I was surprised by some fact of life I'd just never seen before, I learned to keep my stupid mouth shut. Because if I said something like, "Can men be teachers, too?" people would laugh at me, and it would start flying around school on wings of, "Did you hear what the hick farm boy Eddie Walsh said?"

But, I was mighty glad to have a male teacher to talk to about college and not having enough money to go there. Mister C. taught history, and when I spoke to him about my problem, he said, "Have you thought about ROTC?"

"What's that?"

"Reserve Officer Training Corps. All branches of the US military offer ROTC scholarships. Of course, after college, you would owe the Army, for instance, four years of service. Would you be willing to do that?"

I was thinking about the Squeeze. There was at least a possibility she would wait for me for four years, but eight years?

"How does that RO … thing work, Mr. C?"

"Well, the Army, Navy, or Air Force would pay for your four years of college. In addition to the college courses, you'd also have to study various things the military wants you to know. Then, after you graduate, you would be commissioned as an officer."

"Officers get paid?"

"Yes, the US military branches pay their officers and enlisted men."

"A brand-new officer, would he earn enough money to get married?"

"A lot of young ROTC men graduate, get commissioned, and get married."

Mr. C. helped me apply for an appointment to the Army, the Navy, and the Air Force ROTC programs. Surely, one of them would pick me.

The Squeeze's mom, I knew she'd keep pushing her daughter to lasso a doctor. But I didn't have to ask her for her daughter's hand. That question you put to your love's father. He would be happy with a college degree. All that had to happen was the Squeeze waiting for me for four years.

And, yes, I had to get an appointment.

Surely, one of the three services would award me one.

I got home from school one Friday in May, and Mom told me I had a letter from the Navy. I tore it open.

I was the fourth alternate for a US Navy ROTC appointment at the University of Missouri. Fourth alternate? What the heck did that mean? Come Monday, I'd ask Mr. C.

When Pop got home, I showed him the letter and told him my intention to talk to my history teacher.

He hmphed. "Just means they ain't got guts enough to tell you you ain't getting no appointment."

I still intended to talk to Mr. C.

Time Break Goes Here

After I started my junior year in high school, I stopped working for Mr. Horstwessel. His oldest son took over my job. I went to work in the grocery store in town. For that job, I didn't have to get up until eight on Saturday mornings.

But, one Saturday morning in my senior year of high school, "Git up" rousted me earlier. I looked at the clock. It was only seven. Pop was looking at me, getting mighty close to saying it a second time.

We ate breakfast and got in the car. Pop drove us toward the town where I went to high school.

He parked on Main Street and led me into this building and then into the Navy Recruiter's office.

"Mr. Walsh?" the guy in the sailor suit said.

"Yes."

"Got the paperwork filled out. All your boy has to do is sign it."

Sailor Suit had a piece of paper atop his shiny wooden desk. He spun it around and slid it toward me.

"You filled that out like we talked?" Pop said to Sailor Suit.

"Yes, Sir."

"Sign it."

Shanghaied into the Navy by my own father.

And holy crap! Goodbye, college. Goodbye, house with a picket fence. Goodbye, four kids.

And holy crap #2! Goodbye, One and Only Squeeze?

Driving back home, Pop gripped the steering wheel with both hands and stared out the windshield. He didn't say anything. Nothing new there.

From the shotgun seat, I also stared out the windshield. Except I wasn't seeing the road. I was seeing me telling the Squeeze I would be going into the Navy and not to college. I was seeing her hand me back my high school ring and saying, "Goodbye, Eddie Walsh. You know. Like forever."

Where my heart was hurt. It was like the pump and source of love had dropped to the bottom of my stomach and popped out of my belly button, and one of Heiny Horstwessel's cows had stepped on it, smashing it flat and leaving it buried in brown, runny poop.

Growing up, I'd been sick with the flu and a couple of other illnesses that made me feel bad. Contemplating the Squeeze *goodbying* me, "Like forever," that was all the way to abject misery.

> Maybe, Dear Reader, you see it without me saying it. Probably, I should just tell you.
>
> We're at another side bunny trail: How I came to fall in love with The Squeeze.
>
> Between March and May of 1958, junior year of high school, some things happened.

During my junior year of high school, I noticed girls. I mean, Mom was a girl. So was my little sister. Nuns were girls, though that thought took a little coaxing to settle in comfortably. And the other thing I noticed was that girls were more interested in guys with cars than those of us without one. Pop letting me use the car on Saturday evening for a date counted for nothing. Owning a car and driving it to and from school, going on dates in the middle of the week, riding to and from school with a boy in his car, those things counted—the way I saw it—with the girls. Big time.

I told Pop I wanted to buy a car from Ax Axlerod's Used Cars.

"No."

"I got five hundred dollars in the bank, and there's a Ford on his lot for just that amount."

"No. The upkeep will be more than you earn at the grocery store."

"Well then, I can borrow the money from the bank to buy the car and use what I have in my savings account to help pay off the loan and take care of the upkeep. Plus, I'm earning fifty cents an hour at the grocery store."

"And most of that, you blow on your Saturday night dates. You ain't borrowing no five hundred dollars."

"People borrow money all the time to buy cars and houses."

"I don't."

"That's because you're old-fashioned." I stomped away.

The next morning, it was normal quiet, not unusual quiet, at the breakfast table. Pop didn't say anything while he ate and finished his cup of coffee. He hardly ever did. After he placed his empty cup on his saucer, he rose, nodded to Mom, and left to walk the couple of blocks to work.

The door closed on him, and Mom said, "When you called Pop old-fashioned, you hurt his feelings."

I didn't say it, but I sure thought it loud. *Pop has feelings?*

As I rode to school that morning—with Maurice Heffledinger, who had a job in St. Louis and gave me a ride for twenty-five cents a week because it was against his religious principles to let me ride for free—I thought about that hurt feeling I caused. I'd have to take some time off work Saturday afternoon to go to confession.

Once I got to school, though, something else occupied my brain. We got our midsemester report cards, and I had my normal A and B grades everywhere except in Literature.

Sister Mary Mark—guys had nicknames for her. Pimple-faced candy lovers called her Sister M and M. Boys who owned cars called her Sister MM as if Marilyn Monroe could be a nun. About as easy to swallow as nuns being girls.

That preceding paragraph, I point out, was not a side bunny trail. It was a brief aside, see?

Anyway, back to the report card. Sister MM had given me an F in literature. An **F!** A fribble-frapping F. As soon as the bell rang after first period, I stomped into Sister's classroom, up to her desk, and pointed at the obviously mistaken grade.

"Sister. I should have gotten a C."

She looked up, but not at me, through me. "No. You should have gotten an A."

I sure hadn't expected that. I could have gotten an A. I should have.

Another sin to confess come Saturday: the deadly sin of goofing off, or sloth, a more serious literary mind would call it.

Deadly sin. There was a thing to think about in the way I was headed. Settle for a C because my mind was so full of cars, girls, and what we might—

I mention **THE F** because I have become convinced the next thing I'm going to write about could not have happened without the soul-butt kick. And the next thing is **the most important thing that ever happened to me.** The most important. More important than being born.

So, it's May, and getting close to the end of junior year. Normally, I walked a couple of miles from school to where I hitchhiked back home, but on this particular day, I got a ride with Sarah Sissy Sanford. Guys called her Snake because when you said her full name, you sounded like one. Sarah Sissy Snake Sanford was an only child, and for her sixteenth birthday, her parents gave her a Ford convertible. Most days, SSSS gave a ride to three other girls, but that day, she had an open seat, and—Thank You, God—gifted me with it.

Sarah etc. pulls out of the school parking lot—the top's down—with the girls chittering like a tree full of sparrows next to an oat field that's just been combined. I sit there on the back right seat and think about what I would have been thinking about if Sister MM hadn't kicked me. I'm glad she kicked me. Confession is good for the soul, some folks say. Not sinning in the first place is pretty good for a soul, too.

The car comes to a place where the street climbs a hill. There were no sidewalks at this point. I spot a girl walking on the side of the road. She's wearing a school uniform skirt and white blouse. She has books in one arm and a bunched-up sweater in the other hand. The sun glints off her brown hair as if she has a gold barrette fixed on the side of her head.

We pass her.

She looks at me.

And at that moment, Cupid's arrow smacks into my chest and penetrates my gizzard. I know it hits my gizzard because the shaft dislodges a gizzard stone, which gets stuck in my throat.

Just like that, I fell in love with Golden Barrette Girl, and she became my One and Only Squeeze. I confess, though, that it took me a couple of weeks to work up the guts to call her and ask her to go to a movie with me.

"Which movie?"

"Uh, I didn't have one picked out. I wanted to see if you'd—"

I ran out of words. She said, "Pick one and call me back. If the movie's okay, I'll go with you."

Until that moment, I'm sure no human had ever experienced profound euphoria while, in the exact same instant of time, feeling like the biggest idiot to ever walk the earth.

I picked a movie and called back. The movie was okay, and we went together. **And that was the most important thing that ever happened to me.**

It is, to this day, more important than being born. Without me falling in love with The Squeeze, without her loving me, too, I know that the me I would be, I wouldn't like at all. More important, The Squeeze wouldn't care for that me, either.

And looking back on it all, the way I was headed, I'm convinced I would not have been able to fall in love without Sister MM butt-kicking me. At the time, the devil's evil spirits who prowl about the world seeking the ruin of souls were dangling cars and girls and another L-word in front of me. The one ending with U S T.

And in life's rear-view mirror, I can see that butt kick opened my heart to the L-word that ends in O V E. Otherwise, Cupid would have been careless with his shot and missed, or he'd have used a dull arrow, and it would have bounced off my sternum, or some other dumb thing would have happened to keep The Squeeze and me apart.

But, Sister soul-kicked my soul-butt.

Cupid's arrow hit its target.

I loved her.

More important, she—and even in retrospect, it is almost incomprehensible, but even more glorious—loved me.

She loved me.

During the early part of senior year, I got a taste of heaven wallowing in a lake of love, or maybe I just dipped a toe in it. Anyway, I had a plan to keep love alive, and that was through college.

You can see why the above side bunny trail was important. Anyway, we're coming back to the main path now.

We're riding home that Saturday morning after Pop gave my body, my mind, and my soul to the US Navy. Pop's driving, and I'm staring out the window. What I'm seeing is the devil's evil spirits have spitted me on a stick, and they're toasting me like a marshmallow over the fires of hell.

The Navy meant: No college; No marriage with The Squeeze; No kids; No white picket fence; and Not only no happy ever after; but no happy ever. **EVER!**

We got home. I went to work at Klaus's Grocery Store. My main job there was stocking shelves. When required, though, I bagged and even manned the checkout. I had to do the latter just before lunch.

Mr. K. had taught me how to make change. If a customer's bill was $13.62 and they gave me a twenty. I was to say, "Thirteen sixty-two, plus three—I'd hand them three pennies—makes sixty-five plus ten—hand over a dime from the cash drawer—makes seventy-five, and a quarter makes fourteen dollars." Then a dollar from the till made fifteen, and a five made us even. And I could do that drill in my sleep.

Except that Saturday, I couldn't do it wide awake. All I could think of was telling The Squeeze that night I was not going to college, and she not giving me a goodnight kiss, or kiss of farewell. I pictured her looking at me with pity, getting out of Pop's car, walking to her front porch without so much as a glance back, and closing the door on me forever.

My mind movie machine played that scene over and over and over.

Mr. K. heard a woman customer tell me I owed her another dollar. I gave too much change to the next customer. Mr. K. saw her hand back the extra, too.

"Bag."

That job didn't last long either because I'd put a quart jar of pickles and a can of pork and beans on top of some bananas.

Mr. Klaus sent me back to stocking shelves. With a warning. "You break a jar of something, it comes out of your pay."

I managed to make it through the afternoon without breaking a jar. All the items got themselves priced properly, too, but only after checking, double-checking, and triple-checking them.

Every time the store received a box of cans or jars of foodstuff, the price of each can or jar went up or down a penny or two. So, we had to remove the old prices of the items on the shelves and stamp the new prices on them.

Keeping my mind on the business at hand got easier once I decided how I was going to tell the Squeeze that night.

I was sure she'd dump me as soon as she found out I wasn't going to college, so, I thought I'd put off telling her until the end of the date. I could at least watch one more double feature with her and have that drive to and from the theater with her by my side.

After work, though, as I walked home, try as I might to convince myself I could put off telling her, I knew she'd know something was wrong.

She'd know.

Sigh.

TBGH

At her house, I knocked, she stepped out, and I walked her from the house to the car. She got in on her side. As soon as I got in on mine, she said, "What?"

I knew she knew something was wrong, so I told her.

She said, "I'll write to you. Every day."

She scooted over tight against me and hugged my arm. The gear shift was on the steering column, out of the way. That helped. It was also before Al Gore invented seat belts. Of course, he was only eleven years old then.

It was like this time Cupid didn't shoot me with a puny arrow; he stuck an eight-foot-long spear in my gizzard. That evening, sitting in the driveway by her house, I stopped loving a high school girl and started loving a woman.

CHAPTER THREE

We never heard another word from ROTC, so, on August 11, the day before my eighteenth birthday, I was sworn into the United States Navy.

It turned out Pop had wangled two things from that recruiter.

One: If I joined the Nav—now here's an example of how to make Navy more Navy by dropping the Y than it could be by retaining it. The Nav, see? So, anyway, if I joined the Nav before my eighteenth birthday, my enlistment would expire the day I turned twenty-one. So, my term of service would be three years and one day, not four years. He must have figured maybe I wouldn't like it, so I could bail out sooner if that were the case. I never talked to him about it, like I never talked to him about anything, really. Except about getting paid that once. And buying a car and going to college. I guess I could've asked Mom, but "I'll write to you. Every day," those words mattered so much, I just didn't worry about anything else.

Two: As soon as I finished Boot Camp, the Navy would send me to a six-month school to teach me how to be an electronics repair specialist. If I couldn't be an Electrical Engineer, this must have been a good second-best in Pop's mind. Pop was right. And I would have added "again," except I had never stopped to wonder if Pop was right. I just did what he wanted done.

Boot camp. I had no idea what to expect. And, if I'm being totally honest, I might have been a little afraid. But, once we got a couple of days into the program, I felt at home there. Our company commander wasn't much different than a combination of Pop and a nun.

The first Saturday, we woke, hit the head (took care of our morning bathroom business), then mustered; and found out that during the night, three guys had climbed the fence and run away. I figured they had sissy fathers and hadn't had nun teachers, either.

They were quitters. I wasn't.

Navy pay was interesting. Working for Heiny, I'd gotten twenty-four dollars every two weeks. The Nav took taxes off my pay, and every two weeks, thirty-three were left. At home, Mom bought toothpaste, razor blades, pimple lotion, you know, the necessities. But now I had to buy those myself, plus stamps and stationery.

I finished Boot Camp in late October and transferred to San Francisco for Electronics Technician (ET) School. I planned to take a train to St. Louis for the Christmas holidays and visit The Squeeze. I had priced the ticket, and I could afford it. Barely. So, I had to save as much as I could.

I graduated from Boot Camp as a Seaman Apprentice, an E2, the second enlisted rank. And got a pay raise. Now, it was thirty-seven dollars a payday. While I was in ET school, I bought a roll of quarters every other month and called the Squeeze from a payphone booth. My plan permitted the quarters. Barely.

Absence is supposed to make the heart grow fonder. My take on that is, without our letters, without our phone calls, The Squeeze wouldn't have grown fonder of me. Rather, fondness would have dried up and blown away. The way it did for a lot of guys in Boot Camp and in ET school. It was a rare week when someone in the barracks did NOT receive a Dear John letter.

This was in 1959, and the song, *Hit the Road, Jack,* came out the following year, or we'd have probably hijacked, or Shanghaied—being Navy—that title to name that particular kind of letter.

The important thing is I did not get one of that kind of letter.

And my plan worked. Though I only got a week off, and the train trip home and back ate up four-sevenths of my whole leave period. Still, three glorious days with The Squeeze. Too bad I hurt Mom's feelings by being away from the house all day, every day, except The Squeeze came to supper one night.

I remember thinking: *Well, Eddie Walsh, you hurt Pop's feelings that one time. I guess it's only fair that you hurt Mom's once, too.*

Now that I've grown up and matured considerably—please don't ask The Squeeze to confirm that point—I realize I must've hurt my parents countless times. Going there, though, would be a heck of a lot more than a side bunny trail.

Back to Christmas 1959. Each day, more glorious than the one before. Each one, over faster than the one before.

Our last night is when The Squeeze came to dinner. I drove her home with her pressed against me. We arrived at her house. There was a big elm tree next to the drive. I sometimes parked behind the tree in case her mother looked out the front window to check on us. That night, I started to park there.

"Don't," she said.

I stopped the car short of the tree. "Can I kiss you?"

"No."

Here it comes. Two years before the song was even written. Hit the Road, Jack, except she would have sung it for Eddie to hit the road.

But she planted an industrial-strength lip lock on me that took my breath away. Heck, it made it unnecessary to breathe at all. It gushered up such an intense attraction, such a powerful longing, such an all-consuming need—

I reached for her, but she grabbed my forearms. "Don't." She slid across the seat. "I love you, Eddie. More than I love my own life, but I have to go in now. I have to." She got out of the car.

I did, too, and didn't catch up to her until we stood together on her front porch. She took my hands and held them down at my sides … and kissed me again. Softly, tenderly, and then there was the briefest of tongue tip touches.

She broke apart from me and went inside. She left the main door to the house open behind her and stood looking into my eyes through the screen in the storm door.

I went to the door and pressed my lips against the screen. She kissed me from her side of the screen. Then she went in and closed the main door.

I stood there wondering what the heck had just happened. Some of the things flaring up in me had seemed hot enough to have burned me up and left me a pile of ash. But I wasn't ash. Or a puddle of molten Eddie.

Inside that door in front of me was my Squeeze. My Woman. My great gift from Great God Almighty.

I never expected a miracle, but if what just happened to me wasn't one, what in blue blazes was it?

I got in the car and sat there with my hands on the steering wheel. On my lips, I tasted dust and what may have been desiccated bug guts from last summer. I didn't brush my lips off, though. And I was not inclined to lick them off.

When I got home, I brushed my teeth. Toothpaste could eradicate tooth decay. It could not eradicate a miracle. So, if desiccated bug guts got rinsed away with the toothpaste, the miracle was still as miraculous as it had been.

So, we are still on the main path to answering the volunteer question. It is just that I felt I had to explain how Eddie Walsh got to be the man he was when he faced that opportunity. The Squeeze was not just a vital part of who Eddie was. She was the reason he was who and what he was.

The reason.

TBGH

Back to San Francisco and ET School. There, among a few other things I learned, I found out you called San Francisco, San Francisco, or The City. You did not call it Frisco. So, of course, we sailors didn't call it anything else while we were on the Navy base of Treasure Island.

I only went into The City once while I was stationed there. Three ET School buds invited me to come with them. Bus fare to and from and the price of a meal would cost too much stamp and phone call money. "Oh, come on," one of the guys said. "We're pinching our pennies, too."

I don't remember much about that trip into San Francisco. Most of what we did was ride around town in buses. I recall passing Lombard Street, supposedly the crookedest street in any city in the world.

Whatever.

We ate lunch at a place that offered rattlesnake pizza. My buds and I got pizza, but none of us tried snake pizza. And was it rattlesnake meat on the pie, or did the pie come with some venomously hot sauce? We were not inclined to risk money on something we might choose not to finish eating.

Even though it would have been nice to be able to answer the question: "Whadja get to eat?" with "Rattlesnake pizza."

I never found that kind of pie offered any place else, and I think about it now and then and wonder what it would have tasted like.

Oh well.

I liked ET School. The Navy unloaded dump trucks full of material on us each day. It was highly interesting stuff. We also had sessions in a laboratory where my classmates earned nicknames like Sparks, Smokey, and Zap, Crackle and Pop. I never earned one of those monikers.

I liked the lab, too.

Another thing I liked was making E-3, or seaman, or SN.

> A slight aside. Not a side bunny trail. A slight aside. I remember encountering acronymization in Boot Camp. The petty officers in charge of us flung those abbreviated terms at us nonstop, all day and every day. They, the POs (see what I mean?), did not like to be interrupted by questions like, "What does that mean, Sir?" It seemed like everything was acronymized except the word acronym. So, it's hard, see? to tell a Navy story without them.

And E-3 meant a pay raise. Twice a month, they paid me forty bucks. One of my ambitions was to make forty-eight dollars a payday, which was twice what I made working for Heiny Horstwessel.

Note: I had to fight hard to keep Heiny from becoming HH.

WHAT AM I?

I finished ET School with the highest grade in my class and, equally important, no laboratory nickname. And I was then an ETSN. A seaman but with a technical specialty. The Navy gave me orders to a destroyer based on the east coast. Traveling there, I could stop off in St. Louis and see The Squeeze.

That was better than a forty-eight-dollar payday.

The Navy allowed me to take four days of leave during the St. Louis stopover. Which was a day longer than we'd had the past Christmas, but it seemed like it was over even faster than the shorter stay had been.

Leaving The Squeeze this time, again, there was nothing sweet about the sorrow I experienced at our parting. It felt like my heart ripped itself out of my chest and said, "I'm staying here with our One and Only Squeeze. I'll get back in your chest next time you visit her."

I'd taken a train to St. Louis. A Greyhound carried me the final third of my trip to the East Coast. We were barely out of the bus depot when I got out my stationery and started a letter to her. If twelve years of Catholic schools hadn't taught me I had a soul, writing that letter would have. When I turned my back on her and climbed aboard, it was as if a guillotine blade had dropped and severed my connection to her. Totally, and more completely than any Hit-the-road-Eddie missive from her would have. At least in my imagining, that's how I saw it that day. But, as soon as I wrote "Dearest," and that was my standard salutation to her, Dearest, I felt the spiritual bond tying us, binding us to each other.

Decades later, somebody invented cellular telephones. Probably Al Gore. Anyway, look at how the kids are these days with their devices. They are not connected to the earth by their feet being on the ground. They are connected to the world cellularly.

Well, our letters connected The Squeeze and me soulularly.

TBGH

On the second day of the bus trip, I not only thought about The Squeeze, I also thought about checking in to my ship. I pictured myself walking down the pier with a seabag strap over my shoulder and looking like a total goober new guy. Which of course, I was, but I did not want salty sailors to see me looking like one.

Taps at Boot Camp and ET School went down at 22:00—ten p.m. for landlubbers. In the Nav, putting the lights out at that time was standard ashore and afloat. Mr. Greyhound dumped me at the bus terminal at 1800. So, I decided to wait there until taps. Then, I would take a taxi to the Navy base.

Which I did. The taxi dumped me at the main gate. The sailor gate guard told me where I could catch an on-base bus to where my ship was berthed. I arrived there at 23:30. Ships, large and small, lined both sides of the pier. The first one to starboard—for some reason, the Navy could abide civilian "up" and "down" being Navy "up" and "down," but civilian "left and right," well, that just would not do, so, we had "port and starboard"—was a destroyer, but the number painted on the bow was not the one to which I was assigned.

A cruiser lay to port. Twice as long as a destroyer. Her guns twice as big. *That ship is too big*, I thought. It took a couple of weeks to find out how wrong I was.

I continued my solitary trek down the center of the pier. Harsh, glaring pole-mounted spotlights exposed me like a fan dancer who'd dropped her fan. What I felt like, though, was a cockroach on a kitchen floor when, suddenly, someone turned on the lights. In total darkness, the cockroach belongs on the kitchen floor. The moment the lights flash on, though, he doesn't belong even a little bit.

And, I, a boy from a Midwest, hick farm town, did not belong on that Navy pier skittering between all those moored ships just short of midnight. I wished like heck that I had just gone ahead and reported aboard right after I hit town. Feeling like a newbie, I was sure, was better than feeling like a cockroach.

"Wishing for something you coulda' done but didn't, now there's a good use of a man's time."

Pop never said that to my face, but I heard him say it across the distance from the Mississippi River to the Atlantic Ocean. It was near midnight where I was. It was 23:00 back— Home was what I wanted to put next, but—"Fed long enough at the family trough" popped to the front of my brain. Home was a thing I didn't have anymore.

My ship was the last one to starboard. It was moored starboard side to the pier. I walked up the gangway to the quarterdeck, on the fantail, the back end of the boat. The procedure for reporting aboard a Navy ship was to salute the flag flying from a pole mounted to the stern, then salute the Officer of the Deck (OOD), and request permission to come aboard.

The flag only flew between the hours of morning colors and sunset. I knew enough not to salute the flag that wasn't there. The OOD was a chief petty officer and an enlisted man, and normally a sailor would not salute him, but as Officer of the Deck, he represented the commanding officer of the ship. I saluted him and said, "ETSN Walsh reporting for duty, Sir, uh, Chief."

That "Sir, uh, Chief," as soon as I heard myself say it, made me blush so hard I sweated. It would have been appropriate to call him Sir or Chief, but "Sir, uh, Chief" marked me as a newbie, and not only a newbie but a newbie cockroach.

So much for sneaking aboard in the middle of the night and avoiding the newbie business.

Besides the OOD, a third-class petty officer stood Petty Officer of the Watch (POOW). A seaman served as messenger, but apparently, he didn't rate an acronym.

The OOD returned my snappy salute with a sloppy one. Appropriate for a newbie cockroach. Then he told the POOW to enter my arrival time, 23:55, in the logbook. After that. the messenger escorted me to the berthing space which was to be my new home.

The messenger led me forward down the port side, almost to the bow. Then we entered the superstructure to an athwartship passageway. Just inside the door, he pointed to his right and said, "That's the ET shop." Electronics Technician shop. I'd be working there after reveille. We then descended a ladder to the second deck and went farther forward. The lights in the passageway were red. Red light didn't destroy night vision as white light did. But I'd been told red lights were used when a ship was at sea, not in port. I wanted to ask about it, but I felt stupid already, and asking a question would only make me look stupider.

Red lights illuminated the berthing space also. I'd thought the bunks in the barracks at ET school made for crowded living. But that was luxury compared to shipboard berthing. Ships could be berthed, and so could sailors. These bunks were three high and stacked pretty close together. I wondered if a guy in the second or third bunk had enough room to sleep on his side.

The messenger said, "A couple of empty top bunks here."

"Shut up!" welcomed me to my new home.

The messenger whispered, "Sleep in this one and put your seabag on the other one. Otherwise, somebody will get annoyed with it being in the way and throw it overboard."

He left. Left me standing there. Amid the narrow aisles between the stacks of sleeping, a few of them snoring, sailors. *Shipmates I should call them.*

A good bit of the floor—floors were decks in the Nav; *Best remember that Newbie*—space between the tiers of my shipmates was taken up with shoes. The bunks were aligned with the ship's centerline. All the shoes on the deck were aligned that way, too. That seemed like the first thing that made sense. With the shoes aligned that way, it took up the minimum amount of space. I lined my shoes up that way. Then I hiked my seabag onto an empty top bunk, slipped off my dress uniform, and draped it over the seabag.

Before climbing onto the other empty bunk, I looked around the compartment again. The light fixtures in the overhead leaked, not red light, but red dimness, into the compartment and over the tiers of bunks, the tiers of sleeping bodies.

At that moment, I knew exactly how Dorothy had felt when the tornado dumped her and Toto in Oz. I wished I had a dog to talk to.

CHAPTER FOUR

Note to Number Five: I could jump to the volunteering question, but I am presuming the folks who send me those questions are really interested in putting together the story of my life. And answering their questions, which in many ways do not seem to be connected, would be one way to do that. But, since I began working on the answer to this particular question, I have been inspired to see the story as a coherent whole, not as something needing to be pieced together like a jigsaw puzzle of an abstract painting after their shelfful of questions gets fired off and responded to.

And I confess, developing the story as a coherent whole has been a big challenge. I start down a string of recollections, but then my mind says: *Eddie, you forgot to include umpty fratz in the story. It's just not complete without umpty fratz.* So, I go back, stick umpty into the story where it's appropriate, then check everything I've written to that point to make sure everything still flows.

If Pop were still here, and I picture him in the living room reading the sports page, I'd say, "Pop, I want to tell you something."

Through the uplifted paper, he says, "Then tell it."

"You know what's harder than work?"

The uplifted paper remains as mute as a sphinx.

"Writing," I say, "is harder than work."

Pop continues reading his paper.

I am sure Number Five, you see, by this point, that Pop is a spiritual cocklebur stuck to the skin of my soul.

I think **most** of what constitutes the building blocks of my soul comes from your mother, with a brick or two from Sister Mary Mark and my Mom, but every once in a while, Pop pops up as an unignorable entity, and despite thinking I have dealt with him, these instances recur, where I just have to tell him, "My work, writing, is harder than the work you worshipped."

Pop hurt me, and, at times, I want to hurt him back. Which is petty and stupid. He's in heaven, and I can't hurt him there.

Sorry, Pop.

I hope that can get me by St. Pete, the gatekeeper.

Sorry. Time to get back to the first ship to which the Navy assigned me.

"Reveille, reveille. All hands heave out and trice up. The smoking lamp is lit in all authorized spaces. Now, reveille."

That was almost as effective as a "Git up!"

Sailors began spilling out of their bunks, crowding the deck with, it turned out, forty-seven underwear-clad bodies yawning, scratching, moving in all directions. I stayed on the bunk, watching. They were all grabbing towels and Dopp Kits from lockers. After a minute or two, all that aimless motion congealed into a flow forward. Toward the head, I found out.

None of the forty-seven seemed to notice me. But then a guy stopped next to—I almost wrote "my" there but I remember feeling like nothing on that ship was mine at that point—the bunk I'd slept on. "I'm Gutter Mouth," he said. It turned out his real name was Guttermuthe, a seaman assigned to the ET shop. Being called Gutter

Mouth was kind of funky because, besides me, he was the only one of the four dozen of us assigned to that berthing space who did not insert swear words into each sentence he uttered.

"Why don't you climb down?" GM said. "Best we get to the head."

Head is what sailors call a bathroom. Where a woefully inadequate number of commodes, urinals, and sinks was made adequate by an unceasing stream of "Hurry (cuss word goes here) up." "Don't take all (cuss word goes here) day." "My grandpa's slow, but he's (cuss word goes here) old."

Gutter stopped behind a guy at a sink looking at his hair in the mirror. Like he was trying to decide if he needed a haircut. I thought it might have been two days since he'd been to the barber.

"The way it works, Ollie," Gutter Mouth said, "is you don't get prettier the longer you stare at yourself in the mirror. You get uglier."

"(Cuss word goes here) you, Gutter Mouth." But Ollie moved aside, and GM nudged me to take the sink and shave.

Seaman Guttermuthe stayed close to me, urging me to move it, to hustle. The pressure was to complete the morning head business, get to the mess decks for breakfast, return to the head for brushing teeth and any other head business, and get to the ET shop by 0800 for morning muster. The passageways were jammed with sailors going both directions. Like a Los Angeles freeway at rush hour. Like an announcement had been made: "Everybody aft move forward, and all you aft bozos move forward." We made it by 07:50.

The other guys assigned to the ET Shop were already there. Three PO3 (Petty Officer third class), another ETSN, like me, a graduate of ET School. All of them looked at me as if Guttermuthe were a cat and had dragged a half-eaten mouse into the shop.

A vivid memory of my first day aboard my first ship is how like a fish out of water I felt. The most amazing thing, though, is how fish-in-water I felt by the third day. According to Gutter, it took time for a newbie to fit in. Usually. But the first morning, after the down-their-noses looks at me, I said, "I'm the newbie. I expect you to have newbie jobs for me to do. Will one of you explain what I need to do, please?"

The other ETSN explained. The newbie's job was to empty the trash twice a day. Sweep and swab the deck in the shop twice a day. Sweep and swab the passageway outside the shop before reveille and at 21:00.

Aye," I replied, which is nautical, for *I'm all over this.*

I did the first day's twice-a-days and the second day's. After the third day's morning chore, I felt a change in the atmosphere the guys brought into the shop after breakfast.

They treated me differently. Like I belonged there as much as they did. From that, I built the idea that the ship I was assigned to was not the Navy's vessel. It was mine. And I was hers.

I thought it sounded sort of like a marriage. Which, of course, got me thinking about The Squeeze, our four kids, our house with the white picket fence. Always nice to think about her.

Swabbing the deck, I didn't mind that one little bit. Compared to mucking out Heiny Horstwessel's milk barn, my ship's passageway was a pleasure to work on.

But, contrary to what I, and the white picket fence, wanted from The Squeeze, my marriage to my ship lasted two days.

That Thursday night, the ET2 had spent the night aboard. He was up and on the way to the shop early enough to catch me swabbing down the passageway.

"Walsh. You didn't have duty last night, did you?"

"No, ET2."

"Then why are you swabbing the deck?"

"It's my newbie job."

It turned out that the routine established for the ET Shop was that the seaman in the duty section had to clean the shop and the passageway. We stood three section watches. So, I should have been doing that duty only every third day. Not every stinkin', blinkin' day.

At first, I was mad, but then it occurred. I'd asked to be treated like a newbie. And the gang obliged me. Big Time. I couldn't be mad at them. But I wasn't married to my ship anymore. And I wasn't married to theirs either.

It was a lot like working for Heiny. I could claim no ownership of even a square inch of his farm. He gave me a job. I did it.

The Navy gave me a job. On a ship. I'd do it as good as Pop would.

And I wasn't a total newbie anymore. Just ninety-five percent of one.

TBGH

Monday of my second week aboard the destroyer to which I'd been assigned—in lieu of **my** ship—I got up half an hour before the Navy's "Git up," or reveille. As I donned my shower flip-flops, I resolved that, by the end of the day, I'd be no more than ninety-four percent newbie. And so, to the head, to breakfast, to the ET Shop.

Gutter had passageway cleaning duty that morning. He was the only one in the shop.

"Hey, Eddie." He never treated me like a newbie. "Our chief was on leave last week. He'll be back today. He's generally here by 07:50.".

And we had a division officer. An ensign, the lowest officer rank. An O-1. I'd been an E-1 in Boot Camp. As soon as I completed the program, I was an E-2. Like the Navy thought it was important that they give me a promotion as soon as they could justify it. You know, so I wouldn't feel like **the** lowest form of life on earth. Which had been pointed out to me in boot camp that that's what I was as a boot. I was lower than a worm that ate whale poop and lived at the bottom of the Marianas Trench. I'd had very little to do with officers to that point in the Nav. I did know that officers were an exalted species of human. Still, I wondered why I went from E-1 to 2 so fast, and my division officer was still an O-1 after he'd been aboard for six months.

One of the things I'd learned growing up, relearned in school from nun teachers, and re-relearned in boot camp is that I should remove the word "why" from the list of words I might speak out loud. Life was better that way.

It didn't much matter. We saw very little of our division officer. On my—**my** slips in so dad-burned naturally. On **the** ship, while in port, a couple of days each week, we mustered outside and in formation. The ET's station was on the O-1 level amidship. We did see our Div O on topside mustering days. It was the only time we saw him.

On those days, we technicians formed up in two short rows, with the ET2 in charge, at 0745. The chief petty officers, including our chief, also formed up in their own formation on the O-1 level, with the senior among them in charge.

Our Div O climbed the ladder from the main deck to the O-1 level at 07:55.

The ET2 called us to attention, saluted, and reported, "All present, Sir."

The Div O returned the salute and said, "Very well."

The ET2 returned to his place in the front row.

The Div O ordered us to stand at ease.

At 08:00, a whistle sounded over the 1MC, the ship's general announcing system. A cacophony of whistles sounded over the 1MCs of each ship in port.

In our formation, we snapped to attention.

The Div O faced aft and saluted.

On the fantail, the US flag was being hoisted up the pole mounted on the stern. At 0801, three whistle blasts sounded.

The Div O dropped his salute, faced his formation, and said, "ET2, take charge and carry out the Plan of the Day."

ET2 saluted and said, "Aye, aye, Sir."

The ship's office published the Plan of the Day each evening, listing any extraordinary events that would occur the next day, such as, "The ship will get underway at 07;00." Most days, though, we had a Business As Usual Plan of the Day.

That first time we mustered topside, I sure hadn't expected it to, but it moved me. To that point, all my life, that I could remember, I'd spent in school: grade school, high school, boot camp, and ET School. Even working for Heiny Horstwessel was like school: "A boy's gotta learn how to work."

But that morning, I, Eddie Walsh, was part of something in the real world. School wasn't the real world. School was because a person's brain wasn't quite ready for the real world. School helped a mind get ready. It was almost like the mind, my mind, wasn't ready to be born yet.

That day, on … **the** ship, my mind was born. A doctor held me upside down by my ankles and smacked me good on my little bare buttocks, and I started yowling—in my mind yowling—and my mind started breathing on its own.

When Pop told me I'd fed long enough at the family trough, I felt like I didn't fit into the family anymore. I didn't belong anywhere. In both Boot Camp and ET School, I'd felt comfortable, maybe even kind of close to sort of happy. But that morning, I felt like I belonged in the Navy. I wanted to say "and I belong to my ship, and my ship belongs to me." But to coin a totally unique phrase, that ship had sailed.

It couldn't be my ship. But then, Boot Camp had never been my Boot Camp. The same with ET School.

One thing this Navy ship had, though, was a trough with plenty of slop in it to snarf.

This feeling that I fit into the Navy was a thing that blew hot for a while, then something would cool it down. Then hot. Then cold again.

These things I'm relating here may seem like I am avoiding just answering the volunteer question, but these are all paving stones leading to the answer. The most important paving stone was, is, and always will be The Squeeze and loving her. This hot and cold belonging feeling, maybe I even hankered for it to be forever warm, and feel like I found a new home in the Navy after Pop booted me out of the one I thought I had for life. All I can say for sure is, at the time, with another two years to serve, well, I was sure I preferred serving that time feeling like I fit in and not like some kind of eternal newbie.

As mentioned, we didn't see our division officer except on topside muster days. We did see our chief every day, though. Not as much as we saw the ET2. We saw him pretty much all day, every day. We ate with him, bunked in the compartment with him, and worked with him repairing malfunctioning radios and radars. On these jobs, it was obvious the man knew what he was doing.

The chief respected him too. Sort of like you might respect a house-trained dog while the rest of us junior goobers in the division were always leaving messes that needed cleaning up. The chief was sort of like Pop. A menacing presence even when he was absent. Not devil menacing, more like St. Michael the Archangel with the fiery sword ready to slice your gizzard out if you sinned. The ET2 was sort of like

Mom. He ran the shop like Mom ran the house. Except she never swore. ET2 did. And Mom never said, "Don't make me say it twice." When he was showing us how to do something, ET2 said, "Now pay the (cuss word goes here) attention, so I (cuss word goes here) don't (cuss word goes here) have to show this to you again."

And our Div O, he was sort of like the Pope. There, but way, way up there, there.

Understanding how things worked on the ship was a big part of beginning to feel comfortable, to feel like I belonged. Like someday, it really could feel like my ship.

I quickly got into the habit of rising with the first-class radarman in our compartment, getting to the head, doing my business, and getting out before reveille unleashed the hordes. Which got me through the chow line early, too. After eating, I went to the ET Shop and dug out a repair manual for one of the electronic systems on the ship. The systems we studied in ET school were all systems which had been replaced by updated models, but it was explained that it cost money to replace all the teaching material every time a system was upgraded, and studying outdated material was just fine to learn the fundamentals. But I needed to learn how the specific systems we had worked. So, I read the system operating manuals.

One morning, Pop, I mean the chief, walked into the shop at 07:00 and found me sitting on a stool at the work bench and reading a manual for the ECM (Electronic Counter Measures) System. The system could detect enemy radar signals, identify the type of radar, and pinpoint the direction from whence came the signal.

He looked over my shoulder. "I need that."

"The ECM manual?"

His scowl said *Duh!*

I slid the manual down the workbench.

"I need that."

He kind of nodded. His chin might have lowered three-quarters of an inch.

"The stool?"

Duh!

I vacated the object of his desire. He occupied it, slid the manual in front of him, and flipped the book to the front, the table of contents.

Pop and the sports section, the chief and the ECM manual, samo-samo.

I slunk into the back room of the shop, grabbed a manual for one of the ship's radio systems, and read part of that.

After 08:00 muster in the shop, the chief surprised me. He told the ET2 to check out the ECM system. The chief radarman had complained about the system not working.

"And," the chief said, "take HWF with you." The chief left the shop.

"Congratulations," ET2 said to me.

"What for?"

"Chief just promoted you from FNG to HWF."

FNG meant Fairly New Guy. I knew that. "What's HWF mean?"

"Tell him, Gutter Mouth," ET2 commanded.

"It means Halfways Worth a Fart."

Huh! Another promotion. And I hadn't been in the Nav but a year and had already logged three promotions: E1 to E2 and 2 to E3, plus HW—

Another aside: Cussing. Now I will confess that I consider the word F A R T to be crude but not really cussing. It's just that it's too close to that other word, which is clearly cussing. I got this aversion to swearing from two places.

One, Pop. He took me with him to work in the elevator a couple of times in the summer when I was in first and second grades, before I wound up doing girl work all the time. He warned me that some of the guys bringing oats from the farms said bad words. I wasn't to pay any mind to their nasty talk, "But don't you **never** use words like that! Not ever!!"

Pop using two exclamation points in a row, well, his message stuck.

Two: Sister Daniel. She showed up to teach third-, fourth-, and fifth-grade classes when I was in the latter grade.

> Note: My grade school was pretty small. We had three classrooms: Classroom One, where a nun taught first and second graders. Two, where another nun taught

third, fourth and fifth grades. In Room Three, Sister Superior taught sixth, seventh, and eighth grades.

Back to Sister Daniels. The first thing we noticed; she was young. At that point in my education, I didn't know there were young nuns. And she smiled. I couldn't recall seeing a nun smile before, either.

But the real surprise came at noon recess when she played softball with the girls.

Okay. Sorry. This aside is turning into a bunny trail.

Anyway, the surprise Sister Daniel laid on us the next day blew my socks off. She played baseball with us boys. **Baseball with us boys!** And she was the best hitter, pitcher, outfielder, and infielder on the playground. It was fun to be on her team and beat the snot out of our opponents, but it was also fun to compete against her team as well. It made us better baseball players faster than just getting older would. Fourth grader Jimmie Joe Meinerschlagen pointed that out to us.

In our religion class, Sister Daniel emphasized working hard at keeping our thoughts pure, but to work harder to keep our speech clean and free from curse words. Because thoughts wouldn't be an occasion of sin to others, but cursing out loud could lead others to commit the same sin of taking the Lord's name in vain. "And make no mistake," she said, "Curse words violate the third commandment. Even if the Lord's name is not used inappropriately."

Pop and Sister Daniel agreed on that.

CHAPTER FIVE

Mentioning Sister Daniel snapped me back to fifth-grade baseball at recess. The day Sister played shortstop as Jimmie Joe batted. He popped up, and Sister didn't have to move a step. She was perfectly positioned to catch the ball. Jimmie Joe said a word that rhymes with spit. Sister stopped looking up at the ball, pulled off the glove, dropped it, walked off the field, up the sidewalk, and into the side door of church.

Jimmie Joe didn't see what Sister was doing. He was hot-footing it to first base. Even if there was a 99.9% probability the ball would be caught, you always ran out a pop-up. Something could happen. The sun could blind Sister. She could trip on the hem of her habit.

I didn't watch him run or stop. I don't think any of the other players did, either. We were watching Sister.

Jimmie Joe is stuck in my memory, though, as turning and seeing all of us on the field frozen in place, not moving a single muscle, even to close our hanging open mouths, and the only person moving was Sister toward church.

That day, I played third base. As soon as the church door closed behind Sister, I saw Jimmie Joe hang his head for a moment. Then he slunk off the field like ... I don't know. Like a slinker.

Pop's admonition against using nasty words got me to fifth grade as a non-cusser. Sister's example amplified Pop's stricture and carried me for decades with no cuss words escaping from my mouth.

Looking back on my life now, which your question about volunteering has inspired me to do, it is monumentally amazing to see that, at the times when my soul needed a boot to the rear, someone was there to administer the kick.

After fifth grade and through high school, I heard cussing now and then, but when I got into the Navy, I learned what the phrase "cuss like a sailor" meant. Because of Pop and Sister Daniel, though, cuss words entered my ears, but they did not enter my mind nor my soul.

I needed that to be the case when the volunteer question came up. Otherwise, I am convinced I could not have seen it as opportunity.

TBGH

When I started writing the answer to the volunteer question, I sure never expected there to be so many side bunny trails. But then, that's life, isn't it?

Say you're going to the grocery store for blueberries, lettuce, tomatoes, Dove bars, and a gallon of skimmed milk. You take the keys to the pickup from the hook next to the door into the garage, and The Squeeze says, "As long as you're out, pick up the dry cleaning, too, please." A side bunny trail. See?

The eyes of my soul just caught a glimpse of the straight and narrow path to heaven, and it, too, is not pure straight. Although it is pure narrow, and it is festooned with, replete with side bunny trails. What you have to do is, if you veer off, you have to work to get back to that narrow way.

The other thing is, you don't have to take every side bunny trail that presents itself enticingly to you. It is **not** like Yogi saying, "If you come to a fork in the road, take it."

Apparently, if you were driving to Yogi Berra's house, you came to a fork in the road, but both forks led to his house. The devil sneaks in side-bunny trails leading off the sort-of straight and truly narrow, and you don't have to guess where *his* bunny trails lead.

So, I'm offering this as explanation, justification, or just a plain-old excuse, maybe, for the side-bunny trails in this narrative. It is just that all these side-bunny trails had a major bearing on how I responded to the volunteer question.

Back to Seaman Halfway Worth Something Eddie Walsh.

My chief—I can't say was impressed—viewed favorably my digging out system manuals to better understand the equipment we had aboard. Perhaps he saw some potential in me. Anyway, the ET2 took me along to Combat Information Center—CIC, of course—to check out the Electronic Counter Measures equipment. He carried the manual for the system. I toted a bag of test equipment and tools.

The ECM gear had some built-in test functions. Those all checked good. ET2 then had me read test procedure steps from the manual as he used meters and tools from the bag. These tests, too, indicated a perfectly operating system.

"It's one of the antennas or a connection to them," ET2 said. He called the shop and ordered the other guys to come help us.

ET2 and I then climbed a mast on the after part of the ship, which housed three domed antennae. Inside those domes, the antennae rotated and were used to determine the direction from which a particular signal came.

> Note: I called the dictionary I took with me to the ship my William Faulkner dictionary—even though it was a Webster's—because I couldn't read WF's books without a dictionary. And in the dictionary, the plural of antenna is listed as "1. antennas, 2. antennae." Me, I just like #2 better than #1.

At this point, I am twitchy with the desire to spew all kinds of details about the ECM system and how we figured out the problems, but I'll skip the details.

One. We found a malfunctioned part in the base of a rotating antenna.

Two. The cable connection to the antenna was corroded.

The Supply Department on the ship did not carry the part we needed, so we placed it on order.

"Probably take a month for the part to come in," ET2 groused that Thursday.

However, the part came in late Friday afternoon.

"We can do the ECM repair on Monday," the chief said.

Everyone from the shop left to go on liberty except for one ET3 and Gutter Mouth. They had the duty. I didn't go on liberty, either. I did not want to blow the little bit of money I made on what sailors spent money on in port.

Saturday morning, the ET3 and Gutter Mouth entered the ET shop after just-before-the-mess-deck-closed breakfast. Both of them grabbed books from the shelf. Gutter took a Louis L'Amour. ET3 selected another kind of book.

I looked up from the ECM manual. "ET2 tell you to do anything over the weekend?"

"Yeah." ET3 paged to the dog-ear bookmark. "He said, 'Don't do anything stupid.'"

I pondered **stupid** for a bit. "I think we should finish the ECM repair job."

ET3 didn't look up from his book. "That'd be stupid."

"Yeah," Gutter said. "We'd have to climb the mast, remove the dome cover for the antenna, replace the part in the antenna pedestal, and then we'd have to resolder all those wires to the multipin connector. Plus, we'd have to plug several extension cords together to get power to the solder gun."

"That'd be stupid." ET3 didn't look up from his book.

I said, "According to the paper this morning, the weather is supposed to be bad all next week."

ET3 looked up. "I read the paper and didn't see that."

"Cause all you read in the paper is the funnies," Gutter said.

Profane response goes here.

"Well," I said, "I'm going to fix the ECM system, whether you guys help or not."

Extensive profane response goes here.

Aside: The ET3 was senior to me. If he'd said, "We're

not doing the job," or, "You're not doing the job," that would have been a direct order from a superior. I would have complied with the order. But the petty officer argued with me as if he and I were equally ranked.

I strapped on a safety belt, bagged tools for the first two parts of the job I had in mind, and walked out. Before I closed the door, ET3 popped off a curse word. Or two. He and Gutter followed me, though.

By the time I got to the after mast, the petty officer had run out of words to cuss—for the moment.

I asked Gutter Mouth to get someone to open the paint locker and get us a can of primer paint and another of gray. Gray paint and the Navy, they go together like a horse and carriage, like marriage.

The Squeeze. It was as if my mind was a swimming pool, and she was always standing on the side, but give her the least little opening; she'd jump right into the middle of it.

Oh yeah. Paint. Navy ships are made of steel. Seawater eats steel for breakfast, lunch, and dinner. Paint keeps the hungry beast at bay. When ET2 and I had been on the mast earlier that week, he discovered rust along the base of all three ECM antennae. He said we'd treat the corrosion once we had the repair done.

I had a different plan. I'd replace the bad part in the base of the antenna, wire brush away the rust around the base and apply a coat of primer over the erstwhile rusty area. The primer would dry while we ate lunch. Then we would paint gray over the primer and repair the corroded multipin connector. By evening chow time, the gray paint would be dry, and the connector repair would be completed.

How did I figure out how to do things like that?

Pop taught me. Though at the time I had that learning experience, I certainly didn't recognize it as such. Pop was finishing off the upstairs of the house we had moved into when I was in fifth grade. He'd just smeared cement—he'd called it mud—over the nails and seams of sheet rock. Then he got a hammer, a bag of finishing nails, and started to nail smooth floorboards over the rough plywood base. I asked him why he did that, worked on the wall for a time, then switched to working on the floor.

"After you put mud on the wall, it has to dry for a spell. It don't dry no faster if you sit and watch it."

Six or seven years prior, Pop had taught me that lesson, and it finally sank in. That probably doesn't qualify me as a fast learner.

That was the time I asked Pop if I could help him nail floorboards in place, and he said, "You really wanna help?"

For a lot of years, I remembered his, "Then don't help," but not the real lesson: While paint is drying, get another job done.

So, that day on my first ship, the job got done according to Pop's plan.

The next day was Sunday. I went to Mass in the base chapel and returned to the ship. On Sundays in port, the mess decks served brunch from 0800 to noon. So, everybody got a day of rest except for the cooks. And as I was to find out, the mess cooks. Mess cooking in the Navy was KP duty in the Army.

After brunch, I went back up the after mast to treat the corrosion around the base of the other two ECM antennae. Gutter Mouth helped. ET3 slept all afternoon, rising in time for dinner and the evening movie on the mess decks.

TBGH

Monday morning. 07:45. ET shop. Except for the chief, we were all there.

ET2 looked at Weekend-duty-section ET3. "Anything happen over the weekend?"

"Well, uh. You see, uh—"

"We fixed the ECM system," Gutter Mouth said.

"What!" Normally the word "what" expects an interrogative punctuation caboose, but the "what" ET2 had said, and how he said it, was all exclamation.

Immediately thereafter, exclamatory interrogation happened, with ET2 the interrogator. Weekend-duty-section ET3 stammered responses.

Gutter Mouth offered a sentence of explanation. The Interrogator fired another question at the ET3. He pointed a finger at me. "It was his idea."

"So, you, the petty officer in charge of the duty station, took orders from the FNG?"

"Actually, ET2," GM said. "Chief promoted him to HWF."

The door to the shop jerked open. "What the hell is all the shouting about?" The chief's interrogation trumped the second-class petty officer's by a lot of decibels.

Once the chief understood what had happened, he sent the ET2 and the other ET3 up the mast to pull the ECM antennae dome covers to check on the repairs we'd done.

Then, Chief phoned the first class radarman and got an ECM system test organized with another destroyer. "Set up the test for 10:00," Chief barked into the phone. "I have guys checking the antennas. They'll be done by then."

"We did that Saturday, Chief," WDS ET3 said. "The systems from our two ships talked to each other very nicely."

Chief wasn't talking nicely.

"You dumb (cuss word goes here) could have fallen and killed your stupid selves. You could have dropped a tool or an antenna dome and killed some poor duty section bastard just walking by."

"Chief," I said. "ET2 showed me how to use a safety belt to climb and work on the mast. He showed me how to tie the antennae domes to the railing on the mast. He showed me how to secure a tool with a line to my belt so it couldn't fall and hurt someone."

The chief, still rooted to the deck in the doorway, aimed his spotlight of animosity at me. "Get up to Radio Central and test the UHF and VHF radios." (UHF and VHF being specific frequency ranges in which particular radios operated). Chief was staring at me, but he was talking to Gutter and Weekend Duty Section PO also.

We tested the radios and arrived back in the Shop at 11:15. The whole gang was there, including the chief. He looked at us. That look would have stopped a freight train. It stopped the third class in front of me.

Now what? Did they find something wrong with the ECM system?

The chief said to ET2, "Know what we have here?" Chief reminded me of a roller coaster that had just been through the wildest part of the ride, and now was coasting calmly back into the starting/stopping point.

"Uh, no, Chief."

"A one-butt-kick sailor."

The chief, it turned out, believed the first time he showed a new sailor how to do a particular task, there was zero percent probability that the FNG would know how to do it on his own. The next time he demonstrated the job, he always punctuated the lesson with a kick to the butt. An exceptional sailor was one who got the message by the third butt kick.

"So, repairing the ECM system was your idea, Walsh," ET2 said, "and you showed Gutter and Dumb Butt here—hooked thumb indicated Weekend-Duty-Section (WDS) ET3—how I showed you, how to use the safety gear." There was no question in any of that. It was the prosecuting attorney in a pre-closing argument summing up a perp's guilt for the jury.

Chief smiled. Pop smiling would not have been any stranger. "One butt-kick sailor."

"Technically, Chief," I said. "Shouldn't I be a no butt-kick sailor?"

Chief clouded up and sparked inside-the-cloud lightning. "Turn around." It was real clear he was talking to me. WDS ET3 got the heck out of the way. I turned around.

"Bend over," Chief said.

I bent. The chief kneed me in the rear, lifting my feet off the deck.

"Now you're what I said."

Then he sent us to chow, "Before they (curse word goes here) close the (curse word goes here) mess (curse word goes here) deck.

TBGH

After the servers glopped food into the compartments of my aluminum tray, I followed Gutter Mouth to a table with two empty seats. Gutter sat and I was about to when ET2, from behind me, said, "Over here, Butt Boy."

The other two guys sitting with Gutter looked at me. My cheeks—the face ones—got hot all the way past my armpits.

ET2 held his tray in front of his chest and nodded toward an empty four-seat table against the starboard side of the mess deck. I sat against the bulkhead. ET2 sat diagonally across from me. Lasagna waited for me in the biggest section of my tray. I'd never had lasagna before. I was anxious to try it, but ET2 obviously wanted to talk to me. So, I left my fork in my shirt pocket.

Note: The ensuing dialogue has been modified to PG-13.

ET2 sucked in a big lungful of what I've come to believe was patience, but most of it got away from him on the exhale.

"You build a thousand bridges but poot in church once, what are you?" ET2 glared steel needles into my eyeballs. "Say it, Butt Boy. What are you? Are you a bridge builder?"

"I'm a church pooter."

"That's what you did alright. Chief and I were both convinced that what you got the guys to do over the weekend had been stupid and dangerous and probably had not been done properly and that we'd have to do it all over again. But, when we checked it out, the ECM repair had been done properly. As a bonus, you and the guys treated the corrosion on the antenna pedestals. Plus, you showed the guys how to do the job safely and made sure they were safe up on the mast. You know what that amounted to?"

"Uh—" I shook my head.

"You built nine-hundred ninety-nine bridges; then you pooted in church."

I frowned consternation.

"You have no idea how far above your station in life your division chief petty officer is. Did you hear the list of a sailor's priorities in Boot Camp?"

I nodded.

"Onboard this ship, it's not God, country, Navy, family, self. Rather, it's God, division chief petty officer. Period. Nothing comes after, see?"

I frowned.

"Now listen to this next part, Butt Boy, and listen good." He leaned toward me and dropped his voice to just above the mess deck buzz. "Whether you believe that list of priorities is not important. The chief believes it."

He scooped up a big forkful of lasagna, chewed, swallowed, wiped the back of his hand across his mouth, and took a drink from his glass of Kool-Aid. Bug juice we called it. If there was a landlubber term for something, in the Nav, it had to be changed, preferably into something gross, or better still, profane.

"What happened back there in the shop is the chief spent the whole morning discovering just what it is that you duty-section dweebs managed to accomplish. And he was impressed. Then, he climbed down off his high horse to give you a compliment. What you did then—ET2 shook his head—was to, in effect, promote yourself to his equal and make a joke of his praise."

"That's not—"

"What you meant is not important. How the chief read it is."

ET2 took his tray to another table.

I looked down at my food and ate a green bean.

CHAPTER SIX

After my one-bean lunch, I walked up to the 0-3 level (Third deck above the main deck) to the signal bridge. When we'd tested the radios, I'd been up there because some of the radio antennae were mounted there. Everywhere else on the ship, you found hordes. I wanted a quiet place. I had some things to sort out.

No one was there that noon. All still at chow. I leaned on the waist-high railing, looking down at the pier. The way the sailors moved up and down the pier, walking, talking, carrying, it was as if I watched a movie of them. I was disconnected from them somehow. Then I remembered that *soulular* word. That was it, I was *soulularly* disconnected from them, from the whole blinking world at that moment.

I had felt pretty good about what we'd done over the weekend. I felt good about it being my idea to repair the ECM gear.

Seaman Walsh had graduated from Electronic Technician School and turned himself into ETSN Walsh. Then, the repair job gave him the opportunity to show he'd learned something. He'd shown the other two how to safely climb the mast and work on the antenna platform safely.

They even treated the corrosion properly. Then, they tested the ECM system, and it worked. Holy Crap, it worked!

> Note: As I wrote the above part of the story, I, without being aware of it, slipped into third person. It happens

now and again, especially in a first draft. Usually, a writer will correct that kind of error in the editing phase. But here, I am going to ask your indulgence to permit me this narrative person aberration. Simply because slipping from first to third felt so natural in the writing.

Another note: The Holy Crap! In ET School, when Zap, Crackle, and Pop had gotten his nickname, the instructor had said, "GD. Sometimes a man just needs a good GD." Of course, Mom, Pop, and Sister Daniels wouldn't allow Eddie to have one of those. Standing on that signal bridge, though, ETSN Walsh understood what his instructor said. Eddie decided he needed a good … something … sort of like a good GD, but not confessable naughty. A good "Holy Crap!" filled the bill.

Back to first person.

As I was saying, I had done something useful, and nobody had to tell me to do it. I felt pretty good about that. I felt like I belonged to the ET gang, like I belonged to my ship, and that I had an ownership stake in **my ship** as well.

Monday morning, I anticipated some questions from ET2 like, "Did you use safety measures when you climbed the mast?" I anticipated replying, "We did just like you showed me." I anticipated a "Well, okay then."

I thought about Boot Camp. Though it surprised me some, I felt like I had fit in there. ET School, I was comfortable there, too. So, why had fitting in on the ship taken such a sudden turn for the bad, bad, bad?

Then I remembered ET2 saying, "Promoted yourself to his equal."

It was a Holy Crap realization moment, a run around the ship naked, hollering Eureka! Eureka! moment.

But, thank You, God, I restrained myself. I saw what I'd done.

I had made myself equal to Pop and joked with him.

Over the ship's announcing system, and echoed by each ship at the pier: Two dings of the ship's bell, indicating 13:00, followed by, "Turn to. Recommence ship's work."

WHAT AM I?

My inside-the-head light bulb came on. When I'd entered the Navy, I hadn't left Pop behind. He was right here, on my ship, waiting for me. Chief Pop.

I knew how to behave around Pop. Well, except for the time I called him "old fashioned." But I'd learned that lesson.

And Chief Not-Pop, I'd had to relearn the lesson, but I learned it.

"Now, turn to," the petty officer of the watch intoned the third brief sentence of his 13:00 directive.

"Now" seemed to have been extra emphasized.

As I descended the ladders from the O-3 level, I thought about the chief. Would I consider him to be Chief Pop, or Chief Not-Pop? When I stepped onto the main deck and started forward, I decided. He was Chief Pop-Not-Pop.

It made sense at the time.

I also thought I knew how to act around Chief PNP. Around Pop, if he said, "Git up," I never had to say anything. I just had to get up PDQ. Around Chief PNP, it was a little different. If Chief PNP told me, "Git up," I had to spend three-fourths of a second saying, "Aye, Chief," then get up PDQ.

I thought about doing girl work around the house. Mom or Pop told me what to do, and they expected me to do it. So, I did it.

I thought about working for Heiny Horstwessel. He told me how to do something, and I did it.

I thought about working in Mr. Klaus' grocery store. He told me how to do a job, and I did it.

ET2 had told me how to act around Chief PNP. So, I'd just do it.

Eddie, I told myself, *I'm sure glad we got that figured out.*

I dogged the watertight hatch to the weather deck behind me and waited for a moment outside the ET shop.

Eddie, when you were growing up and somebody told you to do something, you just did it. You didn't say anything. The real message here: Keep your stupid mouth shut! You got that, Eddie Walsh?

I sucked in a breath, blew it out, and opened the door.

They were all crowded into the space. Gutter, ETSN, the PO3s, and ET2. And the chief. They stared at me.

"Coupla you Dipwads move into the storage compartment," the Chief barked. "Make some room for Walsh." He beckoned me in.

If I'd have been a dog, my hackles would have stood and tingled. Something was going to happen. There was this sense that whatever it was, I wouldn't like it.

But the Navy had me on a leash. I couldn't run away. I stepped in. The chief smiled.

Another thing to worry about.

"I've thought about this, Walsh," Chief said. "What you did over the weekend showed initiative. That you pay attention. That you do good work. The other two guys were in the duty section. They had to be here, and without you, they wouldn't have done a lick of work. They don't rate anything extra, but you, ETSN Walsh, gave the Navy Monday and Tuesday work on Saturday and Sunday."

His smile had disappeared while he was speaking, but it came back. If I'd been reading this in a novel, what was happening here would be a pause for dramatic effect. I'm telling you, it affected me dramatically.

"Walsh," Chief said, "I'm giving you the rest of today off as well as all day tomorrow."

What?!

(If you're wondering about the double punctuation being a typo, it isn't. What it is, is an exclamatory interrogative.)

The last thing I wanted was a day, make it a day and a half, off. I couldn't hang around the ship while everyone else *Turned to and completed ship's work.* Going ashore was out. It would cost me money buying something I didn't want.

Plus, what I had done over the weekend was the greatest, the most rewarding work experience I'd had in my whole life. I saw work that needed doing and knew how to do it because of ET2's lesson in practical application of ET School learning. And … not I, but **we** got it done without anyone telling us to do it. Whether the two guys in the duty section helped or not, I was going to get the job done.

What I wanted was to get more of that kind of feeling of accomplishment. I did not want a stinkin' day and a half off.

"Earth to Walsh" cut through the fog in my head. The chief was staring, glowering. "By the look on your face, I'd say you're about to puke. Are you? Going to puke?"

"No, Chief."

"What is it then?"

"I, uh, Chief, thanks. Very much, for the day off."

"Day and a half," he busted in.

"Day and a half. But. If it's all the same to you, I'd rather stay here and work."

What happened next felt like I had been standing on Krakatoa when it blew, and, somehow, miraculously, one tiny pillar of stone under where I was standing, remained intact all the way to the ocean floor.

A molten lava explosion of curse words spewed over, around, and at me. It didn't end quickly, but it did. End.

"Walsh. You are taking off the rest of today and all day tomorrow. If you are not in dress uniform and off the ship in fifteen minutes, I will put you on report for insubordination and disobeying a direct order."

He pushed me out of his way and muttered, "Shame they did away with walking the plank."

SLAM!!

After about three each of ticks and tocks, ET2 said, "Fourteen minutes left."

He went with me, and as I changed, he explained what I had done this time, since I obviously was too dumb to figure it out myself.

For the second time within a very short time, the chief had tried to give me what he thought of as a gift, and both times, I threw the gift back in his face. And threw them back in front of the other guys.

ET2 said, "You made the chief look bad. Twice. That's two strikes, Walsh. Think about that today while you're ashore screwing off. Here's your liberty card. Now, get the hell off my ship."

When I got to the quarterdeck, I found my division officer standing Officer of the Deck (OOD). I showed him my liberty card.

"The chief gave you the rest of the day off?" In that sentence, there was not only interrogative but also incredulity.

"Yes, sir. Over the weekend, I wasn't in the duty section, but I worked with the guys who were, and we fixed a problem with the Electronic Countermeasures System."

He handed back my liberty card with a "Huh."

I took the card and saluted. "Request permission to go ashore, Sir."

He returned the salute. "Permission granted. And Seaman Walsh, have a good time, but not **too** good a time. Understand?"

"I understand, Sir."

I saluted again. He returned it. I popped an about-face.

Behind me, the seaman standing Messenger of the Watch snickered.

My about-face had been a tweak too much military formality. Now if we'd been US Marines, it would've been appropriate. US Marines, it was said, had a broomstick rammed up their butts when they reported to Boot Camp, so they looked like they were standing at attention all the time, whether standing, marching, sitting, or even sleeping. The Messenger evidently thought someone had endowed me with a USMC broomstick, and wasn't Seaman Walsh a funny-looking wanna-be Marine?

I hung onto the handrails on the gangway to the pier. You walked a gangway from the ship to dry land. A gangplank, however, was a board to step off and fall into the ocean with anchor chain wrapped around you. Just then, there didn't seem to be a lick of difference between the two.

Behind me, the Messenger sniggered again.

I started walking. If there was a difference between the two planks, it didn't matter.

By the time I reached the end of the pier, I knew what I was going to do first.

I took a bus to the base chapel.

Inside, I had the place to myself. Light through the stained-glass windows filled the place with a warm, yellowish glow. I knelt on the kneeler in a back row pew and felt the warm, solemn silence settle over me. Like I had gotten into a giant bathtub upside down.

The reason I came to the chapel was because I remembered Sister Daniel in grade school. When Jimmie Joe had popped up to Sister, he cussed. Sister walked off the field and into church.

Jimmie Joe knew what he'd done, hung his head, and slunk off the field. The rest of us knew the game was over, and we walked off also. We had nowhere else to go, so we went to our classroom, sat, and waited for the end of recess bell. We boys waited in silence. That silence was electric with **_I wonder how much trouble we're in?!_**

The girls trickled in and sensed the troubled aura. They whispered as they took to their desks. Mildred Hemsath asked what was going on. Jimmie Joe confessed, and then the girls went quiet, too. It seemed strange. As more entered the room, the quieter it got.

The bell rang, Sister walked into the classroom, stepped up onto the one-step-high platform and stood behind her desk. She didn't say anything. She didn't have to. We got the message: **_<u>No cussing on the playground!!</u>_**

She didn't have to say the second part of her message either: **_<u>Even when I'm not there!!</u>_**

Then she commenced teaching as if nothing untoward had happened. But something very untoward HAD happened. At the end of classes that day, I felt like I had left the confessional with the admonition to *Go and sin no more* rattling around inside my empty skull where my mind was supposed to be.

Instead of going home, I entered the church and sat on the bench of a back-row pew. I wanted to see if I could figure out why Sister had gone into the church.

The Navy base chapel was just like our parish church some seven years prior. The harsh, bright colors filtered from the sunlight by the stained glass. The solemn silence.

Fifth grader Eddie Walsh sat there for what felt like a long time. Then he asked: *Are You here, God?*

God didn't answer, but It was like when Sister didn't say out loud: *No more cussing on the fribble-frapping playground*. A kind of telepathy happened. Eddie knew God was there.

Eddie felt good just sitting there. Which was a little weird, because Fifth-Grader Eddie Walsh could not ever remember just sitting and not doing anything. Except of course when he'd had chicken pox and again with measles and with mumps. Then, he had just wanted to sit or lie in bed and try to figure out whether it was better to endure the malaise with his eyes opened or closed.

I sat on the pew bench.

*Lord, I thought it would be a good thing if I fit in, felt at home with the guys on the ship, like it was even **my** ship. Twice this morning, that blew up in my face.*

After thinking about it, I guess they look at me like I'm a newbie, and they have expectations of how a newbie should behave. Actually, not the guys. It's the chief. He definitely has firm ideas as to how newbie seamen should behave.

So, maybe, God, with ET2, I should work at being seen but not heard. With the chief, maybe it's work to be neither seen nor heard.

Sister Mary Mark telling me I should have gotten an A popped to mind. I imagined her telling me, "You can't go all palsy-walsy with the chief."

I'm such a doofus, I told God.

And He answered me!

THERE ARE A LOT OF THINGS MUCH WORSE THAN BEING A DOOFUS.

CHAPTER SEVEN

Side Bunny Trail

A new question from Number Five just hit the inbox: Do you believe in a higher power?

Answer: No. I believe in The Highest Power. From early on, I believed in God and in the Almightiness of Him. That fifth-grade day in church, when He spoke to me, I came to believe in the personalness of Him as well. Almighty and Personal. How could those two things exist side-by-side? He is so Almighty, that He can be personal with each of the gazillions of people He created at the same time.

I hope you don't mind this SBT, but you see how this occurred. We were dealing with this very subject, and what happens? A question comes in with the perfect opportunity to flesh the story out. Could this "coincidence" come to be without God's fingerprints on it?

If I had a bippy to bet, I'd bet it that the Divine Prints were there.

/s/DDD (Dad duh Doofus)

PS: I thought I was ready to get back on the main trail, but I don't want to leave this SBT with you thinking that from fifth grade on, I was a pure, dedicated, unwavering disciple of Christ. I was not. In fact, my commitment to Him wavered before I completed fifth grade.

What happened was that when fall arrived, and we boys started playing football at recess, we thought we'd seen the last of Sister Daniel on the playground until Spring baseball season rolled around again. We played tackle football. Our imaginations were nowhere near powerful enough to picture us tackling Sister Daniel. Or her tackling us and getting dirt and sweat and snot and a little blood even on her white wimple collar. No way!

WAY!!

We'd assembled on the field and were choosing sides when who showed up? Why Sister Daniel. She had two white strips of cloth tucked under each side of the black waist sash around her black habit. When she ran with the ball, we were supposed to grab one of those strips of cloth instead of tackling her.

Flag football was for sissies. But—

"Understand?"

"Yes, Sister Daniel."

Well, we knew Sister could run from playing baseball with her.

What we hadn't seen before, though, was how her long arms made her the most effective straight-armer in the history of football. It seemed to take her team but a heartbeat to have us down eighteen to nothing. Sister received a kickoff. Ran it for a TD. She took a handoff from her quarterback. TD #2. She intercepted a pass Jimmie Joe was trying to get to me. She headed for the goal line and straight-armed three guys. Jimmie Joe was the last one to have a chance at grabbing one of Sister's flags, but she straight-armed him and sat him on his butt on the ground as he watched her score on the interception of **his** pass.

Sister's team kicked off to us. We made a few yards on the return. On the next play, Jimmie Joe called another pass to me. And I am pretty sure he wanted Sister to intercept again. Which she did. Only this time, with Jimmie Joe the last would-be flag grabber between Sister and the goal, JJ ducked under the straight arm and tackled her. There was a cloud of black habit and a little dust, and JJ got tangled up in Sister's dress. Which he got frantic to get free of.

"Jimmie Joe, stop squirming. You'll pull my clothes off."

It was like every angel between heaven and earth sucked in a huge breath of astonishment, so there was nothing left on earth but silence. Jimmie Joe went still. We all froze in place.

Then Sister grabbed the hem of her habit and hiked it up. We could see her ankles encased in black stockings, but she freed JJ, got to her feet, and started brushing dirt from her skirt.

"Boys. Go on with your game. I have to change my habit. I'll see you in the classroom."

Sister started walking away, and I looked up to follow her, and Whoa! What do my elevating eyeballs espy? SS. Sister Superior, the girls called her. The other gender called her Sister Sourpuss. That day, she was SS+.

Leaping to the end, SS+ got SD booted out of the convent. I was stunned and mad at God.

The Saturday after Jimmie Joe cussed on the ballfield, I served at a funeral Mass. The choir sang *Just a Closer Walk with Thee*. And that's what I thought Sister Daniel had shown me how to do: To walk closer with God.

God! How the heck could You let this happen?! You let them un-nun her!

I didn't walk close to God again for quite a spell.

Rejoin Main Trail

Back to the chapel on the east coast Navy base. Peace and calm flowed into the belly of my soul. I knew what I was. I was a doofus, and there were many things that were much worse.

And I remembered Sister Daniel. I thought she was holy enough for God but not nearly nunnly enough for SS++.

I left the chapel, went to the base exchange, bought stationery, took it to the library, and wrote to The Squeeze. After filling three pages on both sides, I checked out a William Faulkner book. I never tried to read one of his stories without a big dictionary to hand. The library's probably weighed thirty pounds.

So, as I was looking up a "Faulkner word," I ran across obsequious.

The word stopped me in my reading tracks.

I thought about holy, un-nunnly Sister Daniel.

I thought about SS+++ and my chief. Maybe chief+++.

TBGH

The base movie ate a quarter that would have gone into a phone during a call to The Squeeze. I didn't eat supper. Spending more Squeeze-talking-time on a burger was not going to happen. Heck, there were times working for Heiny when we had to beat the rain to get hay baled and in the loft before the storm cut loose. "Work," Heiny said. "You kin eat tomorrow." Suffering a little hunger for The Squeeze, just then, not a deal at all, especially not a big one.

I got back to the ship at 21:30, stamped and mailed the library-written letter, and was in my bunk five minutes before taps.

The next morning, I woke at 05:30, hit the head, donned my second dress uniform, obtained a new liberty card from ET2, snarfed down a honking big breakfast, and walked the plank at 06:37. The library didn't open until 09:00, so I spent more Squeeze quarters buying bus tickets and riding around town. I don't remember even looking out the window. What I did was think about the word obsequious and about fitting in and not fitting in.

Just before disembarking from the bus, I thought I understood. Checking aboard **the** ship—definitely not **my** ship—was sort of like when I was in third grade, and third-, fourth-, and fifth-grade boys chose sides to play recess baseball. As a newbie third grader, I was with the ones picked last. After a week, though, the fifth-grader team pickers understood that I could hit and field as good as they could. So, I started getting picked earlier in the selection process.

But the way it worked, I was teammates with a different crew every day. And I fit in with them for the duration of the game. Afterwards, I wasn't particularly close friends with any of them, and we went on about our personal business.

Getting along in the Navy, I also decided, was like getting along with both of Heiny Horstwessel's tractors. One was a Farmall. It had six or eight cylinders and produced power while purring. The other was a John Deere, a two-cylinder machine, and it went *putt putt putt.* The two tractors had different controls to elicit and manage either purr power or putt putt power, and I had to cater to the individual persnicketies of the machines. They did not adjust their behavior to my way of doing business. I had to adjust to theirs.

At the end of the bus ride, I felt like I had gotten something worthwhile out of the trip. I knew how I would approach life on the ship, which was worth way more than mindlessly observing the scenery of a place I really didn't care about.

At the end of the previous week, on **the** ship, I had felt like I fit in and acted that way. But the others thought I was a newbie and should act like that. Like a newbie. Newbies didn't fit in until the oldies nodded and said, "You know. That Eddie Walsh. He fits in now."

TBGH

Wednesday morning. I welcomed the day with open arms, elated that I did not have to take another day off.

EWTLB (Eddie's Words to Live By):

1. Don't speak unless spoken to.

2. You don't have to be obsequious, but you do have to be deferential.
3. Every day, give the Navy a Pop's day of work.
4. Get along with others, like I did with Heiny's tractors.

I didn't see the chief that day. I was pretty sure ET2 orchestrated things, so we didn't bump into each other. Before muster at 08:00, he sent me and an ET3 to Radio Central to work on a faulty receiver.

At 16:30 that Wednesday, ET2 told me, "Walsh, you're a real piece of work. Most sailors need a kick in the butt to impart effective correction. You, you need to be forced to take a day off."

He smirked, shook his head, and went ashore for the evening.

Both Thursday and Friday, I did encounter the chief in the ET Shop. During those occasions, I tried not to be noticed, and I thought he was trying not to notice me.

The weekend loomed as a worry. Was I going to be ordered to go ashore those days, whether I wanted to or not? I did not want to blow any more talk-to-the-Squeeze money.

As it turned out, I needn't have worried. At 16:00 on Friday, the chief stopped by the ET Shop with a message for all of us.

"We're going to sea bright and early Monday morning. Don't none of you dipwads get in trouble over the weekend trying to cram too much fun into too few days. *D'jou* understand that, or do I have to say it again and slower for you?"

"We understand, Chief," one of the ET3s said.

"And Monday morning, I do not want to find any of you hung over." Chief paused for a glower of exclamation. "Especially, you, Walsh. You liberty hound, you."

The guys burst out laughing. My cheeks blushed about one hundred watts of heat into the shop.

The chief walked out. The ET3s and the seamen followed, babbling like four brooks running side-by-side. ET2 stayed behind. He wore his dress whites and could have stepped out of a Navy recruiting poster. Impeccable uniform, standing straight at about five-nine or -ten, and,

WHAT AM I?

I thought, his eyes sparkling with recollections of exotic places the Navy had taken him.

"Walsh. I find it encouraging to learn that you are not nearly as dumb as you look."

He handed me my weekend liberty card, stepped to the door, put his hand on the knob, hesitated, and turned back.

"Don't screw it up."

I almost said, "I won't, Sir." But that would have been a screw-up.

In boot camp, we were taught to salute anything that moved because, at that point, every living creature on earth was senior in rank to us boots. We should salute sea gulls, dogs, snakes. Even maggots were senior to us, and we called everyone and everything, "Sir." Out here, in the real Nav, we called officers Sir. We **never** called senior petty officers—from chiefs to PO3s—Sir. Never.

With a little mind-muscle exertion, I managed, "Aye, ET2."

He smirked, gave me a tiny nod, and left.

I stood in the shop by myself, looking at the closed door, expecting it to tell me something profound. Finally, it did.

EWTLB #5. "Don't screw it up."

I wrote to The Squeeze, ate, and took in the movie on the Mess Deck. Watching a **free** movie spurred extra enjoyment.

Saturday morning, I told the Duty Section ET3 that I'd be aboard during the day, and if he needed any help, I was available.

"Nah. We're just testing the surface search radar. Not expecting any trouble."

"Well, I specialized in communications gear in school. Mind if I watch you guys?"

"Whatever floats your boat."

I interpreted the look he gave me as: "You didn't screw up, but you are stupid."

If to learn something, I had to spend coins of stupidity, I didn't mind. Spending those kinds of coins did not subtract phone-booth minutes with The Squeeze. That's what mattered.

All morning and for an hour after lunch, I observed the duty section guys check the functioning of the radar itself and then ensure each monitor received and displayed the signals properly. The learning experience approximated ET School, only better. I was my own teacher. I'd read the radar manual, studied the steps the manual laid out to check out the system, and watched the duty section guys "do it by the book." I was almost as proud of them as I was of myself.

I left the ship at 19:15. Through our letters, The Squeeze had informed me the best time to call her that weekend was Saturday, 20:00, East Coast time. On Sunday afternoon and evening she had what amounted to duty weekend. For her, this was logging time on the floor of the hospital attached to her nursing school and absorbing how to apply her book learning to actual patients.

On Fridays and Saturdays, it was hard to find an open phone booth, so I left the ship early enough to scout around a bit.

The phone booths near the pier were all occupied and had lines of sailors waiting for a turn to spend quarters. Outside the base exchange, I found an empty one and had to wait fifteen minutes for Mickey's big hand to point straight up before I could call. Calling early risked getting her roommate telling me, "Hi, Eddie, she isn't here." And losing three quarters and accomplishing something worse than nothing! Waiting was hard, but it was free.

Then, Mickey agreed it was time. A quarter clunked, and a dial tone droned, I dialed the number, I entered two more quarters, the phone rang, and "Eddie!"

I don't know. Maybe it was the week I'd just had, but the only thing I could think of was a line from "The King of Love my Shepherd is." My heart was transported on a tidal wave of delight, holy, heavenly, here on earth delight.

"Eddie?"

I cleared my throat and then was able to answer her.

CHAPTER EIGHT

My only disappointment Sunday was, at Mass, we didn't sing "The King of Love" hymn. But my soul refused to let that force it to disembark from the roller coaster of delight transporting it.

That afternoon, I watched the guys check out the air search radar. At 16:30, as the guys were wrapping up the job, the ET3 said, "Walsh, you know what you're really good at?"

I looked at him, knowing some kind of put-down was coming.

"You're really good at watching other people work. You should be an officer."

A couple of return shots popped through my mind, but I squashed them. What he said reminded me of NESEP (Naval Enlisted Scientific Education Program)—a title like that really makes a person appreciate acronyms, doesn't it?

Anyway, here's the background: During World War II, the Navy recruited a lot of college athletes. The thinking was they were competitive and wanted to win. But, during World War II, a plethora of technical things started entering the arsenal of weapons the Navy owned, such as radar, radios, communication, and navigation equipment. And God bless jocks everywhere, but not all of that group were masters of technical subjects.

In the fifties, the Navy decided they needed to infuse their officer corps with some engineering talent. They discovered they had some of that among the enlisted ranks in the technicians who repaired all those high falutin' gadgets with which the Navy equipped their ships and planes and subs. So, the NESEP program came to be.

In Boot Camp, our instructor told us about the program. "To get into NESEP, you have to take a test. It's designed to screen out applicants who'd be unlikely to hack college. Ninety percent of NESEP Group 1 graduated last year. They are ensigns now and performing well in the fleet." Our instructor closed out the lesson with: "If any of you Dumb Butts think you can hack college, put in for it when you get to the fleet. You just might surprise the hell out of yourself, and all the rest of us, and get selected."

What with the ups and downs of checking into the ship, and not fitting in, and then feeling comfortable and part of the ET shop and the crew, and then not again, I forgot about what I thought of as the only way on God's green earth Eddie Walsh would get to college: NESEP.

I resolved to talk to ET2 about it next week. At-sea next week.

I wrote an extra-stamp-required letter to The Squeeze and got it to the ship's post office by 20:45. Mail would close out at 21:00.

We were getting underway at 07:00 the next morning. The ship's mission was to station itself along the flight path of a Project Mercury rocket launch. It would be an unmanned capsule atop the rocket, a test, to make sure the thing would work properly. If it didn't work, we might be able to retrieve the astronaut capsule, or parts of it, so the engineers could figure out what went wrong.

And Eddie Walsh, ETSN and newbie from a hick Missouri farm town, was part of this. Part of the Holy-cow space program! That felt kind of good.

I reminded myself how how bad it turned on me when I let myself feel good about things too soon.

Sleep happened. And then waking before reveille. Normal, except for going to sea for the first time ever. The engineers who made steam for propulsion and the boatswain mates who handled the anchors and the lines securing our destroyer to the pier had had early wakeups. So did some of the radiomen and radarmen. They began standing watches at 04:00.

At 05:00, I reveille-d myself. The Mess Deck was open. I grabbed chow and went up to the 0-1 level to watch us get underway.

I'd asked the ET2 if we had any special duties for getting underway.

"Yeah. Don't get in the way of the Snipes and Deck Apes."

Snipes worked in the Engineering Department, making steam to generate electricity and power the propellors. Deck Apes were Deck Department guys responsible for handling the anchors and mooring lines. When they weren't doing those jobs, they chipped away rust and painted the hull to keep salt water from eating the ship out from under us.

That morning, the Snipes would be working below the main deck. Actually, they always worked down there. Another name for them was Bilge Rats. Everybody got branded with some term of endearment. The Apes would be on the pier and the main deck.

I should be out of the way on the 0-1 level, where we mustered at quarters. Besides me, only two newbie radiomen were there to observe us cutting our tie to dry land.

To starboard, all the ships on the far side of the pier had already departed save for a destroyer backing out into the channel and two tugboats pulling the cruiser from the head of the pier following the destroyer.

On the pier, two sailors, Deck Apes, from our ship stood by each bollard with mooring lines around it that ran to our ship and secured us to shore. A bollard, by the way, is a low, thick steel post affixed to a pier to which mooring lines secure a vessel. The bollard sailors looked like they were waiting for something, like a dog waiting for a man to toss the fetch-tennis-ball.

The ship's announcing system blared, "Now single up all lines."

The sailor pairs on the pier busted out of their anticipatory poses and went to work, freeing up two of the three lines running to each bollard.

Our destroyer had two smokestacks. At the same time the pier sailors sprang into action, the after stack belched a puff of black smoke.

I wondered what was going on down there in the engineering spaces. Did some of the snipes heave a scoop full of coal into a furnace? The only thing I could think of was Western movies showing such activity on locomotives just before the train was robbed by a gang of outlaws.

I decided to ask ET2 to help me get a tour of the engineering spaces, so I could figure out what all those guys did down there.

I sure never expected it to take six years before that would happen. It did happen, though, not until after the volunteer thing.

TBGH

Observing the ship get underway was interesting, even though I kept hearing the ET3's voice in my head telling me I was only good at watching people work. There did seem to be a good deal of work going on, and I was just watching. An inclination oozed out of the pit of the belly of my soul to say something to the spirit of the ET3 that I would have to confess when we got back to port. The spirit of Sister Daniel helped me shove the inclination back down where it belonged.

"Shift colors!" blared over the announcing system.

The signalmen had hoisted a rolled-up American flag to near the top of the forward mast. At that announcement, one of the signalmen tugged on a line, and the flag unfurled. A signal to all that we were underway. At the same time, I knew someone was on the fantail lowering the flag on the stern pole.

Underway. ETSN Walsh was underway. For the first time in his life.

As long as a couple of ferry boat rides across the Mississippi didn't count as being underway. Nah. Those would not count.

A couple of sayings popped to mind. "Sailors are meant to be on ships, and ships are meant to be at sea." From the moment of that "Shift colors," I, Eddie Walsh, was underway. And I was a sailor. Another saying: "Haze gray and underway," which meant you come into port to touch up the gray paint job, then head back out to sea again, where you were meant to be.

The Toto in the back of my head said, "Eddie Walsh, we for sure ain't in Missourah no more."

This Toto sounded like he came from the Ozarks. To get to Kansas, he'd have traveled through Missour … i. So, he'd know about our state, too.

Until that getting underway moment, I viewed the whole US Navy as if ninety-five percent of its sailors were electronics technicians.

I did the math. Bodies assigned to the ET Shop divided by the size of the crew = Poop! We made up less than three percent.

2.6666666666666666666666666666666666 … etcetera, if you are looking for precision.

Which slammed me back onto the steel deck from the lofty heights to which my spirits had rocketed with seeing myself as a sailor and being where we sailors were meant to be. I realized the ship could not have gotten underway without the Deck Apes and the Snipes, but it sure could have without us ETs.

I shook my head to clear it of the world Toto created for me so I could behold the one God had created.

Our ship backed away from the pier, pivoted, and started down the channel. The rest of the Navy piers and the rest of the harbor slid past to either side, and ahead lay nothing but smooth, dark-blue water under a cloudless, light-blue sky.

Suddenly, I staggered a bit. It was as if Poseidon had risen from the deep, shoved against our starboard bow, and said, "Hey! Watch where you're going!"

The ship had only leaned a couple of degrees, and it quickly righted itself. But then it happened again. A roll to port, followed by a return to straight up and down. A pattern, regular as clockwork. Roll to port, return to upright. I walked to the starboard side and saw it then. Swells coasting toward our ship, regularly spaced, not very high, but stretching away farther than I could see.

Understanding what caused that motion helped. It was like: *Oh. I get it. Those things are swells. I read about them.*

I checked my watch. 07:50. Almost time to muster in the shop. The wind had picked up. I removed my Dixie Cup white hat so it wouldn't blow over the side.

After crossing to the port side, I descended to the main deck on the aft-facing ladder. I burped up a bubble of gas, leaving a vinegary taste in my mouth. After muster, I thought I'd get a cup of mess deck coffee. That'd wipe away the vinegar residue hanging onto my taste buds.

Facing forward, I espied the guys from the shop standing by the guard rail outside the door into the athwartship passageway. They were smoking, drinking coffee from paper cups, talking, and laughing.

As I walked up to them, Gutter said, "Hey, Eddie."

The other ETSN said, "Where were you?"

"01 level. Watching us get underway."

The weekend duty section ET3 then told the guys they found out what Seaman Walsh was really good at. "Watching other people work."

They laughed. Someone opened the watertight door, and they started filing into the passageway.

"That Eddie Walsh," one of them said, "a man of many talents."

I was about to follow them when I spun around, leaned on the rail, and power puked up breakfast. I muscled up some spit and spat.

What the crap just happened!

It never occurred that I was seasick. Looking out at the ocean, aside from those not-very-big-at-all swells, the ocean was baby-butt smooth. I'd heard that phrase before to describe a particularly calm sea state.

I stood at the rail, waiting to see if I'd hurl again. Again, I wondered how I could be sick with such gentle seas. There was a rocking motion that I barely noticed. Looking forward, the ship sliced a path through the sea, curling back a big wave from the bow. But it all felt so … baby butt smooth. *What the heck?!*

My wristwatch showed 07:59. Muster.

I didn't think I was going to puke again, at least not right away.

I entered the passageway and dogged the watertight door. I felt not quite right. When I opened the door to the shop, the chief was speaking to the other ETs, and he kept talking as he turned his head to look at me. Then his mouth stopped. For a moment.

"The hell's the matter with you?!" The chief reached out and laid the back of his paw against my forehead. "No fever. They feed you a rotten egg for breakfast?"

I spun around, undogged the door to the weather deck, and

hurried to the rail, leaned over, and my stomach felt like it was trying to turn itself inside out, like I had swallowed a shoe worn by a guy who never washed his feet, and that stinking shoe desperately wanted out of there.

Nothing came up, though, but a vinegary dew coated my tongue and made me grimace, gag, and cough. A hand grabbed my shoulder.

Gutter said, "Chief told me to make sure you didn't fall overboard."

Later, GM told me what the chief really said, which was, "If Walsh doesn't fall overboard, shove him over." And for about a week, I didn't think he really meant it. Of course, the whole of that week, the only thing I thought about was to wish I was dead.

Gutter took me to sick bay. We did not have a doctor aboard, rather a first class hospitalman, like a nurse practitioner today. He told us all he could offer was a motion sickness pill, but generally, for them to be effective, you had to take them before you went to sea.

"But if you want to try it, I'll give you one."

"I'll try anything," I moaned.

He handed me a pill and a paper cup filled with water.

The pill sat on my tongue okay; then I sipped the water.

I had no idea a man could puke water out his nose. You learn something new every day in the Navy.

The rest of the water and the tiny white pill made it into the trash can in a corner of the sick bay.

Behind me, Doc said, "Gutter Mouth, you brought me one seasick sailor. His name isn't Cecil, is it?"

I knew he was referring to Cecil, the seasick sea serpent, from the *Time for Beany* TV show. My sister loved that cartoon. I wished I felt good enough to feel insulted.

I spent the morning and half the afternoon lying on the deck in the storage area behind the ET Shop. Chief found me there and invited Gutter to get me the hell out of there.

Gutter helped me down to the compartment and up into my bunk. I pretty much stayed there. I sure did not want to get up and go to the chow hall. The only good thing about our compartment, it was the farthest forward. The farthest from the mess deck smells, so mouth-watering before "Shift colors!"

I do remember getting up that first night to brush my teeth to get the taste of oily vinegar off my tongue. Colgate and vinegar. That taste combination made my stomach forget it was empty and think I had swallowed another shoe.

After dry "urk, urking" at the sink for a while, I turned to go back to my bunk with a worse taste in my mouth than when I'd entered the head. I felt dizzy and hung onto the sink. My head hurt. The rest of me did not hurt, but there was an intense feeling of something just ain't right here from my Adam's apple to my belly button. My arms and legs felt constructed of weakness, not muscle. I contemplated just lying down on the floor—and I didn't care if the Navy wanted me to call it a deck.

But my brain went to work and dredged up enough revulsion at lying on **that** surface to propel me back to the compartment. There, I had to convince my arms and legs that they were not just along for the ride; they had to get us up onto the top bunk.

Once up there, I collapsed into my two-inch-thick mattress pad and closed my eyes, but there was no sleep to be found behind those closed lids. My mind fired questions:

- How the crap, Eddie the Seasick Sea Serpent Walsh, can you be so sick when the ocean outside is so baby-butt smooth?
- Did anyone ever die from seasickness? If so, God, please let it come soon. If not, please, God, let me be the first.
- Lord, can You let this bitter cup pass from me? On this one, I had to work really hard to append, "But not my will, Thine, be done."
- Two more years to serve out my enlistment; how will I handle two more years of this?

I managed to get up a couple of times at night, when no one else was about, and cup a handful of water at a sink in the head. I sipped just a handful. I didn't want a puddle of water to form in my belly.

I lost track of what day it was. It didn't matter.

Then, a miracle happened.

Thank You, Holy Mary, Mother of God, and Father, Son, and Holy Spirit!!!!"

I was cured!

CHAPTER NINE

I'd been sleeping; then a noise woke me. It came from forward, all the way forward. I recognized it.

The Deck Apes had dropped the anchor. The sound was the anchor chain rattling out the hawse pipe.

"Shift colors," came over the 1MC.

That meant the anchor connected us to land again. The US flag would be hauled down from the forward mast and raised on the fantail pole.

My headache was gone.

Between my Adam's apple and belly button, it felt normal.

And thirsty. And hungry.

I climbed down and hit the head. I brushed my teeth, shaved, showered, brushed again, and donned a work uniform. No way the chief would let me go on liberty. It didn't matter. I had no reason to want to go ashore. I wouldn't be able to afford a call to The Squeeze from San Juan, Puerto Rico. Although feeling dry land under my feet held some appeal. Bottom line, though, I owed the chief five days of work.

My belt, I noticed, cinched tight with a fair amount of extra belt extending from the buckle. I was pretty darned hungry.

Food! Glorious food! And they served **BACON** that morning. Smelling it was almost as good as eating it.

Thank You, God!

WHAT AM I?

The blessings just kept coming that morning.

When I forked up the last morsels of breakfast, I had to restrain myself from licking the aluminum tray. Then, as I placed the tray on the conveyor belt into the scullery, my stomach felt like I had stuffed a basketball in there, but there was not the least hint that my organ of digestion would rather bark up breakfast than do the work God intended it to do. I did step through the door into the midship passageway leading aft. I loosened my belt a bit; then I reentered and passed through the mess deck to the passageway leading forward and to the ET Shop.

I knew I was going to get some kidding from the guys, you know, along the lines of being Cecil The Seasick Sea Serpent. But I felt so dang good! It would take more than a little hazing to smack me down. *Eddie Walsh can handle whatever they throw at him.*

Eddie Walsh opened the door to the shop. They were all there. They all looked at Eddie like he was a Deck Ape or a Snipe. Like he did not belong in the ET Shop one tiny, teensy little bit.

"Well! What have we here?!!" Chief eyed me like he was a fox, and I was the only chicken in the hen house. "You guys ever seen a walking talking boar (crude three letter word signifying a mammary goes here) before?"

> Note: I'd heard the term in boot camp, and before that. Growing up, farmers bringing grain to the elevator used the term when they talked about cows. Mostly.

The chief informed me I was never to enter his shop again; then he ordered me to report to the first-class radarman for compartment cleaning duties starting immediately.

> Another note: On … the ship, seamen (E3) and seaman apprentices (E2) all did ninety days of compartment cleaning or mess cooking (KP) each year. Once you made third-class petty officer, you were exempted from those menial duties. There was one exception to the rule. ETs did not do compartment cleaning or mess cooking.

So, the other ETSN and I did not have to muck out compartments, heads, or the cooking areas. ETs were a small group of specially trained technicians and were not to be wasted on those menial chores.

But, because I got seasick, well, okay, sick when the ocean was baby butt smooth, I was no longer worth a hoot to the chief. Not even worth half a hoot.

The chief glared at me, as if his eyes were trying to fry my orbs of observation.

I stood there trying to figure out what the heck happened to my glorious morning.

I'd seen that look once before. Back in fifth grade, when Jimmie Joe tackled Sister Daniel on the playground, and SS (Sister Superior) had gotten Sister Daniel booted out of the convent; then SS wound up having to teach both sixth, seventh, and eighth grades as well as third, fourth, and fifth. Sister-oh-so-Superior would look at us fifth-grade boys—wearing that ET Chief look—from the step high platform at the front of the room. And I had never known what label to attach to "that look." But then, with chief mirroring exactly SS+++'s look, hate seemed appropriate.

TBGH

I found the first-class radarman in CIC.

"Walsh, your chief told me you are now my compartment cleaner. Follow me. Hustle. I don't want to miss the first liberty boat."

We descended to the compartment. First Class showed me where cleaning supplies were stored and informed me what was expected in terms of overall cleanliness in the berthing compartment and the head, when the announcement came, "The first liberty boat departs in five minutes."

A string of PO1 cuss words goes here. The look First Class laid on me wasn't hate, more like something that started as dismay, graduated to disappointment, and solidified into disgust.

This look I'd also seen before. From Mom. I was in fourth grade. My brother Lenny and I were gathering eggs from the henhouse, and we found a nest full of funny-colored ones. I thought they must have gone rotten.

As Lenny emptied a nest, I threw one of my rotten ones at him. Smacked him right in the middle of his back. "Hey," he said, and reached behind. His hand came away covered with egg mess. He got mad and started firing back at me. I dodged his throws and laughed at him, which made him madder, and he threw more eggs at me.

Mom heard the ruckus we were making, poked her head out the back door, and saw Lenny throw something at me. She saw it splat on the ground and knew what we were throwing.

We both got industrial-strength spankings.

It turned out Mom had Dad get a couple of ducks. She wanted to raise them, and then she planned on, occasionally, serving us duck for supper, instead of fried chicken all the time.

So, we'd derailed the duck-for-supper plan, and busted one whole night's worth of laying work by all the chickens. Six days a week, Mom sold eggs to the grocery store. But that day, she couldn't.

The look she laid on Lenny and me right before administering the aforementioned spankings was the same look the PO1 laid on me for making him miss the first liberty boat.

PO1 did not spank me, but he did say, "This compartment and the head better be sparkling clean when I get back tonight!"

The PO1 stomped out of the compartment. Outside our berthing space, a ladder led up to the main deck. He stomped up that, too. I knew he stomped all the way back to the fantail to wait for liberty boat number two. I couldn't hear that stomping though.

Around me, guys were climbing out of their bunks. A few still slept. A snorer among them. Nowhere near the milling body count after underway reveille. The senior POs in the compartment had already left. They'd catch a ride ashore on the first or second liberty boat. The PO3s might catch a seat on the third, and the seamen would most likely have to wait for the fourth boat. I wouldn't be able to do any cleaning until the guys cleared out of the compartment and the head.

And I hadn't written to The Squeeze all week. I'd just laid in my bunk wallowing in misery or hovered over a commode, and when I wasn't barfing, I wished I could upchuck the misery I felt. But the seasickness itself could not be puked up.

A wave of something like seasickness swept over me. And maybe something like panic. If she didn't receive letters from me, she'd stop sending hers to me. Until it was time to send the "Hit the road, Eddie Walsh" letter.

I took my stationery box from my locker and headed for my bunk. A lot of letters to The Squeeze were written with me propped on my elbows and writing away. That morning, though, with the basketball of eggs, bacon, and hash browns in my belly, that definitely would not work. Chief had told me to never come into the ET Shop again. I couldn't go there.

In the aft starboard corner of the compartment, there was a cranny between some lockers and the bulkhead. Just wide enough for my behind. I took my laundry bag from the end of my bunk and sat on it in that cranny. I wrote "Dearest." Then, I wrote the date at the top. My pen didn't know what to write next.

If I told her about getting seasick, about the chief not wanting me to be an electronics technician anymore, she'd think: *Eddie Walsh, he's not an electronics technician. All he knows how to do is be a janitor. Marry him? Not only* **no,** *but* **HECK NO!**

If I didn't write about it, it was the same as lying to her. A sin of omission.

A picture formed in my head. I saw Moses hand me a two-page stone tablet. On one page was written: Thou shalt not lie to The Squeeze. The second stone page contained: Not ever.

Pop told me once, "Before a man starts a job, he oughta' think about it for a minute."

I always thought that "a" between "for" and "minute" needed to be **A.** A minute. Not a minute plus a tick or a tock. That'd be the biggest waste of time there is.

I wrote: "I got seasick."

Then I proceeded to spill my guts—sorry, but it's staying. I also wrote that the thing I felt worst about was not writing to her for five dad-burned whole stinking days. I filled up the front side of a page. When I started writing on the back side of the sheet of paper, I was back into my writing-a-letter-to-The-Squeeze space.

I finished the second side of the sheet and noticed the bodies/square foot of deck space ratio had diminished quite a bit. There was room for me to get about cleaning the compartment.

Stash stationery in locker. Rehang dirty laundry bag on bunk. Get push broom.

I stood at the cleaning gear locker for a moment.

Congratulations, Eddie Walsh. After completing grade school, high school, boot camp, and ET School, you are now right back to where you were in third grade. Doing girl work. Except now it's for four dozen guys, not just your weensy little family.

Then I remembered Pop giving me to Heiny Horstwessel, and I learned that man work could be even messier than girl work, and how messy it was didn't matter. Getting the work done mattered.

A voice in my mind told me, "Think for A minute."

There was no need to say, "Yes, Pop." That'd be the biggest waste of time there is.

Sweep half the deck in the compartment. Swab half the deck in the compartment. While the deck was drying, clean the commodes and urinals in the head. By that time, it was almost lunch time. The basketball in my stomach had reduced to volleyball size, and I wasn't sure if I was hungry or not.

I had an urge to use one of the shiny clean commodes and discovered that seasickness is a gift that keeps on giving. If I were to measure the severity of my seasickness on a scale of one to ten, I'd had an eleven. I had had nothing to eat since Monday, and what I'd eaten that morning came right back up and out the same portal through which it went in. Also, I had had very little to drink. Water had stuck around my stomach for the same length of time as the food.

What I wound up with was constipation registering on the misery scale between eleven and thirteen point five.

Note: The reader will be spared further clinical details regarding this particular discomfit.

TBGH

Saturday night. 2300. I was sleeping when the sound of someone barfing woke me. It was the biggest guy residing in the berthing space. A six-foot, three-inch seaman. Drunker than a skunk. Two of his buds had been trying to get him into his middle bunk in the stack of three, when Skunk Drunk power puked. He fouled his own bunk plus the one above him and the one below him. And that one was occupied.

Probably a third of the bunks were occupied. The rest of the compartment dwellers were still ashore.

One of the awakened accused Eddie Walsh of having puked all over the compartment, which elicited a litany of curses aimed at me. It made me mad, being blamed for somebody else's barf. Time was, when I heard, saw, or smelled vomit, I'd engage in sympathetic activity of the exact same sort. But that night I was mad. When I'd been seasick, I worked hard to not make a mess someone else would have to clean up. Just then, I was automatically blamed for **someone else's** mess of extraordinary magnitude.

Heck yeah, I was mad.

Some of the guys climbed out of their bunks, pulled on pants, all the while cussing me, and left, still swearing. Some rolled over and snugged their pillows over their heads.

Git up, I told myself, before any of those who lived in the dark corners of my mind could say it.

I climbed down. *Don't put on pants.* For what needed doing, that'd be the biggest waste … you know.

"How about getting out of your liberty uniforms and help me get him to the head," I sort of asked, sort of ordered Skunk Drunk's buds.

We parked SD (Skunk Drunk) on his butt in one of the showers. Then we took off his fouled shoes and uniform and tossed everything into the other shower stall. We turned the water on SD.

I asked Bud1 to rinse out all the dirty clothes in the one shower, and to Bud2, "Try to keep him from drowning."

Then, I checked on the two commode stalls. One in pristine condition. The other, not so pristine. SD had befouled the stall walls and the deck. It didn't look like he got even the tiniest morsel of upchuck in the commode. **Of course. Why would I expect anything to be easy?** The commode would have to wait.

I went to the compartment and cleaned up the mess there. It took a half hour for the smell of cleaning solvent to rise to eye-watering level and exile the other stench.

We got SD dried off, into clean skivvies, onto his clean bunk, and left him there snoring like a Paul Bunyon chainsaw.

The Buds told me SD had also fouled the passageway outside the compartment. They cleaned that while I went back to the head.

By 0200 that Sunday morning, we had the berthing compartment, the passageway, and the head smelling chemical rather than biologic. I wasn't very mad anymore. Mostly, I was grateful to SD's Buds. They'd helped. A lot. While everyone else beat feet out of the compartment or went back to sleep. Those who stayed probably mouth-breathed.

Bud1 said, "(cuss word goes here), Walsh. I don't know what kind of ET you are, but you are one hell of a compartment cleaner."

Bud2 said, "He does know something about puke."

TBGH

Sunday. 0500. My eyes popped open. *Skunk Drunk?*

I climbed down from my top bunk and checked on him. Most of us in the compartment kept a red lens flashlight in the glovebox-sized storage space attached to our bunks. In case the ship lost power, we wouldn't be blind. That's what I'd been told.

The red light showed SD on his stomach, still zonked. He looked like he could easily sleep until Wednesday. He was breathing. The **most** important thing was he hadn't puked again.

Besides SD, Monday's POD—Plan of the Day, in case you've forgotten—was on my mind. It said: "Underway at 08;00."

I had two motion sickness pills to take that Sunday, so I headed for the head to pop the first one. I opened the door, and it was as if someone hurled a big bucket of puke smell on me. More liberty hounds had come back to the ship drunk, just not quite skunk drunk.

Dear God! Enough with puke—.

I stopped that thought dead in its tracks and formulated the eleventh commandment: *Thou shalt not fuss at God. Not ever.*

CHAPTER TEN

The first thing I did was go to a sink, the cleanest of the three, pop one pill into my mouth, cup up a handful of water, and swallow.

My stomach welcomed its visitors. The pill and the water behaved themselves.

And, so, to the mess of others.

Someone had barfed into one of the commodes but hadn't flushed it away. I flushed six times. The bowl still needed a scrubbing out, but at least nothing had gotten on the deck. In the next commode, wads of bloody toilet paper floated in that bowl. Two flushes swooshed that away. A couple of dull red blops stained the deck.

Flushing that first commode hadn't diminished the vomit smell one tiny bit. Then, I found it. Somebody had barfed into a urinal. If I flushed that, it would flood all the vomit and a fair amount of seawater onto the deck making a not-very-big job honking big.

To the cleaning gear locker and then to work.

I was mucking out the urinal when the first class radarman, the senior man in the compartment, entered. "JudasPriestgagamaggot!" The way PO1 said it, there were no spaces between the words.

He hadn't uttered a single curse, though. I found myself being disappointed. I couldn't swear, and normally, sailor talk made me uneasy. But that vomit-filled morning, I found myself wanting a proxy cusser. Someone who would swear for me so I would not have to commit the sin myself, but I'd still get all the benefits of having cussed other people's puke to kingdom come. That made sense to me all the way until I started writing to The Squeeze that evening.

That's when I figured out adopting a proxy cusser made me guilty of not only my sin but the cusser's sin as well. As soon as we got back to homeport, I was going to have to confess to vicarious cussing. It occurred to me that my conscience was better at its job when I felt connected to The Squeeze, even through writing a letter to her.

Back to that Sunday morning, It turned out the PO1 had been rousted from sleep in the middle of the night by the messenger of the watch because one of his subordinate sailors had been involved in a fight in a bar in town. He was being held by the Shore Patrol (SP). PO1 and his division officer had to go to town and get their belligerent rowdy released into their custody. The two of them had left the ship before the Skunk Drunk episode and returned after the Buds and I had cleaned up the messes. The sailor who'd bled in the head was a signalman. He'd gotten away from the scene of the fight before the SPs showed up.

The PO1 shaved while I cleaned. Before he left the head, he noticed the bags of soiled laundry and bedding stashed in a corner behind the showers. He asked about them, and I explained.

"When I got back to the ship this morning, I thought I smelled cleaning solvent. I was totally pooped, though." PO1 shook his head. "One of the problems with a division full of newbies, is that this is the first outside-the-US port they've pulled into. They all act like they can get away with anything once they're away from the US of A. And they all have to learn by experience that just because they are on foreign soil, that doesn't mean their bodies can handle more booze than they can back home."

PO1 stuffed his shaving gear into his Dopp Kit and looked at me. "Walsh, I'm halfway, sorta, almost glad your chief sent you here to clean the compartment."

I wasn't quite so enthusiastic about the assignment.

TBGH

Monday morning, I got up and went to the head at 05:00. The first thing

I did was to thank God that the guys coming back from the beach the night before had not imbibed to the level of the Saturday-night excesses.

I set to giving the space and its appliances a quick cleaning, so the first users had a clean spot to shave, make a deposit, or shower. After reveille and the invasion of the unwashed, I went to the mess decks. There I ate one piece of bacon, a small bite of scrambled eggs, and a piece of toast. And, I drank some water.

After eating, I returned to the head and cleaned up the mess the guys had left. It was a puke-less mess, and I appreciated the heck out of that.

Just as I finished the second cleaning of the head, the anchor chain started clanking in the hawse pipe. Raising the anchor, the chain passed through the hawsepipe slowly, like: *Clank,* pause, *clank,* pause. When we'd arrived in San Juan and the deck apes dropped the anchor, it rattled out the pipe like a freight train rolling down the tracks at seventy miles an hour.

I remembered being on my bunk still feeling sick as a dog when the anchor rattled out, signaling we were attached to land again.

And I had experienced a miracle. I'd been cured!

That had to mean the seasickness was some misguided thinking going on in my head, didn't it? So, I hadn't really been seasick. I only imagined it. If I knew I had only imagined being sick, I should be able to squash that imagined malady flatter than the pancakes they'd served at breakfast.

*I am **not** getting seasick again!*
Eddie Walsh had decided. Eddie Walsh had spoken.

> Note: Above I could have written, "I, Eddie Walsh, had decided" to avoid a total slip from first to third person. But do you see how very appropriate those two short sentences seem in third, vice wasting two letters I and four commas?

There was a vibration through the hull. It meant the ship was swinging about to head out to sea. A moment later, the vibration stopped. I sensed the ship moving toward the open ocean. We'd been underway about an hour when I developed a headache. It wasn't a big one, but a dull ache like someone had gently hacksawed into my forehead about two inches. A general feeling of uneasiness filled me from my sawn into brain down to below my belly button. One thing was different this time. The overall distress was not strange to me.

In one other way it was different from when we left homeport. Then, I hadn't felt bad until after I barfed. And it surprised the heck out of me. This time I expected to blow chunks (despite my resolution), but so far, I hadn't. I was into cleaning the head and feeling bad was no excuse to **not** get the job done.

After the head, I started on the berthing compartment. Like a week ago, the overall feeling of unwellness intensified, and I thought all I wanted to do was to lie down. But, last week, lying down had not made me feel any better. And I had two years to do in the Navy. They would not let me spend it in bed.

So, I cleaned. And I learned I did not have to let feeling miserable keep me from getting my job done.

I thought about what I had eaten and where it resided. *Stomach, you do not have to feel bad because all the rest of us body parts are miserable for you. So, you don't have to feel that way. We are doing that for you, and all you have to do is to hang onto that tiny little breakfast. Easy peasy, see?*

Mr. Stomach *urped* a burp flavored with a hint of vinegar.

I told my brain to remind all my body parts that we hadn't really been seasick on the trip to San Juan, that it had all been imagined. I will confess that with my brain feeling like it had been hacksawed, I wasn't sure it would be effective controlling a misbehaving imagination. But, I gritted my teeth, just like I'd done my second morning facing Heiny Horstwessel's runny cow poop, and I resumed cleaning the compartment.

This time at sea, the ocean was not baby-butt smooth. Our berthing compartment was the farthest forward. The ship rose, and I felt something press me down, like I was pulling Gs. This lasted some seconds. Then the bow fell, and I felt like I almost floated on the air. It made it hard to walk and awkward to work. It made me mad.

I paid attention to how the ship moved, and I figured out how to time the risings and fallings. Working was slower, but it was still getting done. With a few other lessons to learn, like not using more than a half bucket of water.

At 1130, I'd finished cleaning. I went up to the O-1 level to check the ocean. Yep, a long way away from smooth. White capped waves rolled at us relentlessly, ceaselessly. A stiff breeze tugged at my shirt.

Off to port, another destroyer plowed through the waves. It had a sharp, pointy bow compared to the ship I rode on. Oh, phooey. I'm just going to say **my** ship. My ship had a bulbous bow. Sharp-pointy-bow ship rose on a wave, then plunged, and sometimes the bow buried itself under the surface. Then the bow would come shooting up out of the water again flinging a great cloud of seawater into the wind, which ripped it aft.

Just beyond the destroyer bobbing about like a toy boat in a bathtub with two rowdy boys, sailed a larger ship, a cruiser. It rode the waves serenely, sedately, steadily, so unbothered by the sea state. I imagined the larger ship saying: "Waves? I don't see no waves, Man."

Eddie wondered: *If I'd been assigned to the cruiser, would that have kept seasickness at bay?*

Wishing for a big boat when all you got is a small one, why that's the biggest waste of time there is.

Eddie shook his head to clear Pop out of there.

Shaking your head to clear me outta—

Yeah, yeah, Pop!

Eddie watched the destroyer plowing through the waves, then noticed how his ship would rise on a wave, but after passing the wave crest and falling, the bulbous bow kept it from sinking below the surface. *If my ship had had that sharp pointy bow, I'd be soaking wet now.*

Watching all that was interesting. For a moment, I'd forgotten about not feeling well. But the headache, the nausea, they came back.

The most amazing thing was I hadn't puked. Now here I confess a **yet** is desperate to hang on the end of the preceding.

It was lunchtime, and I really was not hungry, but I had determined I could not go another week without anything to eat. And I had to get water down to keep Mr. C. away. (Mr. C. would be constipation.)

On the mess decks, I made three one-piece-of-bread-folded-over peanut butter sandwiches. One, I forced myself to nibble the whole thing down. The other two I wrapped in paper napkins and took with me. If I puked, I was going to make myself eat a sandwich and try to keep it down. It seemed like a good idea to have a spare for that plan.

I made it back to the head forward of our compartment before the PBS (Peanut Butter Sandwich) came back up, which I neatly deposited into a commode. Before I flushed, though, the bow rose exceptionally high, on what must have been an above-average-height wave. I staggered but stood against the extra G-force going up. Then at the top of the rise, the bow seemed to hesitate there for an instant, then it plunged, and I felt like I'd go airborne, but I braced myself against the walls of the stall. I leaned over while the bow fell.

Suddenly, a geyser of flushing salt water, with pieces of PBS along for the ride, shot out of the commode and into my face. The bow started another but gentler rise. A spike of panic shot through me.

I imagined someone seeing me and spreading the word. "You should have seen seasick Eddie Walsh. He puked into a commode, and the commode puked it right back on him. The look on his face, man!"

I looked around. No one was there. *Thank You, God.*

But the mess from the geyser commode—I named it Old Faceful—included bits of PBS stuck to the overhead. I had to use the mop to clean that. Using a step ladder sure wouldn't work the way the ship was moving.

Old Facefull erupted a couple more times that afternoon, but it was just sea water and so the mop got a workout.

That afternoon, nobody used the head. The PO1, I found out, had warned the newbies in our compartment about Old Faceful—though he didn't call it that, and I sure wasn't going to tell him I did—and they used facilities farther aft where geysers did not erupt.

What happened, Gutter told me, was when the bow rose on a big wave, the exit port for the commodes sewer pipe in our head was normally below the surface, but in heavy seas, the exit port rose above the surface, and all the water in the sewer pipe drained out. Then, when the bow crashed back into the water, it caused sea water to gush back into the sewer pipe and erupt out of the commode. Rather forcefully. Understanding the physics of what happened did nothing to assuage the disgust I felt over the commode puking on me.

Another chore I had to do that afternoon was to retrieve the sacks of clothes and bedding from the ship's laundry. After dragging the bags back to the compartment, I tossed the clean items onto the owners' bunks. Note: All the items had a sailor's name stenciled on it somewhere. Underwear, dungaree shirts and pants, the white dixie cup hats. The name was printed on the inside of most items, like the hats. Socks went into a small mesh bag with the sailor's name printed on that. A couple of times during that chore, I forgot to feel bad, but the illness never moved far away.

One thing I thought I learned that afternoon was that keeping busy at something made bearing the unsettledness somewhat more bearable.

Suppertime surprised me. On the way to San Juan, time dragged as if so much agony hung from the big hand of my watch, it could barely move.

So, for supper, I ate the other PBS. And an apple. I did not want to catch scurvy on top of seasickness. And I drank water. Mr. Constipation could just stay the crap—maybe heck would be better here—away.

The residents dribbled back into the compartment during the evening. They made me think of the Peanut's character, Pig Pen. They didn't trail a cloud of visible dust, but they left messes in their wakes. Cleaning up after them took me to 21:00.

Then I climbed up onto my bunk and lay on my stomach to write to The Squeeze. I worried about laying on my supper, but it was the best position from which to write. I was not going to go another week without completing at least one page each night.

At 21:50, I stashed the two pages I'd written in my locker, brushed my teeth, and climbed back up onto my bunk. The bow was still rising, hovering at the peak, then dropping back down. Over and over and over again. It wasn't like rocking my sister when she was a baby, but throughout the day, it was something that couldn't be fought. Not fighting it wasn't anywhere near to liking it, but, at some point during that day, I stopped trying to fight it.

Fighting something you couldn't beat, why, that would be the biggest waste of time there is.

I rolled onto my back and closed my eyes and was halfway asleep when taps came over the 1MC. As soon as that clicked off, I fell the rest of the way into dark, delicious sleep.

TBGH

Panic ripped me wide awake. I was falling. Like a ton of lead. Like I'd stepped off the end of the world. I was trying to decide whether to scream or not when I noticed the overhead above me in the dim red light.

On the ship.

Then I hit bottom. The bottom was soft, well, Navy bunk soft.

A rattling of buckets came from the cleaning gear locker. Curses rattled from all over the compartment, many of them beginning with: "What the—."

Next came a round of quite colorfully phrased invitations to the newbies in the compartment to kindly be quiet and go back to sleep.

This was followed by the announcement from the bunk below mine: "Oh God! I wet the bed."

It was 0330. I was pretty sure I was done sleeping for that night. I was right.

It was hard to walk in the compartment. The bow pitched and fell and rolled side-to-side as well. You had to hang onto something to stay upright.

Three of the guys staggered and struggled their way to the head to puke. One of them was me. The other two headed to the commodes and puked and the commodes geyser puked right back at and over them. I **barfed** in the trashcan under the sinks. Then I rinsed my mouth out and swallowed a little water. I said, "Urk," but the water stayed down.

That familiar misery occupied my body, from my half-hacksawed brain to my belly button. It felt like a solid log of misery with my ears and arms stuck on the sides, and my legs dangling from the bottom. All I wanted to do was to crawl back up onto my bunk. I was pretty sure I wouldn't be able to sleep. I just wanted to feel miserable **there.**

A boy don't hafta feel good to work!

CRAP! Then I worried Pop could hear me think: Crap.

I helped Geyser Puke guys, one at a time, shower and make it their bunks.

Bed Wetter had peeled off his skivvies and left them on the deck. I attended to his mess.

The sea was rough all the rest of the day. There was plenty of work to do, and though the log of misery forming the core of me was there, I got the work done. And I did not throw up again. The roughest sea state I'd ever experienced, and it was only a One Puke Day.

Holy crap!

I mean: *Thank You, God.*

The next day, the sea had calmed down considerably, not all the way to baby-butt smooth, but a heck of lot more peaceful than the day before. My log of misery didn't totally disappear, but it diminished to something like a headache you have for so long you forget you have one. It was a no puke day.

All the way back to homeport, my days were like that.

CHAPTER ELEVEN

After two weeks in port, we went to sea again to support another Project Mercury rocket launch. This one had a live monkey aboard. On the previous test, we were a hundred miles away from where the astronaut capsule splashed down. All of us aboard hoped we'd get to see this spaceship. *Andthemonkeywouldn'tthatbecool!*

Now I wrote "All of us aboard," and of course, I never talked to an officer, or a chief, but the guys in our berthing compartment were hyped up. Deck Apes and Snipes, I heard them talking on the mess deck. A general air of excitement over this mission at sea was palpable. It was sort of like being seasick. Even when I wasn't puking, the feeling of being unwell took up permanent residence in the core of me, from my brain to my belly button. This general air of excitement was like that, always there. Except if there were a meter that registered feeling good to feeling crappy, Space Monkey would be on one end of the scale, grinning and eating a banana. The opposite end of the scale would show Cecil the Seasick Sea Serpent looking like if anyone had a right to be colored green, he did.

Being seasick and **not** puking was better than feeling sick **and** puking. For four days since leaving port, I hadn't barfed once.

That day, NASA would launch the monkey, and he'd fly up, kiss the edge of space, and ride his rocket ship back to earth under a big parachute. If the capsule landed close to our destroyer, we were to put a boat in the water, motor alongside, and attach extra floatation gear to it. It was supposed to float, but you can't be too careful when a monkey might drown. The plan was for a helicopter to pick it up and transport it back to an aircraft carrier.

But, if a helo did not show up, we were to hoist the monkey conveyance aboard our ship until a helicopter could come.

I was in the compartment swabbing the deck when the 1MC blared, "Man all capsule recovery stations. Man all capsule recovery stations."

Get to the 0-1 level. Hurry! You'll miss it.

That thought engendered every bit as much urgency as the GQ alarm.

> GQ: General Quarters: the call to man battle stations. When the GQ alarm sounds: *Gong! Gong! Gong!* It opens a firehose of adrenalin shooting straight into your heart. Enemy ships, subs, or planes are shooting at us, torpedoing us, or bombing us. And maybe all three things are happening at once, so get the crap to your battle station!
>
> Okay, the chance to see a monkey in a space suit is not quite that adrenalin-laced an event. Even so, it could be a once-in-a-lifetime thing.

Still, I took thirty-seven seconds to stow my cleaning gear before hustling up to the 0-1 level.

I climbed the ladder from the main deck on the port side. Topside, the 0-1 level was crammed with sailors, as was the 0-3 level and the fantail. On the 0-1 level, everyone stared to starboard.

The ship had stopped dead in the water, and it wallowed from side to side as waves paraded toward us and rocked us like a baby cradle. When the starboard side dipped on a roll, I caught a glimpse of the monkey-mobile. A parachute with alternating orange and white panels lay draped over the shiny conical shape as it bobbed on the white capped waves.

I made my way aft along the port railing, then pushed through the sailor jam to the after mast. I climbed up a couple of steps and had a clear view of the capsule.

We had a boat in the water, and it was headed for the space monkey but still had a way to go, when the sound of a helicopter approaching from aft reached us.

The helo came pretty fast, descending, and looking like it would land right atop the capsule. I saw the guys in our boat all turn and look at the Navy chopper. One crewman waved his fist at it. Another stood and started throwing things at the descending whirly bird.

Bananas! The boat crewman must not have had anything else to throw.

None of the yellow missiles came close and did nothing to slow or dissuade the helo in its determined descent to just short of **our monkey**, where it nosed up and hovered. A swimmer dropped out the side door and some ten feet into the water. The helo rolled to its right and arced away.

The swimmer resurfaced, swam to the capsule, climbed onto its side, reached up and released the parachute attached to the top. The orange and white cloth disappeared beneath the waves.

The helo, meanwhile, completed a circle and approached the capsule again, trailing two cables in the water. The swimmer attached one to a ring on the top of the capsule and the other to himself.

The guy in our ship's boat must have run out of bananas to throw because all he could do was shake his fist at the guys who were stealing **our** monkey.

Somebody near the starboard railing hollered, "Hey, you (lengthy string of curse words goes here) Flyboys, he's our monkey. We got here first."

Onboard our ship, all we could do was watch the flyboys. The swimmer was hoisted up and in through the open side door. Next, the chopper hovered directly over the capsule for several seconds, then the monkey container came out of the water. The helo headed back to its carrier and started climbing.

On our ship, guys emitted a group discontented mumbling and started going below again.

I have a stored memory, of my own manufacture, I admit, of the monkey looking wistfully out a window in his capsule and wishing he could have come with us because we had bananas.

Side Bunny Trail Happens Next

I wrote about the monkey that night. To The Squeeze, of course. I didn't write home to Mom and Pop much. That "fed long enough at the family trough" continued to bother me. With that phrase, Pop had disowned me. Well, I disowned him right back and the family to boot.

But, of course, when I went home on leave, I stayed with the family and snarfed from their trough. Maybe when I went home, my head was so filled with The Squeeze I couldn't see my two-faced moral self.

I confess, Kid Number Five, it took me to my mid-twenties before I realized what I was doing, and I finally got over my feelings being hurt by how Pop told me that it was time for me to get a job and start making myself financially self-sufficient. It was time for me to grow up.

I have tried to imagine Pop saying something like, "Eddie, you are pretty close to all growed up now. You need to be thinking about finding a job and supporting yourself. Coupla years from now, you and your girlfriend might want to get married and have a family of your own." I have tried to imagine Pop smiling, sort of wistfully, like the Space Monkey hankering for a banana and looking at me like his father looked at him at that growed-up-now point in Pop's life.

That's when my imagined mind movie blows up, and I picture what most likely did happen.

Grandpa most likely told Pop, "You fed long enough at the family trough. Pack some clothes. You'll be leaving first thing in the morning."

And Pop would have understood "first thing" meant

before breakfast. And Grandpa would not have smiled. I can't remember ever seeing him smile. And I'm not sure I ever saw Pop smile, either. What I figured, though, was as he grew up, Pop didn't get any smiling practice.

One last thing in this rendition of Pop receiving the "fed long enough" speech, I picture Grandma slipping Pop a sandwich as he left by the back door.

Once again, Kid Number Five, your own father proves he was not a fast learner. It took me to age twenty-five to understand that "family trough" speech was not an original creation by my pop. And I also appreciated how effective those particular words were. "Fed long enough," with no possibility it could be a joke. Like, "Don't let the doorknob hit you," which engenders a smile of appreciation for what was a pretty good joke. I mean, it had been a pretty good joke before it got trite.

The other thing I appreciated there at age twenty-five was how much of the good that happened to me in the Navy, was directly due to the work ethic Pop inspired, or instilled, or crammed down my throat.

Confession: Even though I appreciated what Pop had done for me in that regard, I never told him thanks for that "a boy needs to learn how to work" of his in the summer after seventh grade.

I regret that.

We slow learners probably pile up more regrets than those quicker on the pick-up.

Side Bunny Trail Rejoins Main Path

After the Space Monkey Mission, we visited San Juan, Puerto Rico, again.

This time, when the anchor chain rattled out the hawse pipe, I was not sick in bed. I was cleaning the deck in the compartment. But the sound of the anchor dropping sure took me back to the first time.

I had no trouble recalling the depths of the misery I felt lying in my bunk, and then the miraculous cure, the sound of the ship attaching itself to shore again and snapping me from agony to *Boy-do-I-feel-good-now!* From one heartbeat to the next, I'd been cured.

Once again, I thought this meant seasickness was all a matter of an imagination running down a side bunny trail, not the main path where truth abided. If that were the case, and I knew it was, shouldn't that knowledge have been my seasickness cure?

I reminded myself that I had been really seasick only once on this trip to San Juan and hadn't been the only one. A couple of other guys got sick and puked, too.

The rest of the time, I can't say I felt good, or dry-land normal. I had a minor headache most of the time underway, and not much appetite. But I made myself eat something at each meal. And I drank water. I did not want another case of industrial strength constipation.

This time in San Juan, I went ashore on Sunday and attended Mass at the cathedral. The Latin prayers were familiar, comforting, and made me feel like I belonged. I appreciated the Spanish homily as well. I didn't have to try to pay attention.

I had taken a pew near the back, and I stayed after Mass ended. As the people filed out in reverential silence, they all glanced at me. At first, I thought their looks meant they considered me to be a stranger and had no right to be there. But the children, curiosity was the only thing coloring their faces. One little guy, about five, smiled and raised his hand in a wave.

It made me think of "Suffer little children, and forbid them not, to come unto me." And here were these children who suffered me, a stranger, and did not forbid me to enter their house of worship.

As the people filed out, up front, altar boys snuffed candles. Throughout the church, ushers moved through the pews straightening prayer books and hymnals. Finally, that was all done, and it was just God and me.

I thanked Him for how good I felt being ashore. And I admitted I'd felt good ever since the ship anchored, but there was something, an extra dose of feel-good from being ashore. Another indicator that seasickness was all in my head, that if it weren't for my screwed-up imagination, I'd feel just as good at sea as I did ashore.

I didn't ask God to help me get over my imaginary illness. I needed to figure something else out. The Naval Scientific Education Program, NESEP. Getting sick had pushed that out of my mind; now, it was time to deal with it. As things stood at that point, I owed the Navy another two years. I figured I could do that, sick or not. If I got NESEP, the Navy would send me to college. That would be ashore. But then, I'd owe them four more years of service, and I was sure most of that would be at sea. And I'd be an officer.

A seasick officer.

Would it be fair to the Navy to take their ride through college, and then, as I paid them back for that, trying to do my officer job while feeling like puking all the time?

My imagination reminded me of something it had told me before in a voice that sounded like Pop's: "A boy don't need to feel good to work." And then imaginary Pop added: "And *neether* does an officer."

I thought about the first-class radarman in charge of our compartment on the ship. He'd praised me a number of times for the job I did keeping the berthing space and the head clean. And I hadn't felt good through much of that.

And if you, Eddie Walsh, do not go to college, The Squeeze will marry a doctor.

That voice was all mine, and it pushed me over the edge.

I was going to apply for NESEP. If God wanted me in that program, I'd get it. If He didn't, we'd just have to see what happened then. But thinking about no college made me consider no Squeeze in my life, and I could not imagine that. Without her in my life, how could I live? It would be like Eddie Walsh getting unborn and no trace of him left to indicate he'd ever been on earth.

I knelt and looked up at the altar.

Please, God, NESEP.

Please, God, The Squeeze.

But, not my will, but Thine be done.

Thy will was the hardest prayer I ever prayed. I considered repeating the two Pl*ease, Gods,* and ending with an "Amen." Removing that invitation to The Almighty to exercise His will. As if He needed my recommendation to do so!

I repeated *Thy will be done* on my knees. After the sign of the cross, I rose and raised the kneeler, stepped into the aisle, genuflected, left the cathedral, returned to the ship, and wrote to The Squeeze:

> Tomorrow, I will go to the Ship's Office and figure out how to apply for NESEP. It will probably take me a couple of days. But I should have it done by the time we get back to homeport.
>
> I'll call when we get in, and that'll happen before you get this letter. One other thing will happen when we get back. I will complete my ninety days of compartment cleaning and can go back to being an Electronic Technician again.

I restrained myself from equating compartment cleaning to girl work in the letter.

The trip back to homeport was my first no-puke at sea period. Though I kept a bucket close.

CHAPTER TWELVE

At 15:30, the 1MC blared, "Moored! Shift colors!"
It meant were no longer underway. At least one line secured the ship to the pier in our homeport. Signalmen would be hauling down the flag from the main mast. The quarterdeck watch would be hoisting another on the pole on the stern.

I, seasick but not puking, seaman Eddie Walsh was in the berthing compartment swabbing the deck. "Moored" registered with my body by the immediate cessation of the buzzing in my head and the queasiness in my stomach. The buzzing was like a bumped hive when only a few of the bees were home. And the queasiness was like somebody, for a joke, slipped a little vinegar into the Kool-Aid container on the Mess Deck.

It was kind of funny. The bees buzzing in my skull and the ubiquitous vinegar aftertaste did not annoy me. What annoyed was, when we tied ourselves to the pier, the aggravations magically disappeared. The seasickness, whether at puking or non-puking level, was all in my head. I knew that to be gospel true. Still, I couldn't convince myself the sickness was not real. That annoyed me.

Just get over it already!

But I couldn't get over it. Did this mean my flesh was strong, but my mind was weak?

The main thing, though, was that regardless of how I felt at sea, the Navy got a Pop-sized day of work out of me every day.

Even though I had convinced myself the day before that it was morally okay for me to apply for NESEP, Pop was up there in my bean box going at me. I imagined Pop telling me I had to change my last name. A son of his who took something of value from an employer, then didn't pay him back with good, honest labor, well, that sort of man could not walk around bearing the Walsh name. I pictured Pop telling me that and then going back to reading his sports page.

But, I had learned how to handle the buzzing and queasiness and still deliver a full day of honest labor day after day after day. So, if I applied for NESEP and got it, I wouldn't be cheating the Navy out of their payback, even though I might puke now and then while doing so.

I hoped I wouldn't have to plow through this issue every day. Then, I pictured Sister Daniel smiling a little smile and nodding her approval at how I worked out the morality of applying for NESEP.

It was the first time any spirit in my head ever argued my Pop spirit into submission. *Thank you, Sister Daniel.*

I was able to move on.

NESEP meant college, and college meant marriage to/with The Squeeze. For the first time, The Squeeze and me together, forever and ever Amen, seemed real, solid, attainable. My imagination cranked up this picture of Mr. and Mrs. Eddie Walsh together, so I couldn't stay annoyed with it for not curing my seasickness.

I was going to call her that evening. I had two rolls of quarters, extravagant but absolutely necessary with the path to our future now looking solid, looking like a main path and not some side bunny trail meandering off into a wilderness where reality and wishful thinking intersected and where you couldn't tell one from the other.

Looking back on that day, on that moment, from the here and now, I know I did not even consider the Navy not approving my application. After all the wrestling my conscience muscles had done over the issue, after the struggles to get myself to say, "Thy will be done," in the cathedral in San Juan, after finally deciding I would not be cheating the Navy out of their payback for college, I said to God: *You know, Lord, even Heiny Horstwessel decided to pay me for working for him after*

Pop said he didn't have to, surely You won't let the Navy disapprove my request. Right, God?

Guys started thundering down the ladder from the main deck and into the passageway outside the compartment. With the ship moored, signalmen, radiomen, radarmen, and the other ratings in the Operations Department were all released from their posts and were coming to change into dress uniforms to go ashore.

I took the water bucket and the puke one into the head and stored them in the cleaning gear locker there.

The first-class radarman in charge of our compartment found me. "Walsh," PO1 said. "Congratulations. You did a heck of a job as compartment cleaner."

He handed me a sheet of paper. An enlisted performance appraisal form. It had an X in all the highest-grade boxes along the left side of the page. The remarks section included:

> "Hard worker. Attentive to detail. Self-starter. Sees what needs to be done and does it."

"Thanks, PO1," I said.

"You earned it, Walsh. I'm sure your chief will be glad to get you back in the shop."

That caused me a moment of angst, but I was sure Chief hadn't meant it when he said he did not want me in the shop anymore.

I returned to the compartment, found ET2 donning his dress uniform, and showed him the application form for NESEP I'd filled out during the trip north from San Juan.

ET2 studied the form. He looked up at me and shook his head. "Try as I might, ETSN Walsh, I cannot picture myself saluting you."

PO1 stepped out from behind a tier of bunks. "Well, ET2, college takes four years. You'll have that long to get used to the idea of saluting Ensign Walsh. By the way," he clapped me on the shoulder and turned back to ET2. "I'm sure you and the chief are happy to get Walsh back in the shop. Best damned compartment cleaner I've had. He keeps the space in ready-for-inspection condition most of every day despite three dozen slobs living here."

Surprise burst over ET2's face. "Getting him back?"

"Yeah. His ninety days of compartment cleaning are up." PO1 frowned. "You didn't know?"

"(Curse word goes here)"

"If you don't want him, I'll keep him and make a radarman out of him."

PO1 walked away, muttering how, sometimes, even Deck Apes were smarter than ETs.

The compartment cleared out quickly. I crawled up onto my top bunk and read until chow time. After supper, I went ashore. The pier, an attachment to dry land, conveyed me to the real deal, the real blessing. Dry land itself, not just an attachment to it.

There was a saying: Sailors are meant to be on ships, and ships are meant to be at sea.

Wherever Eddie Walsh was meant to be, he appreciated the heck out of dry land for several reasons. The top of the list read: Phone booths grow on dry land.

TBGH also switch to third person goes here

The call with The Squeeze was the best phone call they'd ever had. Ever! She felt that way, too. He knew she did.

He told her about applying for NESEP. He told her he could see college, could see them getting married, could see them living in a house with a white picket fence to corral their four kids.

"Before," he said, "it was a dream. Like during a baseball game, when Harry Carey says over the radio after a Cardinal batter hits a long fly ball, 'It might be, it could be, It **is** a home run!' Now it's like we're in the 'might be, could be' part. And the main thing is, Harry never ever said, 'Oh shoot! Not quite.'"

"I love you, Eddie. More than I love my own life."

Baseball analogies did not float the Squeeze's boat, but her profession of love floated Eddie. There had not been a proposal, rather a profession of deep and abiding love. Heck, a formal proposal would have required a conversation with the Squeeze's father and a ring. A ring might cost a whole stinking year's pay, and talking to her father made his Adam's apple bob just thinking about it. But they'd committed themselves to life together during the call. That was how Eddie understood it.

He floated back to the ship, floated through teeth brushing and other stuff, floated up onto his bunk, and floated into sleep, dreaming over and over and over, "It might be, it could be. It IS! Marriage to The Squeeze."

TBGH also switch to third person goes here

What the heck?

Someone was shaking me. My heart started hammering.

"Walsh! Wake the (cuss word goes here) up!"

"What's wrong? Is the ship on fire?"

"No, (Cuss word goes here) for brains. Get out of your bunk, now."

It was ET2. He was insistent.

My feet splatted on the linoleum.

"Get dressed. You need to report to the mess decks chief ASAP."

"What for?"

"You're mess cooking. And you're late checking in."

"I just finished compartment cleaning!"

Normally, a seaman or seaman apprentice was assigned to **either** mess cooking **or** compartment cleaning for ninety days out of a year. You did not get assigned back-to-back stints of those menial duties. It wasn't a law, but everybody believed it to be true.

"You're late. Check in with the chief cook." ET2 started to leave and stopped. "Chop-chop! And do put on a work uniform first."

ET2 returned to his duty station, the quarterdeck where he was Petty Officer of the Watch.

I stood there stunned, trying to understand what the heck happened from the dream of marriage to the reality of now. My mind seemed incapable of bridging the gap. Then Pop's voice kicked my mind in the butt. "If you are less than ten minutes early to work, you're late."

WHAT AM I?

My body got itself dressed. My mind tagged behind like a kid in a wagon pulled by a big man, unable to see where the wide-butt adult was taking him.

I found the chief on the mess deck at 0500. He was behind the serving counter talking to one of the cooks about eggs. When they finished their conversation, I told the chief I was reporting for duty.

Chief Cook scanned me down and back up again. He was my height, but what I remember most about him was his face, eyes in particular. ETC's eyes had the shades down with *You ain't seeing into my soul, Dirt Bag!* written on them. Chief Cook's eyes, I remember being like Mom's. A little, anyway. Mom's eyes sort of said, *This is my beloved son, no matter how many times I have to spank him.* Chief Cook's eyes said, *This is my Mess Cook. I halfways come sort of close to trusting him to be a good one. Almost.*

Chief Cook said, "Being an ET, I guess you never did a stint of mess cooking before."

"I worked in the Bread Locker in boot camp, Chief. It was just a couple of days, though."

"The second class from your shop said you are a hard worker and showed initiative. I'm going to put you in the Vegetable Locker. The kid there completes his tour of mess duty next week."

The guy I worked with was an tall, skinny Snipe. He was busy peeling potatoes. Actually, the peeler was busy. The Vegetable Locker peeler had a rotating barrel, sort of like a cement mixer, with a very rough interior. As the barrel spun, the rough surface skimmed the skin from the spuds.

"Of course," Tall Skinny Snipe said, "we still have to cut the eyes out. But this morning, since they are serving hash browns, and we grind them, we don't have to be too particular with getting out all the potato peepers."

He showed me how to load the peeler, how long to let the spuds get tumble-skinned, how to un-eye them, how to use the grinder, and how to deliver the ground taters to the cooks. He showed me and then watched me finish the job.

Next, we carted up cases of bananas and grapes from the walk-in fridge a deck below.

Fifteen minutes before the Mess Deck opened for breakfast, we got to eat. A fringe bennie of being a mess cook. Actually, **the** fringe bennie.

Note: Looking back on it, I am a bit surprised at how often **bold letters** need to be used to describe my life as a seaman. The necessity just keeps popping up.

We went from *Prepare for breakfast* to *Clean up the mess you made preparing for breakfast.*

At 08:00, the 1MC invited, "Turn to. Commence ship's work."

"Us mess cooks commenced work three hours ago!" Tall Skinny Snipe hollered over his shoulder.

Chief Cook stood outside the door to the locker. "Only one more week to go, Fatso. Then you can join the ranks of slackers, no-loads, and goof-offs."

Skinny-as-a-rail guy, what else would you call him? "Fatso," of course. *I'm worried about you, Eddie. This kind of thing is beginning to make sense to you.*

Tall-skinny-snipe called Fatso said, "Eddie, how about stashing the cleaning gear and bringing up a carton of carrots from the frig?"

Newbie mess cook Eddie Aye, Aye-d the authoritative interrogative.

Eddie made the trip and plopped the box of bunny food on the counter in the Vegetable Locker. Skinny Fatso ripped open the carton and took out a carrot. "Cut off the top and check each one for bad spots and cut them out. Then pile them next to the slicer." TSS held up a wooden paddle. "Use this to push the veggies through."

But TSS pushed the carrots into the blade with his finger.

I watched. His finger came close to the blade. Eddie Walsh was going to do what he said. He definitely was **not** going to do as he did.

Leaving Fatso to the slicing, I went a deck below for a carton of apples for lunch. Lugging the sizeable box, I reentered the Locker just as TSS pulled his hand away from the slicer and howled, "Ow! (Several cuss words go here) I cut my finger off!"

He hadn't cut off his whole finger. It was only the tip with most of the nail sliced away. The wound bled enthusiastically. I grabbed a rag, which didn't seem to be too dirty, and handed it to him.

Chief Cook poked his head in the door, heard the slicer motor running, looked at it, looked at the bloody rag on the index finger of Fatso's upraised hand.

"Walsh, take him to sick bay. Then get back here and finish slicing the carrots. Do I need to tell you to use the wooden paddle?"

I shook my head.

Fatso didn't seem to be able to do anything for himself but use his good hand to elevate the wounded one. He also moaned and mumbled cuss words.

I grabbed his good arm and led him to Sick Bay, which was just aft of the Mess Deck.

Hospitalman First Class unwrapped the finger, examined the damage, and applied clean gauze around the wound. "Where's the end of his finger," he asked me.

I shrugged.

"Find it. Fast. And bring it to me."

I hustled back to the Vegetable Locker and looked for the aluminum container TSS (Tall Skinny Snipe) had used to catch the sliced carrots, but it was missing from behind the slicer. Out in the kitchen, I asked one of the cooks if someone had taken the sliced carrots.

He pointed to a counter by a pot of steaming water.

I hurried to the container and probed through the raw slices. There. The fingertip.

A half-full coffee cup sat next to the carrots. I dumped out the coffee. One of the cooks hollered at me.

"I need it," I said.

"What you need is a kick in the ass, Mess Cook!"

I rinsed the cup in the sink, placed the finger in it, and took it to Sick Bay.

The hospitalman tweezered the fingertip from the cup to a plastic bag filled with ice cubes. Then he hustled his patient and the severed digit out the door and aft down the midship passageway.

I returned to the Vegetable Locker. The chief entered behind me.

"We need tomatoes sliced. Gotta do those with a cutting board and a knife. When you use a knife, first thing you gotta do is sharpen it. A dull knife is worse than no knife at all. Understand?"

I said I did.

He sharpened. He sliced one tomato. He handed me the knife.

I dried the knife with a rag and sharpened it.

Chief Cook smiled; then he watched me slice one. "Fill the plater," he said. "Then take it to one of the cooks."

He had his hand on the doorknob when he stopped and turned. "And Walsh, If you cut your finger off, I ain't taking it to the hospitalman in a coffee cup. I'll throw it over the side."

He left, and I sliced.

Carefully.

CHAPTER THIRTEEN

On the Mess Deck, breakfast was breakfast. Lunch was lunch, but the evening meal wasn't dinner or supper. It was the evening meal.

All three meals, for the most part, included some form of potato: baked, sliced skin-on or sliced skin-off and fried, mashed, or ground for hash browns. There was a job to be done, and no one to do it but Eddie Walsh. So I did it.

> Sorry. An irresistible Side Bunny Trail popped up. When I was in Boot Camp, I worked in the galley for five days. In the Bread Locker, we passed whole loaves through the slicing machine. We kept a large box near the slicer and dropped the heels into the box. Sometimes, the slicer would mangle a loaf and we'd toss the disfigured pieces into the box as well. When we had two boxes of messed-up bread, a cook would make bread pudding for dessert. Once, one of the guys stomped on the contents of the box to make more room. I still don't eat bread pudding.
>
> Time pressed on all of us hustling through preps for three meals a day for a thousand people, and we were messy, but there wasn't much time to spend on cleaning, so the deck wound up covered in pond-scum-looking

goop a good bit of the time. After serving began, we cleaned. One day, while carrying a box of sliced bread to the serving line, I observed two guys sliding this huge tub of mashed potatoes toward the same place I was. Suddenly, the tub tipped over, and the potato mush spilled onto the yucky deck. A deck-cleaning tool we had was this huge squeegee contraption on a push broom handle. We used it to herd slime toward deck drains. The potato spillers grabbed a squeegee, squeegeed the mashed spuds back into the tub, and took it to the serving line. That's when I stopped eating mashed potatoes.

That was a sort of fringe bennie of an assignment to the mess deck. You learned what not to eat. I've always wondered if the Nav decided ninety days of mess cooking was the right period of time to be sentenced to such duty. Serving a longer term might mean you would have nothing left to eat.

At any rate, I had some experience with food preparation from Boot Camp. Plus, there was an echo of Pop saying, "You're working for Heiny now." *Whatever he tells you to do, do it!* He didn't have to say that part, or the next one: *If you don't do what he tells you, you will* **not** *like what happens to you a lot more than the work you didn't want to do!*

Just as I finished cleaning up the Vegetable Locker after the evening meal, Chief Cook poked his head in the door. "Walsh. First day on the job, most of it by yourself. Pretty close to kind of halfways, sort of decent job."

He started to leave and stopped. "Tomorrow, you prove to me that today wasn't some sort of beginner's luck. Hear?"

"Aye, Chief. Uh, do you know how Seaman Smedlap is doing?"

Note: In boot camp, my company commander used to use "Seaman Bertie (No Middle Name) Smedlap" as the name of a generic and "unsquared-away" recruit.

Such as: "Seaman Smedlap forgot to call me Sir. Know what happened to him? So, I can't remember Tall Skinny Snipe's real name, and I wouldn't use it if I did, thus Seaman Bertie NMN Smedlap lends his name to this telling.

PS: Sorry if this character winds up with three names: Bertie NMN, Fatso, and Tall Skinny Snipe.

Chief Cook told us, "HM1 (Hospitalman First Class) said the docs at the hospital sewed the tip back onto Smedlap's finger. If he is real careful, doesn't bump it, bang it into things, it may grow back onto the end of Mr. Nose Picker. The Snipes are giving him a couple of days off, but then he's back to work with the other Bilge Rats.

"By the way," Chief Cook continued, "the cooks said all the guys really liked the peas and carrots we served for lunch. So, the next time we serve that, I may ask you to contribute a fingertip to the recipe." He laughed and departed for chiefs' quarters.

Finally, I had time to worry about my NESEP chit being disapproved. At lunch that day, Gutter Mouth told me the chief had disapproved my request to apply for NESEP.

Just then, I missed not being a member of the ET gang anymore. In the evenings, I could write to The Squeeze on the workbench in the shop. I was getting tired of having to write propped on my elbows on my bunk.

But that's what I had.

I wrote a page, read it, and tore it into confetti. I'd spilled my guts, all the anguish I felt over seeing NESEP as the path to realizing my dream to marry her and then having ETC smash it to smithereens. Nothing but anguish on the whole page.

I started over and wrote how she often said, "The Lord won't give us a challenge we can't handle." Pulled along by that locomotive of thought, I filled up a page, read it, and made more confetti.

In the next attempt, I wrote about formulating a new plan. I had two more years to serve. She had two more years of nursing school. I figured I'd get a job as a TV repairman, and she'd be a nurse. I figured we'd both work for another year, and then we'd have enough money to get married. I had filled two pages and didn't feel the need to tear them up.

Then my mind realized something I wished it hadn't: I had a lot more practical experience cleaning urinals and slicing carrots than I did repairing electronics. And Chief ET would keep me in the kind of job that would **not** help me realize my new plan.

I filled out the request form to take the NESEP test, and I never wondered if it would be turned down. My mind saw the form stamped "Approved." Then, college. Then, marrying The Squeeze, kids, and picket-fenced house. And I'd seen it all as 101% probable.

A boy shouldn't count his chickens before they's hatched.

I wondered if that was my guardian angel. *And if so, why did he talk to me in Pop's voice?*

Because you listen to him, the voice said.

What do I do now? I asked the voice.

It's bedtime. At bedtime, a boy says his prayers; then he sleeps. So's he kin work come mornin'.

At some point, sleep happened.

The next day, work in the Vegetable Locker happened.

That night, a phone call happened.

I told The Squeeze about applying for NESEP, that it had been disapproved, and that I would not be going to college.

I told her if she wanted to marry a doctor, I would learn how to live without her. "All that matters is that you are happy."

"Eddie Walsh! Have you found a girlfriend there in your homeport? Maybe you found another one in Puerto Rico!"

It was a good thing I brought two rolls of quarters into the phone booth that night.

After stammering out denials of her accusation and assuring her that I loved **only** her and always would and what I wanted more than anything was what was best for her. Even if she would marry someone who **did** go to college, like a doctor.

"Eddie, every time we talk over the phone, I end the call with, 'I love you.' And it is said just that way. Not as 'I love you, but only if you go to college.' In every one of our precious letters, I write it. Every time we are together, I don't say, 'Goodnight, Eddie.' Rather, I say, 'I love you, Eddie.' Do you want me to say, 'I love you, Eddie, unequivocally?'"

The lump in my throat was as big as one of the potatoes I loaded into the peeler. The joy that flooded my heart was almost enough to blow the pump to smithereens. I tried like heck to speak, but the spud was stuck.

The phone demanded my last quarter.

"Eddie, are you okay? What's the matter? Unequivocally. Is that a dangling participle?"

I kind of snorted. I was pretty sure that had not been a dangling participle. And how I rid myself of the Idaho potato clogging my throat out through my nose, well, it was a miracle.

"No, Sweetheart, it is not a dangling participle. At least, I don't think so. If I had a grammar book, I'd look it up when I get back to the ship. And, Dearest Person on Earth, I love you unequivocally."

"Eddie, one of the gifts you will get for Christmas is an English grammar book. And I love you—"

The last second of our time my last quarter bought had expired.

As I walked back down the pier toward the ship, I was sure she'd said "unequivocally," only the phone chopped the word off. As if it had been a dangling participle.

I was pretty sure it wasn't. Danglers of any kind didn't fit on the end of: "Dearest Person on Earth, I love you unequivocally." That last word absolutely fit in that statement.

Did I sleep well that night!

Two days later, Chief Cook entered the Vegetable Locker. "Your division officer wants to see you."

"Chief, I have a lot of carrots to slice. The cook is after me to get them done."

"Go see your Div O. I'll slice the carrots."

"Remember to use the wooden paddle, Chief."

"Get the hell out of here, Wise-ass."

Now what?

I headed aft in the midship passageway. With each step, I wondered what kind of bad news whammy waited for me. Maybe my Div O was a sadist and wanted to see me squirm when he unloaded another dose of disappointment and shame on me.

I entered after officer's country, walked to the aftmost door, took a deep breath, whoofed it out, knocked, and said, "Seaman Walsh, Sir."

"Come."

I opened the door. The ensign sat at one of two gray-painted metal stacks of drawers with a fold-down lid that served as a desk. Bunk beds filled out the space against the bulkhead on the port side of the room.

All this space for two guys!!??

Actually, two officer guys.

Actually, guys were guys and officers were officers, unequivocally.

"Have a seat."

He watched me sit ... uncomfortably.

"You're probably wondering why I asked to see you."

Yeah. Maybe you want to tell me the ETC convinced you I should walk the plank the next time at sea and that I should be put in the brig until then?

"I have a face-to-face with all the people in my division once a year."

Most of my mind wondered at how young my Div O looked. He appeared to be younger than my brother Lennie.

"I see by your record that you scored high on your pre-entry-into-the-service test. You did well in ET School."

What? I almost asked him to repeat what he'd just said. Please. Sir?

"Have you thought about what you want to do next after this assignment?"

Yeah. Get out of the Navy.

He waited a couple of ticks and tocks for a reply, but none came.

"You might want to think of C School."

> Note: ET School might be considered junior college, while C School might be the real-deal college.

"Actually, Sir. I applied for NESEP, but Chief turned me down."

"What? Did he say why?"

"Sir, he said he had already approved a request for the program from ETSN Smedlap (the only ETSN in the ET Shop since I had been banished), and he was only approving one request."

> Note: I learned from Gutter Mouth that Smedlap had not applied for NESEP until after the Chief received my request. Then the Chief told Smedlap to fill out a request "Now!" Smedlap did. The Chief approved that request; mine he disapproved. I didn't mention this to my Div O. When Gutter told me this, the fact that he'd basically ordered ETSN Smedlap to fill out a request was, to me, a bit of nasty gilding on an already maximally ugly occurrence: disapproval of my chit. Chief ET. A sling of outrageous fortune. I didn't want it to be an arrow. The only arrow I wanted stuck in my gizzard came from Cupid's bow.

My division officer shook his head. "Nonsense. I'll talk to the chief. I have it from the PO1 in your berthing compartment that you are the best compartment cleaner he's ever had work for him. That you do a good job even when you feel seasick. I also talked to the Chief Cook. He said he was mightily impressed with how quickly you picked up things in the Vegetable Locker when the kid who was supposed to show you the ropes got hurt."

My Div O looked at me. "Smart, fast learner, hard worker. The Navy needs people like you." My Div O leaned forward a bit. "I'll talk to the chief. Don't worry."

As I walked back to the Vegetable Locker, all I did was worry. The ETC already had it in for me. Now, he would look at my visit with Boy Ensign—that's how I remember him—as going behind his, ETC's, back.

So, I worried. And waited for the payback.

Nothing happened, though, except a good thing. Two weeks later, I was allowed to take the test for advancement to third-class petty officer. ETC had turned down my request for that as well.

There was only one explanation: Boy Ensign had pulled my bacon out of the fire.

The week after the test for third-class petty officer, we went to sea. The ship was assigned to a formation, and we operated in the north Atlantic and even went above the Arctic Circle. The seas were pretty rough up there. I was pretty sick, but I got my work done in the Vegetable Locker with a puke bucket to hand.

The day after the ship poked its nose above the Arctic Circle and smartly turned around, me and my puke bucket took the NESEP test. ETSN Smedlap also took it. We sat at the fold-down desks in Boy Ensign's stateroom. He monitored the test taking.

Smedlap didn't puke. I did. But only once. Boy Ensign wrinkled his nose and told me to empty the bucket in a commode in the officer's head. I did, came back, and finished the test. Without needing the bucket again.

I figured Smedlap passed the test. I figured I failed. Because I'd felt so crappy. As far as I could tell, nobody on the ship knew when the test results would be announced. And what did it matter if I'd flunked it?

We returned to homeport for two weeks. Then, we departed for a six-month deployment to the Mediterranean Sea. Sailors called it the Med.

CHAPTER FOURTEEN

On the Project Mercury mission, our ship had sailed alone, independently. Most of the time, though, we sailed as part of a formation of ships. Prior to entering the Med (Mediterranean Sea), our gaggle of destroyers, cruisers, oilers, supply vessels, and an aircraft carrier sailed north to the latitude of northern Scotland. There, we participated in exercises with our European allies. After a couple of days of that, we sailed south to the Azores and conducted more operations with allies. After two weeks practicing for the next war, we were ready to enter the Med.

Through those fourteen days, I learned all the above through nightly reports from the radarmen in the berthing compartment. I, of course, was not preparing to go to war. I sliced carrots and peeled spuds to feed the guys who **were** preparing to go to war.

I'll also mention logging a couple of days where I had felt ashore-normal. Most of the time, though, my body knew we were at sea and did not want to be there. To let me know, my stomach manufactured vinegar and forced it back up the sewer pipe to my mouth.

I wondered if The Squeeze would taste that vinegar if we kissed, especially a French kiss, which, of course, we would not do until after we were married. Thinking about kissing her was a more effective seasickness medication than the pills HM1 gave me. Unfortunately, the cure only lasted a few moments.

So, we passed through the Strait of Gibraltar.

A day later, the ship anchored off the coast of France with a view of the Riviera and the city of Cannes. I, however, did not go ashore to visit the exotic port. I had an infected ingrown toenail. So, I spent all my in-port time on a large repair ship. It was called a destroyer tender, or a tender, and dedicated to providing intermediate-level maintenance to destroyers.

> Note: In the Navy, there were three levels of maintenance: Operational, Intermediate, and Depot level.
>
> Operational (O level) was what the sailors assigned to a ship could perform themselves. It was impressive to see what Deck Apes, Snipes, and Electronic Technicians could do to keep their ship operating properly. It reminded me of Heiny Horstwessel. There were a lot of repairs to his machinery Heiny performed himself. A few things, like changing the oil in a tractor, he taught me to do. That was O level maintenance on a farm.
>
> Intermediate (I level) The destroyer tender had been built to and did provide the next level of maintenance above O level to Navy destroyers and cruisers. The destroyer tender carried a specially trained crew and was filled with test equipment we had no room for on our destroyer. I Level on Heiny's farm was Ernie Emanthaller's garage. When one of Heiny's tractors needed something significant, like when Heiny's John Deere would go *Putt, sputter, putt, sputter* instead of *putt, putt, putt,* Heiny, or sometimes I, *putt, sputtered* the Deere to Ernie's.
>
> Depot level repair was where a ship underwent extensive modification and repair, such as removal of an out-of-date gun mount and reinstallation of a more modern one. For Heiny, Depot Level Maintenance meant buying a new piece of machinery. The Navy, however, had shipyards for that highest level of maintenance.

Back to the I-level repair ship. Besides extensive equipment repair capability, it also carried advanced human repair capability. They had a doctor aboard. He supervised the removal of my ingrown toenail.

The removal of the toenail procedure surprised me. I expected the hospitalman to use some kind of fancy nail clipper. But he brought in a slender thing like a chisel with a scalpel-sharp blade on the end.

After giving my big toe a couple of injections to deaden it, the hospitalman held the chisel in place at the edge of the nail, told me to stiffen my leg, and whacked the chisel with the palm of his hand a couple of times.

It seemed crude, like something a carpenter would do during the framing of a house. Not something delicate, like finishing work, or a surgical procedure. I wished he'd suggested I not watch what he did to me. Fortunately, it didn't hurt. The numb job was effective.

I had to stay in bed the day of the nail-ectomy. The next day, though, I was able to walk around a bit with a cane and go up on deck to view the French Riviera. Before I left the recovery ward, the PO1 in charge told me, "If you stub that toe, we'll have to amputate your left leg clean up to your bottom rib."

The PO1 employed the literary device of hyperbole, and maybe it was even exaggerated hyperbole. Still, I knew packed behind the embellished language was a truth: *You stub your toe, and whatever discomfort and inconvenience you're experiencing now, it will be worse post-stub.*

I'd been in the Nav long enough to know how to read those subcutaneous messages. I was *dad-burned* careful.

We were anchored a far piece offshore, maybe a mile or a good chunk of one. The day was bright, clear, sunny with a blue sky a slightly lighter shade than the sea. Rumor had it that French women sunbathed topless there.

I knew that on the signal bridge on my ship, the signalmen had honking big binoculars for seeing signal flags displayed on distant ships. My imagination had to expend no effort to see how those devices were being employed at that very moment on each of the half dozen US Navy ships anchored near us on the tender. I imagined the signalmen charging guys a buck a look. I imagined the guys paying the buck without thinking about it even for a second.

I thought about The Squeeze over there on the beach. I could not imagine her topless. But, I was seeing someone like My One and Only, over there on the beach, but French and doing what they did and considered normal, sunbathing topless. I did not want people ogling The Squeeze, or my mind-manufactured French version of her, either.

As I gazed across the sea and past the anchored ships to the distance and haze-dimmed beach, my mind stopped seeing those things, and saw instead, Eddie Walsh in his junior year in high school.

It was when girls became **GIRLS**, you know. And I wanted to win one. Like playing baseball and hitting an RBI single to win the game. Winning a girl, like she was a thing, an end-of-the-year-trophy awarded to the guy with the most RBIs.

At that moment, I could see that the way I had looked at women when I was a high school junior, had never been erased and **totally** replaced with something more … graceful and egalitarian. Something holy and sacred, as in *What God has joined together, let not man put asunder*. I had to admit, deep down, I had looked at The Squeeze that way, too. And the way I looked at **GIRLS**, and what we might do together, there was nothing, not one stinking, blinking thing **for the female** in these imaginings.

When Cupid stuck his arrow in my gizzard, I was smitten. I had never been smitten before. I was drawn to her like a nail to a honking big magnet. In retrospect, now I know I was in love with her. But back then, as a goober high schooler, girls and cars attracted me. And I, Eddie Walsh, knew not one stinking, blinking thing about love.

But The Squeeze taught me. My enthusiasm for her kisses, her embraces were … enthusiastic. She drew a line, though, and I had just enough sense, or maybe my Guardian Angel did, to not cross that line by even a micrometer.

Eddie Walsh, slow learner extraordinaire, picked up that lesson on the second date. Thinking about it now, I'm pretty sure if I hadn't gotten the message, the one she'd have sent me would've been: "Hit the road, Stupid Eddie."

There I stood by the railing on the main deck of the tender, with a crutch this day under the arm on the side of my bandaged big toe, looking off toward the beach on the French Riviera, and I'd dredged up a sin I'd stuffed deep in the belly of my soul years prior.

That I had such thinking buried down there surprised the heck out of me. And the next thought: Get it out of there! Like, now!

One other thing the tender had was a priest aboard.

Is confession good for the soul? I can tell you that one was good for my soul.

Afterwards, I formulated a new EWTLB (Eddie's Words To Live By): Treat other women the way you want others to treat The Squeeze. She most certainly is not some trophy to be won. She is absolutely a gift from God the Father, something to be cherished, something to give to, and never to take from.

Another EWTLB: When you examine your conscience, Eddie Walsh, examine the crap out of it right where you are. Don't put off such deep morality dives until you come to the Riviera again and have an ingrown toenail removed.

I spent five days on the tender. The day before I left, one of the hospitalmen accompanied me to the ship's store. There, I bought a pair of tennis shoes. We returned to the recovery ward where the hospitalman took a scalpel and cut a hole in the left shoe for my bandaged big toe to stick through.

The next day, a first-class hospitalman told me I was discharged and should return to my ship. "I recommend you **not** go ashore today. Take it easy. Tomorrow, you can go back to work, but be (cuss word goes here) careful. You bump that toe, it could get infected bad, and then we'd have to take your whole leg off."

Yeah, yeah! I already heard that one. Still. a picture of a peglegged, seasick Eddie Walsh formed in my bean box. I promised the PO1, and myself, I was going to be real careful.

TBGH

Monday morning, I reported to the galley at 0430.

One of the mess cooks said, "Look at Walsh, Chief. I think he shot himself in the toe so's he could get out of work. You know, he didn't want to hurt the whole foot."

The other six mess cooks laughed.

Chief Cook looked at my bandaged big toe sticking out of my cutaway tennis shoe and snuffed out the giggles. "Listen up, you Dip- (cuss word goes here). Walsh is now officially back at work. If one of you clumsy (cuss word goes here) steps on his toe, I will—Chief picked up a cleaver—I will chop off one of your small appendages. And it won't be a finger or a toe. Now, get the hell to work! Walsh, stay."

If I had been a dog, I'd have squatted on my haunches looking up and eager to hear the next order my master gave me.

The chief handed me a plastic bag and a rubber band. "Put the bag over that foot. Won't do for the bandage to get wet. Also, mid-morning and mid-afternoon, go see the HM1 (Hospitalman First Class). He's expecting you."

He nodded, which clearly meant: *Now get the hell to work.*

I confess KN5 (Kid Number Five), I didn't respond to the Chief's release command as eagerly as a hound would have to, "Fetch," a thrown ball, but I was glad to be back to my ship and doing normal work.

> A backtracking sidenote: Another instance of your dad being a slow learner. It took decades before I appreciated my time on the tender as an opportunity. A chance to stand in silence, looking off toward the coast of France and just think about things. Some people might call it meditation or contemplation. I find myself not wanting to stick a label on it. What I came to appreciate was finding quiet in time and place, and using the time part of it to cut my mind loose to think about things the world won't allow, cause it's got you tied up dealing with all the crap it throws at you all day every day. I'll come back to this before I type **THE END.**

We were at sea for a month, the longest string of consecutive days at sea I'd experienced, and a strange thing happened. I experienced my normal feelings of headache and minor nausea for a time, but then, and I didn't even recognize it at the time, I began to feel ashore-normal **while we were underway.** I need to append when the sea state was "Baby-butt-smooth."

Being in the Med, conditions were calmer and smoother, by a fair amount, than up in the North Sea. Even so, we did encounter a storm, which made me sick, but, again, sick Eddie Walsh got almost as much work done as un-sick Eddie.

At the end of this almost amazing month at sea, we pulled into Beirut, Lebanon, for a couple of days. I signed up for a bus tour of some of the historic sites around the city. I don't really remember much of that tour. I do remember two things:

One: I stepped onto the pier, and it felt like the concrete paved attachment to the country was rocking and rolling like a destroyer at sea. I staggered.

A mess cook, also making the tour, laughed. "A salty sailor like you, Walsh, you should know it takes some time to get your land legs under you."

The guys always talked about "getting their sea legs under them," when we left port. Me, I was always more concerned with my sea stomach. But stepping onto Lebanon, and appreciating that I took those first steps with **sea legs** under me, not land legs, was a revelation. Maybe, just maybe, I didn't have to picture myself as hopelessly sick all the time and looking as green as Cecil to my shipmates.

Two: I appreciated being close to Israel on what I looked at as my **first real** visit to a foreign land. I was disappointed to find we were not close to the Tigris and Euphrates Rivers. Still, we were close to Israel and not **that far** from those two Biblical rivers. Being there, it felt sort of holy. It connected me to the Bible like I'd never felt before. Before, Bible books and stories always seemed as far away from me as heaven was/is from earth. It wasn't a matter of faith for me, rather, a sense of proximity.

Before Lebanon, heaven and the Bible stories were so far away in time, I could barely comprehend it. But, me and my newly acquired

Lebanon-land-legs figured out that if I lived to be a hundred years old, it was only twenty lifetimes to back when Jesus walked the earth. Twenty lifetimes against a universe that was—I'd read somewhere—five billion years old. Twenty lifetimes against five billion. A drop in a cosmic bucket!

When I wrote about it to The Squeeze that night, I discovered that in writing to her, I was also solidifying my experiences into learnings.

Some lessons in life are easy to learn. Like, touch a hot stove, and you will burn the crap out of your hand. Some things are more subtle and require the expenditure of mind-muscle sweat. Writing to The Squeeze, considering the words to use, making sure those words conveyed the right things the right way, nothing was more important than that. Those letters held us together and saved me from a *Hit the Road, Eddie,* missive.

But writing to her also helped me find meanings in experiences that would have floated away from me if I hadn't gone to my Eddie's-writing-to-his-One-and-Only-Squeeze space, and spilled ink on pages. Like finding that sense of proximity to the Holy Land, sensing the proximate presence of Father, Son, and Holy Spirit.

When I figured out that writing to her gave me something, too, it made me uneasy. I felt like before I sealed the envelope, I took some of what I'd written **for her** back for myself.

CHAPTER FIFTEEN

The only thing better than writing to The Squeeze was getting letters from her. By the time I got them, they might have been written ten days prior, but they carried with them a sense of right here, right now. I felt her love, in one way, more than I did in a phone call. Standing in a phone booth, the clock ticked a death sentence on the moments a quarter bought. During some of the phone calls we had during Boot Camp, the end of our talk time expired before we said, "Good night, I love you." We learned to start our conversations with "Hello, I love you." It was important to get those words in during a call, and that's how we resolved to do it. With the letters, that running out of time threat was absent.

There was a problem with the letters, though. We both wrote every day. Except during that first seasick time. So, the letters piled up. My storage space was limited. After we departed Beirut, I tore up about six months of written love and tossed them off the fantail in their own weighted garbage bag. I did not want to commend her letters to the deep, mixed with ordinary garbage.

Besides writing and disposing of letters, there was work to do. While we'd been in port, the ship, to save money, had purchased some locally grown vegetables. Chief Cook had us wash the veggies in a tub of water with a bit of bleach in it. Chief Cook explained, "The Supply Officer doesn't want to spend those savings on extra toilet paper."

Eddie's mind started to build a picture of three hundred officers, chiefs, and sailors all suffering gastrointestinal distress of extraordinary magnitude simultaneously while confined to the not-so-big destroyer. Then he flexed his mind muscles and shoved the half-formed image aside and began to sing, *Hi ho, hi ho, it's off to work I go, hi ho, hi ho.*

Eddie almost, but not quite, sang it out loud.

TBGH

After seven days at sea serving vegetables and fruit to the other two hundred ninety-nine well-behaved digestive tracts aboard, the ship pulled into Izmir, Turkey. I took another tour. This one to the ruins of Ephesus. I remember being impressed with the design of the city. There were sewers under the paved streets, and I remember the guide telling us about how the streets had been designed to accommodate chariots and that carts had to be no more than chariot-width wide. I guess I'd harbored the notion that we modern humans are a lot smarter than those ancients. It made me appreciate their intelligence. Made me wonder if not having conveniences spurred their brains to innovate, to create them. Maybe we moderns have so much handed to us that we wind up being dumber than the two-thousand-years ago dudes and *dudesses.*

> Note: In dredging up, resurrecting these memories, every once in a while, Pop says something like: *Whilst dredging up memories, a boy oughta also dredge up a little humility ever now and agin.*
>
> Note on the note: I've noticed that the older Pop gets, the wordier he gets.

That tour also took us to the house where St. John and the Blessed Mother lived, before she was assumed into heaven. This dwelling for the mother of the Son of God, for the Queen of Heaven, was **not** a bazillion stories high, with rooms as numerous as the stars in the sky. Rather, it was a highly humble abode.

Again, standing by that house, I was overwhelmed with the sense of transcending time, with my mind connecting to that two-thousand-year-old place, but also to that two-thousand-year-old time and to the holy inhabitants of the dwelling.

That feeling was **not** like: Hey BVM (Blessed Virgin Mary). It's You and me, right? We're buds, right?

No. So much awe filled this time-transcendent experience, there was no possibility of such a familiar and sacrilegious way to look at it. And I imagined Sister Daniel telling me: "Finally, Eddie, you know and appreciate what it means to adore and worship."

And, of course, Pop had to put in his dollar and two cents after amending his previous intervention: *A boy needs to add a big spoonful of humility onto his plate for breakfast, lunch, and supper.*

Then the tour bus driver tooted the horn. He'd told us, "Horn toot, you run back, or you get left (cuss word goes here) behind."

Which brought me back to earth as abruptly as a space monkey capsule without a parachute.

TBGH

Back on earth, we went back to sea. I went back to carrots, spuds, and Brussel sprouts. We'd gotten into a routine of Brussels sprouts for lunch and evening meal every blinking day for more than a week before we visited the Blessed Virgin's house in Izmir.

The crew was getting tired of the pygmy cabbages. They'd walk into the Mess Deck, smell the offensive greenies, and walk to the serving line holding their noses. Chief Cook gave the guys a day without them; then it was right back to twice-a-day sailors sliding their trays along the serving line with one hand while holding their noses with the other.

One of my duties was to dump the after-meal-cleanup bags of garbage off the fantail. The bags looked as if not even one sprout had been consumed. I also knew a good bit of the freezer compartment on the ship was filled with Brussel sprouts. I'd also found out, from the guys working in the galleys for Officer's and Chief's messes, that the stinky veggies were not served in those two dining rooms.

Tall Skinny Snipe, the guy who'd worked in the Vegetable Locker before me, the guy who'd sliced off the end of his finger, came to see me just before the Mess Deck opened for lunch. He asked me to get him a big bowl of Brussels sprouts. Which I did.

Later, I found out Tall Skinny Snipe had snuck into after officer's country and left the bowl on the fold-down desk in the Supply Officer's stateroom. Stunk up the room a bit.

The Supply Officer was torqued. He unloaded on Chief Cook. Chief Cook told us he knew, to a ninety-nine percent probability, that mess cooks had committed the foul deed. Just before dinner, Chief Cook assembled all the mess cooks. "Next port we come to, not a one a you is going on liberty."

We mess cooks knew Tall Skinny Snipe was more guilty than even me, but nobody said anything. Getting rid of Brussels sprouts was all that mattered.

The next time we pulled alongside a supply ship, we transferred several pallets of frozen Brussels sprouts back to them. For days after, the guys would parade through the serving line and tell Chief Cook, "Nothing beats string beans." "The peas sure are good, Chief." "Best (cuss

word goes here) carrots I ever et."

Four days after the sprouts departed, Chief Cook posted a sign on both doors into the Mess Deck: If anyone mentions a vegetable to me, any vegetable, the Brussels sprouts are coming back."

Nobody mentioned (unmentionable word goes here).

A couple of days later, our routine-routine had reestablished itself. At mealtimes, sailors paraded in, filed through the line, sat at a table and ate, deposited their trays in the scullery, and went back to work. No need to say anything to any of the cooks, especially not Chief Cook.

TBGH

Now, Number Five, what I have to report next is going to be … mind blowing. It's going to blow your socks off.

This is going to flip your lid!

CHAPTER SIXTEEN

Most of the chapters in this extensive response to the question about volunteering have been about ten pages. The preceding chapter, though, needed to be cut short because what happened next sure opened a new chapter in my life.

It was about 1000, and we were getting ready for the noon invasion of voracious appetites when Gutter from the ET Shop rushed into the mess deck. He found me scrubbing pots and pans.

"You made third class and you got NESEP," the seaman practically shouted.

It was strange. I heard what Gutter said, but it didn't really register. My brain was filled with my job. What Gutter said took a moment to elbow aside the veggie prep and scrubbing pots and pans business to appreciate what "making third class" and "accepted into NESEP" meant.

Then it hit me.

The realization blew my socks off.

I flipped my lid!

Until that happened, I hadn't known my mind wore socks or that it had a lid.

NESEP meant:

- College.
- College meant marriage to The Squeeze.
- Happy ever after, house with white picket fence, four kids.

After all the ups and downs of the last couple of months, was it for real this time?

"Earth to Eddie," Gutter said. "Didn't you hear me?"

"I heard." Chief Cook grinned and clapped a wet hand on my shoulder. "Walsh, you are relieved from mess cooking."

I said, "Chief, I owe you at least the rest of the day."

"You're going to be an officer. Get the hell out of my kitchen." Chief Cook laughed. "I always wanted to tell an officer to get the hell out of here. This is as close as I'll ever get to it. So, I say again. Get the hell out of here."

It was the third biggest day of my life. I made third class petty officer, got off mess cooking, and was accepted into NESEP.

The second biggest day was getting born. The first biggest thing was Cupid twanging an arrow into my gizzard when I saw your mother walking along Elm Street in St. Charles, Missouri, in May 1958.

So, see, Number Five. This development rated a new chapter.

> Dad, the slow learner, learns something new at last, and yet again. It occurs, after fifteen chapters, although, you, Number Five, asked the question, by proxy, that started this story, I am also talking to your Siblings. Sorry about that Sibs.

I had wanted to apply for NESEP, but I'd gotten seasick and ET Chief thought I was worthless. He was **not** going to let me take the test for third class or the one for NESEP.

Then, my division officer, Boy Ensign, intervened. He saw something in me which might be of use to the Navy in the future, whereas Chief ET saw me as useless as Brussels sprouts, something to be dumped overboard, which even garbage-eating sea life would turn their underwater noses up at.

All you holy angels and saints, thank you for Boy Ensign.
Holy Mary, Mother of God, thank you for Boy Ensign.
Father, Son, and Holy Spirit, thank You for Boy Ensign.

"Before you get the hell out of here, Walsh," Chief Cook said, "you and Gutter Mouth can eat with the mess cooks."

We grabbed trays and went through the serving line. Fried chicken, green beans, and apple pie for lunch that day. Chief Cook served me Brussels sprouts in place of the menu veggie.

I ate them. Without holding my nose. Even the stinky little cabbages tasted good that day.

Then, the strangest four days I ever spent in the Navy followed.

I had no duties to perform. Chief ET refused to allow me in the ET Shop. Chief Cook, the same with the mess deck. Another compartment cleaner had been assigned to the berthing compartment. First Class Radarman told me, "Walsh, if Dumb Butt has a question, answer it. But let him do the work. Got it?"

I got it.

What did I do? I read a novel, wrote to The Squeeze, and ate my three squares served to me by mess cooks.

Not doing anything felt like something I should confess. If it wasn't a sin, it felt close enough to being one, that just to be safe, I decided to confess it. Confess the sin of Goofing Off, Malingering, Failure to Do My Duty. Whatever it was and should be called.

One goof-off day, we took on fuel from an oiler, then food from a supply ship, and ammo from—what else?—an ammo ship. I watched those evolutions from the 01 level. I was sure I was the only guy on either ship, the one passing gas, the ones supplying groceries or bullets, and my ship who was committing the sin of goofing off. In the midst of a couple of thousand sailors in the fleet we sailed with, all of them worked hard. Only ETSN (actually ET3 only not formally promoted just yet) Eddie Walsh did not work at all.

That pronouncement by the duty section ET3 some months prior came back. Eddie Walsh was good at watching people work.

Why ain't you workin'?

I don't have any work to do, Pop.

No work to do! A boy's always got work piled up waitin' fer him. Even on Sundays. Chickens need to be fed. Eggs need gathering. Grass needs mowing.

Keep holy the Sabbath.

The way Pop looked at it, however holy the Sabbath was, it could be made holier by doing a little work.

One thing wrong with watching other people work, it allows too much time for too much thinking.

TBGH

Four days after the third biggest day of my life, my ship brought Goof-off Eddie Walsh to La Spezia, Italy. There, ETSN—but ET3 selectee—Walsh disembarked with orders to complete a two-month college preparatory class at Bainbridge, Maryland, and then to attend Purdue University (PU) in the fall.

SBT

A few words about the Naval Enlisted Scientific Education Program. Two hundred ninety-nine sailors, plus me, had been selected to start college the fall of 1961. Seventy-five of us NESEP-ers would go to Purdue University as Electrical Engineering candidates. The other selectees were scattered around the country in various colleges, pursuing science or other engineering degrees.

My recollections of leaving the ship have gotten fuzzied up some over the years. At the time, I think my mind was arguing with itself over whether all the good fortune that came with making PO3 and NESEP was real or a hallucination, a mental trick, like an upside-down seasickness. In this case, the delusion made me feel good instead of lousy.

Could this good feeling be based on reality? I know I was suspicious of the answer and scared of it, too.

At any rate, after we moored in La Spezia, Gutter Mouth accompanied me to the ship's office. There, a yeoman third class handed me an envelope containing my service record, health record, and orders. YN3 also gave me a slip of paper booking a seat on a bus that would convey me to an airport. There, I'd catch a ride on a military plane for the first leg of my trip back to the US.

Back on the quarterdeck, Gutter and I shook hands and said goodbye.

> Note: If this were to happen today, I'd hug Gutter. Back then, hugging a guy, in public or private, was a mighty big no-no. It'd have been like hugging Pop. My mind might be able to build imaginary illnesses that felt so real I barfed, or mirages of feel-goodness, but it could **not** create a picture of me hugging Pop, or any other male.

I showed my orders to the Officer of the Deck, saluted, and requested permission to go ashore.

"Permission granted."

I slung my seabag strap across my shoulder, and, with orders in my left hand, I saluted the flag with the other and departed … Gutter's ship. After a few paces along the pier, I stopped and turned. Gutter was still on the quarterdeck watching me. I saluted him. He waved. I went to find the bus.

Our conveyance to the airport looked like a school bus that had been painted blue, Air Force blue, not Navy. Chicken wire covered the outside of the windows. About half the seats on the bus were occupied. The driver instructed me to put my seabag in the rear with the others. Then, I found a seat a couple of rows ahead of the luggage. A few minutes later, a PO2 sat next to me. I asked him about the chicken wire over the windows.

He leaned forward and looked at my seaman stripes and the insignia marking me as an electronic technician.

I interpreted the look on his face as meaning: *I wish I'd parked my seabag on a seat and sat next to it.*

He said, "Most ports we enter, bar and brothel owners are happy to see us come to town. The rest of the citizens would just as soon we visit someplace else. Sometimes, those other citizens throw bricks at a US military bus."

That news surprised me. At the time, I thought after World Wars I and II and Korea, the people of the free world would appreciate that the US had fought for them as well as for itself.

Eddie Walsh, maybe you got stuff to learn besides Reading, Writing, etc.

A book, *The Ugly American,* had come out just before I graduated high school. I decided to get that book.

I and my seatmate traveled without exchanging another word. The bus stopped in Pisa, and we got an hour to visit the tower and grab lunch.

The tower leaned alright.

The bus ride continued. Nobody sat next to me on this leg of the journey. We entered a military airfield, and the bus took us to a passenger terminal. Inside, we checked our bags, and we were hustled to board a plane.

This was my second flight. The first one had taken me to boot camp. I remember looking out the window, watching the wings bob up and down in bumpy air. I thought the blinking things were going to snap off.

We're all going to die!

I remember thinking that, and about The Squeeze, and about her marrying a doctor.

On my second flight ever, departing Italy, I did not sit by a window. I sat in a middle seat and wrote to The Squeeze. I had a lot of things to say, and I ink-said them.

The trip back to the States was a two-legger. The first leg lasted a couple of hours; then we stopped at Port Lyautey Naval Air Station, Morocco. I put four stamps on The Squeeze's letter. I did not want my Morocco post-marked missive getting bounced for insufficient postage.

The layover lasted long enough for a trip to the chow hall and a visit to the base exchange. I found a paperback copy of *The Ugly American* there.

The flight across the Atlantic seemed long—long enough it made me wonder if the plane could carry enough fuel to get us all the way.

Running out of gas! Wings snapping off! Airplanes seemed like dangerous conveyances.

> Note to daughters: You know I became a Navy pilot some six years after that second plane ride of my life. But that comes after the end of this story, you know, the answer to the volunteer question.

As it turned out, we did have enough fuel.

But I discovered another thing during the flight. Eddie Walsh has a lot of trouble sleeping on airplanes. I for sure would not have wanted to miss it if the wings snapped off or the plane ran out of gas. And I got more than halfway through *Ugly*.

The book opened my eyes a bit. As mentioned, I always thought the nations the US saved from tyranny would be grateful. The book, though, let me get a tiny glimpse at how we Americans appear in the eyes of those **we saved**. Apparently, some of us Americans behaved like the saved didn't act near grateful enough, and we became ugly. Furthermore, if we look at World War I, we Americans did not want to get involved in another European war. We were not interested in saving anyone. Well, not interested in declaring war to save anyone. We did, of course, provide supplies to those fighting Germany. So, we did pick which side we wanted to be on, but we did not declare war until if became a fight, if not for our survival, to protect our interests. We were fighting for ourselves much more than fighting to save others.

So, we had no business acting ugly when we visited our allies. That was my conclusion after slogging through the book without taking even a weensy little nap. And it helped me understand the chicken wire protected windows on the Air Force bus.

As we deplaned, I felt like a Zombie. I retrieved my luggage because everybody else retrieved theirs, boarded a bus because somebody told me which bus to board, and debussed at Prep School because everybody else did.

Unfortunately, we arrived at 08:00. We couldn't take a day off to rest and let our body clocks begin the adjustment process. That would be the biggest waste of time, etc.

The arrivals, including Zombie Eddie, dumped their bags in a barracks and were told, "Bring your health records," before boarding another bus to the on-base medical facility. There, about a hundred of the latest arrivals were subjected to a rigorous physical exam, including the drawing of copious quantities of blood.

I normally, hate needles. Especially when multiple samples of blood needed to be taken. On that day, the seaman hospitalman had a lot of trouble finding the target vein. After multiple failed attempts on the left, he targeted the other arm and eventually captured the elusive fluid.

Normally, I would have passed out after the first couple of jabs, but in my altered state, I just stood there until someone told me to move. Of the hundred in my group, I was the only one with red cotton balls taped to both arms.

Lunch was restorative.

That afternoon, there was a physical fitness assessment: pushups, sit-ups, a sprint, a mile run, and an obstacle course. I scored middle-of-the pack on the first three tests, but the shortest time on the mile run.

I began running during third grade. Run home, gobble lunch, and hump it back to school and arrive so as to **not** miss a single minute of recess. PhysEd in high school kept me in shape. I jogged on my own during ET School. Since checking aboard the destroyer, I hadn't run much, but my legs and lungs apparently remembered how to do it as if recess depended on them.

The Navy saved the Obstacle Course for last. I did okay jumping hurdles and crawling on my belly. At the rope-climb wall, I went up it like a monkey and didn't fall coming down the other side.

Thank you, Heiny Horstwessle's hay bales, for the upper body strength.

At evening chow, the guys talked about calling me some kind of ape. Deck ape wouldn't do. "How about Scalded Ape. He went up that wall just like one."

Somebody else opined that I was too short to be an ape. Rather, I should have a monkey name. Just before dessert, I became Real Deal Monkey.

The next day it changed to RDM, which riveted the moniker to me until the end of Prep School.

Right after evening chow, I returned to the barracks and hit the sack and slept until reveille.

After breakfast the next day, we started classes. At the kindergarten level. But the most important thing was calling The Squeeze that night.

Surprised the heck out of her. She didn't know I'd made third class, been selected for NESEP, and come back to the good old US of A. None of my letters about that had had time to reach her.

My call surprised her, but it did not blow her socks off. She did not flip her lid.

I wondered at her bland reaction. *Doesn't she appreciate what a big deal this is for us? Can't she see that the path to our dream got a major dose of solidity added to it?*

I mean, what the heck, Squeezie! Doesn't this grip your gizzard even a little?

I was just smart enough to hang onto my happiness at my … **our** good fortune, and to shove those questioning thoughts aside and see that The Squeeze was joyed. Not overjoyed as I was. But joyed.

The Squeeze. Her faith in God was strong. Stronger than mine. She believed God wouldn't let bad things happen to us beyond our capability to handle them. She'd told me that any number of times. When bad things happened, she didn't get mad and pop off like I had: *God, how the heck could You let Sister Superior boot Sister Daniel out of the convent? How could You?*

She, on the other hand, would have lifted some of the burden up to God, and said, *Father, right now, the slings and arrows of outrageous fortune, the vicissitudes life has flung at me are a bit too much to handle by myself. Please help me with this part of it.*

If she had been dealing with what happened to Sister Daniel, she'd have said: *But more than my wants, please be with Sister Daniel. She has a beautiful soul. Help her keep it that way.*

Mulling all this, I began understanding the difference between being joyed and overjoyed that night on the phone call.

Back to the phone call. As I was wrestling with *why she didn't seem as happy as I did* with NESEP and being back in the States, I'm sure my guardian angel nudged a memory out of the back of my mind to the front. *The Squeeze believes God wants us to be together.*

That thought led me to dismount from my high horse of self-righteousness, and to wallow in being joyed, and to not be disappointed in not being overjoyed.

We completed a marvelous phone call.

TBGH

The next morning, it was back to classes and another visit to the O Course.

All week, the classes were indeed kindergarten-level RWA, Reading, Writing, and Arithmetic.

The weekend arrived, and Eddie felt as if he had returned to his destroyer with nothing to do but goof off.

After goof-off Saturday and Sunday, Monday arrived with pre-college calculus. A PO1 said, "It's the way the Navy does schools. They give you a couple of days of kindergarten-level stuff and then dump you into college-level classes. Like elementary and high school, who needs those?"

Yeah! That'd be the biggest waste of time there is.

CHAPTER SEVENTEEN

At Prep School, Eddie and one other guy were nineteen. All the rest of the three hundred were older. A couple of guys were really old—thirty even.

The fogies needed a fair amount of help with the academics. In a kind of ironic reversal of roles, the youngsters wound up helping the oldsters tone up their atrophied academic mind muscles. With the efforts expended helping the ancients learn the course material, Eddie realized his own learning wound up being enhanced as well.

A couple of days of check-in and physical and medical screening, followed by a couple of days of kindergarten, followed by seven weeks of challenging academics, and closing out with a couple of days of formalizing the selectee's enrollment in NESEP. Two hundred eighty-seven, including Eddie, completed Prep School.

Six of the non-selects could not hack the academics. Seven of them rejected the program rather than the Navy rejecting them.

"Four more years of this studying (CWGH{Cuss Word Goes Here})! To be a (CWGH) officer! No way! I'm (CWGH) outa here!"

A PO1 Eddie'd helped with his studies told the bellyache-er, "I don't care if you go away mad or not, Smedlap. Just go away." (Smedlap, not his real name, just a term used by Navy folks to denote a typical sailor whose name the speaker didn't care to know.)

Smedlap went away with his shoulders hunched up around his

neck, mumbling. And, of course, cussing the PO1, us selectees, and the whole (CWGH) Navy.

Eddie Walsh wound up being torqued off some, too. During Prep School, the NESEP-ers took a lot of tests. Which of course, were graded. Eddie wound up with a final grade of ninety-five-point-something. The kid who was a couple of months younger than ETSN Walsh scored ninety-seven-point-something. That rankled. But, the PO1 Eddie had helped with his studies, he knocked down a ninety-six-point-something. That flat torqued Eddie off.

His mind futzed with the notion that, in the future, he was going to only help people who were dumber than himself. But then, how The Squeeze would have handled the situation elbowed its way into his bean box.

She would have thanked God for the ninety-five-point-something. And thanked Him, too, for the good fortunes of the boy NESEP-er and the antediluvian one.

> Antediluvian. I'm not sure if William Faulkner used the word in one his books or if Eddie came across it looking up a word Mr. F. did use. Eddie liked having ink-word arrows like that in his quiver to fire at a page when an appropriate or semi-appropriate opportunity presented itself.

The Squeeze was L O V E in my life. She was also right and wrong to me. I have often pictured my guardian angel making a status report to God: "Lord, thank You for putting The One and Only Squeeze in Eddie Walsh's life. Without her, I know I would be here telling You I'd failed to help him save his soul.

Eddie tried to be like her, to say the thank Yous she said, but no matter how many times he said her words, they just didn't settle in, to where they took root and became **his** belief.

Until he went to the chapel one Thursday evening and sat in the solemn silence. Finally, the words settled in, and he finally took them on as his own.

That's one of the differences between Eddie and his One and Only Squeeze. She carries a balloon filled with quiet around with her, and whenever she needs to, she steps inside it.

Goober Eddie has to look hard to find where the world hides the stuff.

Finding silence of the solemn kind is important because it is a lot easier, especially for a goober, to find God in silence rather than looking for Him in the clamor of the world.

SBT in first person

What new question just hit my inbox? You'll never guess. So, I'll just tell you: "How did you decide where to go to college?"

In high school, I thought I'd go to the University of Missouri on a ROTC scholarship. That didn't pan out; then Pop shanghaied me into the Navy, where ET Chief wasn't going let me go to college. However, Boy Ensign overruled him. Maybe Boy Ensign sort of, in a way, decided. At any rate, isn't it funky that question hits my in-box at this point?

I heard The Squeeze in my head. "Eddie, NESEP happened for you, for us, because we prayed for it, and He answered our prayer."

Maybe I should do like the Squeeze, and quietly, calmy, thank Him.

I did.

TBGH and shift to third person happens

Rejoining the main trail.

Friday carried in some significant items for ETSN Walsh.

One: He signed a piece of paper and was discharged from the Navy, even though he had almost another year to serve.

Two: Thirty-seven seconds later, he signed another paper enlisting for six years. Another signature promised he'd sign a two-year extension onto that enlistment when he was halfway through college. Word was that a number of NESEP-ers dropped out in the first two years of college. The party scene got them, or college just was not for them. That's what the word said.

Three: ETSN Walsh received a reenlistment bonus of nine hundred fifty dollars. At the time, the Navy paid bonuses to retain schooled and experienced technicians.

> Note: ETSN Walsh had been selected for ET3, but his promotion date was still a month and a half in the future. If he could have reenlisted as an ET3, his bonus would have been forty percent larger.

Four: The ETSN hadn't known he'd get any bonus, so he thanked God for the unexpected blessing, and harbored not one iota of begrudging that he couldn't wait to reenlist until after he was promoted.

Well, perhaps a single iota of ingratitude festered in the pit of the stomach of his soul, but there for sure were not **two iotas** of the pus oozing from the tiny soul wound.

Five: He had two weeks of leave before he had to report to Purdue.
Two Weeks. With the Squeeze!

The only disquieting thought: *A lot of good things happening, too many, maybe.*

In the recent past, as soon as good things started piling up and elevating his spirit to overjoyed status, Chief ET or something else smacked him back to earth. And Eddie did not have Boy Ensign around to pull his bacon out of the fire.

Still, he manufactured some quiet around him, and from inside it, he thanked God and muscled out a *Thy will be done,* and an *Into Your hands, I commend my … our future.*

After doing so, he was joyed.

TBGH

There was the bus trip home. Eddie determined it would be his last bus trip. He had a plan. With his bonus, with the money in his savings account back home, and with another five or so hundred dollars, he figured he could get a new car. His plan called for a new car. He remembered guys having bought used vehicles and then spending time and money on getting them to run right, or to run at all. He was going to be a college student and wouldn't have time to be messing with a crippled car. He'd need reliable wheels to convey him across the three hundred miles from Purdue University to St. Charles, Missouri, and The Squeeze. Part of his plan was a minimum of one weekend home per month.

Eddie arrived at the Greyhound terminal in St. Louis at midafternoon. His next younger brother Lennie picked him up with Pop's car. During the ride home, he asked Lennie if he had any money in the bank.

Lennie nodded and glanced at his older brother.
"How much?"
"Nine hundred and probably thirty dollars."
"Can I borrow it?"
Another Lennie glance. "You'll pay it back?"
"Yes."
"With interest?"
"I'll pay you nine-hundred-fifty back."
Lennie smiled.

Eddie smiled. His plan was coming together. Asking Pop for a loan, that'd be the biggest waste of time, etc. And he did not want to borrow from the bank. They would not be flexible with how he paid them back. And he needed some time to figure out expenses at college. With the third class pay raise on the horizon, he was pretty sure he'd be able to handle the cost of living with a bit left over to pay Lennie back.

Pretty sure

TBGH

His first night home, Eddie borrowed Pop's Plymouth to take the

Squeeze to a movie. The second evening, the same automobile conveyed The Squeeze to his house to celebrate his twenty-first birthday.

Also, the Walsh family considered half that night's celebration belonged to Lennie. He was leaving for Navy boot camp.

The next day, Eddie, Mom, his other two brothers and his sister drove Lennie to the airport in St. Louis.

Two years prior, the Walsh family turned their oldest son over to the Navy at the same part of the airport. This time, Mom's eyes watered. Eddie wondered if Mom had had watery eyes when he went away.

That night, Eddie posed that very question to The Squeeze.

"Eddie, you are very intelligent. You are also very dumb. Your mother lost three babies before she had you. Of course, she had tears when you left for the Navy."

It took Eddie a while to figure it out. In his family, they were not given to public or private displays of affection. Mom, as best he could recall, hugged him once. Maybe, or even probably, when he was little bitty. Oh, and she hugged him and showered him with affection when he was in fourth grade.

He'd walked home from school one afternoon with Jimmie Joe Meinerschlagen. They talked about their recess baseball game. They laughed about Large Louie. He was an outfielder. A pop fly was hit to him. He didn't even have to move, and the sun wasn't in his eyes. He hollered, "I got it. I got it." He raised both hands toward the ball, and his glove hand turned back and forth on his wrist. The ball sailed down between his hands and smacked him right in the middle of his forehead.

"He didn't even say ow," JJ said.

Eddie laughed. "Funniest thing I ever saw." Eddie laughed some more.

A hand, a huge one, clamped onto Eddie's shoulder and spun him around. Then, lights exploded in his head.

He kind of woke. Sitting on his butt in a ditch full of cold, muddy water. His mouth hurt. He raised his hand to his lips and examined his fingers. Bloody. And muddy.

Large Louie stood at the edge of the street laughing his fool head off and pointing at Eddie. "Funniest thing I ever saw," Large said. Then he turned and walked away.

Large Louie had been behind JJ and Eddie as they descended the concrete steps leading down from the top of church hill. They were so busy talking about him, they didn't pay attention to who might have been behind them.

So, Eddie sat in the muddy water feeling his face with a muddy, bloody hand. The right side of his jaw hurt. The lips on that side hurt as well.

Jimmie Joe reached out a hand to pull him out.

He shook his head and stood, his tennies sinking into the mud, then stepped out of the ditch, each shoe making a "*splurp*" sound as he pulled it free. Eddie was half mad at Louie. Then he looked at Large Louie walking away, back toward Church Hill. Beyond him, those concrete steps rose to the top of the hill as if inviting someone to climb them and go to church. At the top, to the left of the stairway to heaven, the nun's house, and just past it, the church. From below the hill, where they were, it looked as if the point on the end of the steeple was high enough to poke a hole in the bottom of heaven, and that a person could get there by scaling the spire.

The half of his brain that wasn't mad told him: *You shouldn't have made fun of Large Louie.*

Eddie turned his back on Church Hill and started walking toward Main Street again. A couple of times, JJ said something. Eddie didn't respond. He just wanted to get home and put on some clean clothes. And dry underpants and socks.

The idea that he'd been wrong to laugh at Large Louie filled his head, and he didn't quite know how to handle the notion. Growing up, Eddie managed to get into mischief not infrequently. Many times, his younger brother Lennie got blamed. And spanked for something Eddie pulled.

At Main Street, Jimmie Joe turned right. He lived in the last house on that end of the street. Eddie turned in the other direction. His house was the last one on that end of town, right before the Main Street Bridge crossed Crazy Woman Creek.

Eddie walked past the funeral parlor and Mrs. Hemsath's house and came to the vacant lot next to his own building. He cut diagonally across the lot aiming for the rear corner of their ground-floor apartment, toward the kitchen. Mom would be there. Halfway across the lot, he cut loose yowling, crying like wolves were tearing his left leg off.

Mom came out the back door, saw Eddie, grabbed him, and pulled him into the only hug from/with her he remembered well and clearly.

Looking back on it now, Eddie wondered what drove him to start crying at that point, when fundamentally, after the punch, he'd sat in the ditch for a spell, walked home for about a mile, **then** started crying?

It made him wonder if he'd done that sort of thing to shift blame for his bad behavior onto innocent Lennie, to earn Lennie all those spankings for Eddie's misdeeds.

When Pop walked into the house after work, Mom told him what Large Louie had done.

Pop looked at his oldest with those eyes that could see inside Eddie all the way down to the insides of his feet. "What'd you do to make him mad?"

Along with a lot of stammering and stuttering, Eddie confessed.

When he shut up, heavy silence filled the kitchen. Pop's stare didn't make any noise.

Now, with hindsight, looking across seven decades, Eddie sees that one well-remembered hug was just chockful of unquestioning love and concern. She didn't care if he provoked the beating. She just wanted to take some of his pain and blood onto herself.

And Pop, his stare contained a message: *Son, you're lucky that lesson you just learned didn't cost you a whole mouthful of teeth. And don't* **never** *laugh at a guy who's bigger'n tougher'n you are when he can hear you.*

This was a Side Bunny Trail I didn't know I was on. Sorry

Anyway, Lennie left to join the Navy, and with the Squeeze's help, Eddie learned Mom and Pop had loved him. Though it took a while to get it.

KN5, your dad, the **fast** learner.

CHAPTER EIGHTEEN

I'd established a checking account to go with the savings one Pop'd had me establish after Heiny Horstwessel decided to pay me for working for him. I deposited my reenlistment bonus in the checking, along with the money Lennie loaned me and all the money from my savings except for one hundred dollars.

My plan was to buy a car as soon as I could wangle a deal, but longer range, I would need to buy an engagement ring. I would drop at least five bucks a month into savings until I could afford a ring.

The car was first.

I had an uncle who lived in St. Charles. He owned an automobile repair garage. His oldest son, Orville, had gone into the Navy, served four years, and now worked for his dad. I used Pop's car to go and talk with Orville about buying my own.

Orville was a big help. I wound up buying a Plymouth Valiant. My checking account covered the cost of the car and the first monthly payment for car insurance, with a couple hundred dollars left over. My wallet still held about half the travel money the Navy gave me to get to West Lafayette, Indiana, and Purdue. I also carried about half of my last paycheck.

All of this left me feeling rich. Not like the rich kid in town with whom I'd gone to grade school, but with enough money so I could feed from my own trough.

And KN5, I'm pretty sure my brain entertained the thought: *So there, Pop! You didn't think I could make it on my own. I guess I showed you!*

Anyway, I parked the Valiant on the grass next to the graveled driveway at our house. When Pop came home for supper, he didn't say anything about the car. My two youngest brothers and my sister sat around the table. Lennie, of course, was away at Boot Camp. Normally my three youngest siblings chattered away like crazy, but that night's meal was consumed in an unusual and deep silence. As if everybody, including Mom, were waiting for Pop to explode over the car. But he remained just as silent as he always was.

TBGH

The Squeeze had a couple of weeks off from nurse's training, and I took her to a movie in St. Charles. I was not ready to expose the Valiant to St. Louis traffic just yet. We went to the regular theater, not the drive-in. As I understood it, her parents had laid down dating commandments for her on two figurative stone tablets. Her father had inscribed one tablet: Thou shalt not go to a drive-in movie if there is even one boy in the car, and, further, thou shalt not meet up with boys at a drive-in.

Her mother had chiseled several rules on the other page of rock. Before leaving the house, The Squeeze was to obtain a **be home by** time from her mother. After the date, if her boyfriend brought her home before the expiration of permitted date time, Boyfriend could **not** park his car behind the large elm tree in the front yard, which would shield the car from the front window of the Squeeze's house.

After the movie, we had root beer floats; then I took her home.

Back at her house, the Valiant wanted to park behind the elm, but I forbade that.

The Valiant had its gear shift buttons on the dash. Pop's Plymouth had the gear shift lever mounted just under the steering wheel. What you did not want was a floor mounted gear shift lever. That kept your date from sitting snuggled up next to you. Made me glad I never used Heiny's car to date a girl. Floor mounted gear shifter. That's what his car had. It was in his car I learned to drive.

My car, though, permitted, maybe even invited, her to sit snuggled up against me. Which she did, and that felt so much better than owning my own car.

After I parked and turned off the engine, we kissed—until she pushed gently on my shoulder. I figured her mother's tablet contained something like: A girl has to control how much hugging and kissing is okay. A boy doesn't know how to do that and doesn't want to know.

She rubbed her hand over the dashboard. "I like your car, Eddie."

"It's our car." I didn't tell her that Lennie owned 43.18% of it.

"We're not even engaged, Eddie."

That was a big bucket of icy water dumped into an ardor-hot heart.

"Well, uh, I, uh, I have been thinking about it, and I wondered if you'd like to go with me tomorrow to look at engagement rings? I won't be able to buy one right away, but we should pick out one you like, and I'll start saving for it."

"I'd like you to pick it out, Eddie, but I would like it to be an emerald cut."

Eddie felt just like when he'd been five, and Pop had taken him to the creek and said, "Paddle with your hands and kick with your feet." Then, he'd been picked up and tossed out into the stream.

Eddie sputtered, coughed, and flailed.

"Paddle! Kick!"

Eddie made it to shore.

Pop pulled his son in and stood him on the muddy bank. "Hold your nose," he said, and threw the boy in again.

Eddie came to the surface.

"Let go of your nose. Paddle. Kick."

After the fifth repetition, Pop said, "That's enough. From here on, though, you best remember you still don't know much about swimming. And a boy don't need to learn how to drown. That comes easy."

Eddie jerked himself back to the driveway, the Elm, the window with her mother looking out.

"I have to go in now, Eddie."

As he drove home, he thought about the swimming lesson The

Squeeze had given him. "We're not even engaged." That **"even"** meant: *But it's high dad-burned time we got that way.*

We'd been going steady for three years at that point. Dates during senior year of high school tied us together, Then, during two years in the Navy, letters and rolls of quarters maintained the binding. The Squeeze had told me she loved me, and I believed her. Now she was telling me her finger needed something else on it other than Eddie Walsh's high school ring with the adhesive tape wrap to make it fit.

Slow learner Eddie Walsh picked up on **that** message PDQ.

The next day, I went to a jewelry store in St. Charles. It turned out the store was owned by a relative of the Squeeze's family. He knew I was dating his niece twice removed, or whatever she was to him. I told him about the emerald cut requirement.

"That'll be a little more expensive than a round stone."

I asked him how much more. He thought we should go for a half carat stone. My Adam's apple bobbed when he told me how much more the emerald cut would be. Then, he started asking me questions about my financial situation.

"I understand you are just about to start college. Can you afford that and a ring?"

"Yes, sir. I'm in the Navy, and the service is paying for college, and I draw my regular pay. Plus, I get an allowance for rent."

"The Navy is paying you to go to college? How'd you wangle a deal like that? Did you sell your soul to the Devil?"

I wanted to tell him that the Devil had sent one of his evil spirits—Chief ET—to try and keep me from going to college, but I replied, "I heard about this program in Boot Camp and applied for it. I was lucky and they picked me to go to Purdue."

"You owe anybody any money?"

Another Adam's apple bob, but I wasn't going to lie to the man. I told him about owing Lennie nine hundred and fifty dollars.

"Do you have your finances figured out? You know, money coming in each month and how much will go out?"

"Yes, sir. As best I can, but I won't know for sure until I get there.

"Okay, Mr. Walsh—

Holy crap! **Mister** *Walsh. I had never been called that before.*

—can you make a fifty-dollar down payment?"

"How about twenty-five, sir? I'd like to get to Purdue and make sure I've anticipated the expenses properly."

"Thirty."

"Yes, sir. Thirty." I pulled out my wallet and counted out thirty dollars.

That night, I told the Squeeze about the ring. She said, "Eddie!" in a voice that spurred my toes to start dancing the Hokey Pokey, and then she laid a kiss on me that would have steamed up the windows of the Valiant—if they'd been up—so thick her mother would not have been able to see what we were doing even though we weren't parked behind the elm tree.

I loved the Squeeze with all my heart and all my soul. I wrote it to her. I said it to her. All of both belonged to her.

That kiss. It was as if my heart and soul were balloons and **that kiss** blew my heart and soul bigger, to the point where just the weensiest bit more air and both those parts of me would have gone **Blooiee!!** The heart and soul expansion stopped just short of the explosion, but in their growth, I knew I loved her more than had been possible before the "Eddie!"

That kiss, though, so full of passion and love and invitation, sat me back on my heels while my toes kept right on dancing. But then, enthusiasm for that smooch turned into another balloon blowing up. The Squeeze unlocked her lips from mine and pushed on my shoulder to separate us.

"I love you, Eddie. So much that I have to go in now."

Wait a pea-picking minute! How did that make sense? She loved me so much she had to get away from me?!!?

I was wrapped up in those questions as I drove home. She loved me so much she had to get away from me? *How did that make sense?* And the kiss. The most wonderful kiss out of the one hundred and eleven thousand kisses we'd shared since the end of junior year in high school, and as soon as I started kissing her back the way she was kissing me, she pushed me away! *How did that make sense?*

Then! Holy Mary, Mother of God, pray for us sinners now and at the hour of death, amen!

I jammed on the brakes, and the tires screeched. Dead Man's Curve. The highway, about halfway between St. Charles and where I lived, hooked a left turn of almost ninety degrees. Off the edge of the pavement stood this massive oak tree. Over the years, any number of cars had plowed into the tree. Mr. Acorn Producer barely lost a patch of bark in those encounters, but the drivers and passengers were hurt bad or killed.

The Valiant got itself slowed and righted with the road.

I could have been killed!

Worse! I could have wrecked the Valiant!!

Let me tell you, I concentrated on driving the rest of the way home.

After I parked on the grass next to the driveway at home, I got out, walked to front of the car, and imagined what that massive oak would have done to the Valiant.

As I was thinking, the car said, *"Eddie, when you're driving a car, drive the car."*

The vehicle hadn't said *"When you're driving me."* It said, *"Driving a car."* The unselfishness of the Valiant's statement struck me.

Behind the steering wheel, from that day forward, Eddie Walsh let nothing but driving occupy the center of his bean-box brain container.

Most of what we did on dates was go to movies. The next night, we were going to see a double feature at the Fox Theater in St. Louis. As we hit the highway heading east, she said, "I say something to you, and you grunt a response. Don't you want to talk to me?"

"We can talk." I kept my eyes doing their jobs, though. Checking ahead, to the sides, the mirrors. I kept both hands on the steering wheel. Before Dead Man's Curve, I used to rest my right hand on the top of her thigh, not gripping it or anything confessable. Just resting it there as she pressed close to me.

"Eddie, would you prefer I not sit so close to you?"

"I like you to sit close to me."

The odometer clicked off a few silent miles.

"What happened, Eddie?"

The dad-burned woman! *Sure won't do to try to hide anything from her!*

I confessed Dead Man's Curve. I could feel her thinking about what I'd told her—but I still had 96.5% of my brain on driving.

"There's a lesson in your story for me and my driving. Thanks for sharing."

Dear God in heaven! Had she had a close encounter also? If she were killed, that would be the worst thing in the world.

No, Dumbbutt! The absolute worst thing in the world is if you make a mistake driving and kill her.

My mind ratcheted to 98.5% concentrated on driving.

CHAPTER NINETEEN

Eddie figured the drive to West Lafayette, Indiana, would take six hours. It took six. The first night in the town that would be his home for the next four years, he spent in a motel. When he checked in, the guy behind the counter, probably a college senior, said, "that'll be $27.56. Please."

Sarcasm gilded the "please."

Eddie frowned. "The sign says the rooms are $22."

"The rest is city and state taxes and fees. You want the room or not?"

Eddie blushed and paid for the room plus the 25% markup. He felt like he knew more about Beirut, Lebanon, Izmir, Turkey, and San Juan, Puerto Rico than he did about his own country.

There was a phone in the room, but he was sure the motel would gig him for taxes and fees if he used it for a long-distance call. He found a phone booth outside a restaurant and spent four quarters on calls to The Squeeze and to his mom to report his safe arrival.

The bed in his room was almost as comfortable as his bunk on the destroyer had been. Plus, he wasn't seasick, and that ashore-normal feeling rubbed off some of the corrosion of the 25% markup.

The next morning, he drove to the Navy ROTC building to check in. He arrived at 07:00. The place didn't open until 08:00. *Judas priest! Half the day's wasted by then!*

For his birthday, Mom and Pop had given him a brief case sort of thing. It was big enough to carry a bunch of books. At that point, though, it contained his records and orders, his William Faulkner dictionary, a paperback grammar from The Squeeze, and a novel. It also contained stationary. So, he wrote to The Grammar Gifter for one half hour and read for another. At 08:00, he looked out his windshield toward the door into the ROTC unit. Two guys waited there. Eddie got out of the Valiant and got in line behind the two waiters. One was a First Class, the other a Second-Class Petty Officer. They were both members of my NESEP group of seventy-five freshmen Electrical Engineering students.

Finally, at 08:10, a sailor in a dress white uniform, an E-4 yeoman, opened the door.

"Sign says you open at 08:00," the First Class said.

The yeoman shrugged.

"Shore duty sailors!" the Second Class said.

"You check in at the Admin Office. Left side of the hallway, halfway down."

"Left, is that port or starboard?" the Second Class asked the First.

"Hallway, I forget, is that what landlubbers call a passageway?" The First asked the

Second.

"Maybe," the yeoman said, "next year's crop of NESEP-ers will show up with some new material."

In the Admin Office, we deposited our service records, health records, and orders. Then, we were directed to take a seat in the meeting room at the end of the **hallway.**

The in-processing reminded Eddie of Boot Camp. A mass of people herded along through a process that treated everybody equally, but it made a person feel like he amounted to nothing, and nothing can't be equal to anything, not even another nothing.

A general meeting of the NESEP class of 1965—that's what we were called and when the Navy expected us to graduate—had a general assembly scheduled to start at 08:45. As we filed into the Meeting Room, a yeoman directed us to a table against the wall to the right.

"It's a (cuss word goes here) bulkhead, (Cuss Word Goes Here)," someone said.

A chief petty officer had been standing in the port corner of the compartment. He elevated his voice to bullhorn level. "Listen up, College Boys, you ain't in the Navy anymore. You are in an institution of higher learning and surrounded by civilians. They don't know what a bulkhead is. So, start practicing saying and **thinking** floor, ceiling, and wall. Another thing. Cussing. Knock off the cussing. Civilians don't talk that way, and you will have women in almost all your classes."

Somebody groused, not at bullhorn level but intended to be heard, "(cuss word goes here), in Boot Camp they took away my tightie whities. Here they take away my language."

> Note: In Boot Camp, on the first day, we wound up stripped down to buck naked as we paraded through a series of medical exams. The clothes we wore upon arrival were bagged and would be returned after we completed the program. Nobody asked if we wanted tightie whities or boxers. They issued us white boxers. Loosie Whities, some of the Tightie guys called them.

From his corner, Chief Bullhorn bellowed, "No (cuss word goes here) cussing!"

A hear-a-pin-drop silence filled the Meeting Room. For a tick and a tock. During which, no one moved. Then someone sniggered, and the Class of '65 NESEP-ers started moving again.

Chief Bullhorn, he knows how to orient a bunch of salty sailors into a college environment.

The group picked up their packets and took seats on desktop chairs like Eddie used in grade school. Of course, the Navy ROTC desks were larger than the ones Eddie had in his upper-three-grades classroom. Once seated, everyone opened their packets. Inside were a map of the campus and a schedule for the next three days. Classes officially started for the fall semester on Thursday.

The seventy-fifth NESEP-er entered the Meeting Room at 08:42.

He grabbed his packet and headed for the back of the room. Before he found a seat, "Attention on deck!" startled the entire room full of sailor-to-student transition-ees. We'd entered as sailors, were told we were students, and got comfortable with that notion. Then, Chief Bullhorn jerked us right back into full immersion Navy.

A Navy lieutenant, the officer in charge (OINC) of the unit entered, stood behind a podium, put us at ease, and bade us sit.

We sat.

Our OINC—pronounced oink—welcomed us for about three minutes. As he spoke, Eddie looked at Chief Bullhorn in his corner. Eddie was sure he had deliberately orchestrated the group's welcome to leave a message: Don't let yourself get too comfortable too fast. *Aye, aye, Chief B.*

And there was another lesson for Eddie. If you have words to live by, live by them. Duh!

After the lieutenant departed, a first-class yeoman took over and explained a number of things, like the ROTC library contained books for all the courses they'd take while at Purdue and how to check them out. A little later that day, Eddie found out how much some of those books cost. Judas Priest! The books for one semester's work could cost as much as an engagement ring! *Thank You, Father in heaven, I don't have to spend ring money on books!*

We broke for lunch at 11:15. I, a car guy, drove three guys to a fast-food place.

Next, we met in the auditorium in the Purdue Electrical Engineering building for our welcome there. Then I checked into the dorm that would be my home for … who knew how long?

The room was good-sized, larger than the room Boy Ensign occupied with another officer on my destroyer. In it were two beds and two desks. A bathroom down the hall served the residents of the floor. The guys on my destroyer would have paid money to be able to use it. My roommate wound up being this six-foot-nine dude. The ends of his legs hung over the foot of his bed. He wound up being "Goliath" in the dorm. Guess what they called Eddie. In case you can't guess, I was David without a slingshot.

I found out there was a first-class petty officer in my group who had an acquaintance in last year's Group Five NESEP-ers. I attached myself to him for the rest of the process of getting registered for classes. He tolerated me.

In addition, he was married and had two children. There was a lot I could learn from him about being married whilst in the Nav. Of course, at that point, I couldn't even buy an engagement ring to cement the path to marriage. Still, I was sure I should not waste the opportunity to learn from him for the time when The Squeeze and I were able to marry.

The first day of classes was also my date for promotion to third-class petty officer. That pay raise, to me, was more important than the rise in rank. I had an engagement ring to save for.

NESEP-ers carried a heavy load of classes. We were being paid to go to school, and the Nav wanted to get its money's worth from the investment. My days = classes + studying + a letter to The Squeeze. And, of course, eating, doing laundry, and washing the Valiant.

I liked all my classes except one. Speech. I hated getting in front of the class and arguing that women should not be allowed to vote. In the first place, arguing for something I didn't believe in rubbed me the wrong way. It made me feel like I had to go to confession after delivering my argument. I got an F on that assignment. The professor told me I didn't get it. It was an assignment. And it was meant to be a challenge, to build a believable argument for something you did not believe in.

The following month, I got an A on the assignment to argue for the right of women to vote.

In my mind, the professor didn't get it. Arguing for something you do not believe in? It would have made me feel ugly, slimey, dirty. So much so that The Squeeze couldn't and wouldn't love me anymore. At any rate, I wound up with a C in the class. I knocked down As in all the rest.

It felt good being back in school studying engineering, math, and science. Problems in those courses had one solution, not like that stupid Speech class where we were supposed to learn how to lie better.

Even with that one stinker class, I figured I had a good first semester.

The ROTC OINC called me in to review my report card. He wanted to know about my C grade. I explained.

"Walsh, going forward from here, you want to be careful with how you deal with your professors. Arguing with them over how they choose to teach their classes, you could wind up with an F. If you fail a class, the Navy requires you to retake it, and if you flunk on your second attempt, you'll be kicked out of school and sent back to the fleet. Understand?"

I understood the Speech professor was probably a nephew of Chief ET from my destroyer.

"Think about this," the lieutenant continued. "If your job is to argue before a deciding body that women should have the vote, wouldn't you be able to do a better job presenting your case if you understood what kind of arguments the other side would put forward?"

I glanced down at my hands on my lap and back up. "I should have seen that myself, Sir. Thanks for the kick in the butt."

As I walked back to the dorm, I thought the OINC's butt kick was a lot easier to take than the one from ET Chief—almost a year ago. I wondered if I'd ever outgrow the need for one periodically.

TBGH

The first weekend in October 1961, I made my inaugural monthly trip home to see The Squeeze.

I attended my 13:00 class but skipped the next three. I'd talked to my profs and told them what I was doing. They shrugged.

I wished one of the ones I was cutting was stupid, stinking Speech, but no such luck. A guy who lived in my dorm came from St. Louis. He agreed to split the cost of gas for a ride home. Dropping him off cost me twenty-five extra minutes before I could see The Squeeze. But chopping the cost of the trip home in half, well, that threw a few extra shekels into the engagement ring piggy bank.

An elective I took that semester was Sociology. One of the concepts covered was deferred gratification being a hallmark of the middle class. Middle-class young people took the time and scrimped to make it through college so they could land good jobs paying a decent wage.

I arrived at the Squeeze's house at 21:45, parked, walked up the sidewalk, and knocked. One and Only let me in to find her parents watching TV. They would not be going to bed until after the ten o'clock news, and I recognized the necessity for deferring the gratification of reunion.

Finally, the news concluded, and the *Tonight Show* came on.

Her father said, "Goodnight," whilst skank eying the crap out of me.

Her mother said, "Goodnight, Dear," to The Squeeze and kissed the top of her head.

Then, they took turns in the bathroom. The TV was still on with the volume turned down to a whisper, but we weren't watching or listening. We were deferring, she patiently, me not so much.

Finally, her parents finished their business and closed the door to their bedroom. I kept looking at that door.

"Eddie???" she whispered.

"I'm afraid one of them will pop out and go to the kitchen for a glass of water or something," I whispered back.

She grabbed my chin, turned my face, and locked her lips onto mine. Gratification that's been deferred, once it no longer resides in that category, sure tastes sweet. But, The Squeeze managed that gratification and kept a major part of it in the "not just yet" closet. And that was, in my mind, right and just. I came to that conclusion after I parked the car beside the driveway at Mom and Pop's house. During the trip home, I had kept my mind on driving. But, like I'd done on the destroyer tender when I'd had my ingrown toenail removed, I took some time to sort out The Squeeze and me, where we were, and how we got there.

I said, *Thank You, Father in heaven, for The Squeeze and for where we are headed. Oh, yeah. And thank You for the Valiant.*

Then I went inside without locking the Valiant, though I locked the doors in the dorm parking lot at Purdue. I didn't have a house key, either. Those doors were never locked. As I climbed into bed, I thought of Lennie in Boot Camp, and I said a prayer for him. Then I slept like a log.

Sunday night, The Squeeze and I watched *Bonanza* before I headed for St. Louis to pick up my rider. The show ended at 22:00. At 22:03, The Squeeze kissed me goodbye. Chastely. Her parents were watching the news.

During the six-hour drive back, my rider and I took turns driving hour-and-a-half shifts.

I attended all my Monday morning classes.

Before I made the next monthly trip home, my rider found two other Purdue students from St. Louis, and they paid for the gas for the round trip. Extra bucks in the engagement ring piggy bank. Still, filling the piggy was slogging along at a pretty slow pace. I was also putting a few bucks into Lennie's account to pay him back. I had a long way to go to settle that debt, too.

During the school year, the weekend trips home did not require me to take leave. Over Christmas, I had to use half my annual thirty-day allotment for the two-week break. But I still had plenty of days on the books. When we got married, I thought I better have two weeks saved up for, you know, the honeymoon.

The second semester at college went pretty well for Eddie Walsh. He disliked none of his classes, as he had stinking Speech. The monthly trips home with his three riders paying for the gas continued. At the end of freshman year, he had one hundred fifty dollars in the piggy bank, and he'd paid seventy-five dollars into Lennie's account.

At the end of the second semester, Eddie made a change. He'd moved into an apartment in town with three other NESEP-ers. They had second-story rooms above the widow-lady landlady's house. Rent split four ways was cheaper than the dorm fee. Groceries and cooking for themselves also saved a bit.

TBGH

The Navy required its NESEP-ers to take classes during the summer. Eddie quickly grew to dislike the summer session. Even though the course load was half that of a normal semester, the summer program flung material at students at a frantic pace. Eddie still got good grades, but he didn't take a weekend to see The Squeeze. Saturday and Sunday study were required to knock down A grades.

At the end of the summer session, Eddie took off a week and drove home, having to pay for all the gas himself. The Squeeze still had classes to attend, so Eddie worked at Ementhaller's Garage during the day. Changing oil, checking brake fluid and antifreeze, tune-ups, and tires he knew how to handle. After instruction, he worked on carburetors. He dated his student nurse each night. The last evening Eddie was home, he parked outside her dorm, turned off the motor, and reached for her.

"I'd like to talk to you, Eddie."

His heart coughed an ice cube into his lungs. He sat back.

Dear God in heaven, please?

"Before we get engaged, we should date other people to make sure we are really committed to each other."

"But I am committed to you. I could not be more committed. And I could not be more sure." Eddie drew a breath. "You're not sure? About me?"

"Eddie, I love you. You know I do. But, we haven't dated anyone else for almost four years now. I just think it would be wise to date a few other guys and for you to date some girls, just to be sure."

"Are you dating ... other guys?"

"No, Eddie. I wasn't going to until I told you and made sure you are all right with it."

All right with it!!!!! Judas fribble frapping Priest! I hated the idea.

"Someone has asked you out though?"

"Yes."

"A doctor?"

"A med student."

"A doctor."

I don't remember saying goodnight to The Squeeze. I don't remember if we kissed goodnight. I remember the drive home. I remember telling myself over and over and over: *Keep your mind on the road, Eddie. Drive the stupid Valiant, Eddie. Pay attention to the road. Pay attention to the speedometer.*

I talked to myself to keep pictures from forming in my head of

My One and Only Squeeze on a date with some goober med student, sitting close to him in his Corvette with the top up, her arm tucked under his, as he drove. But then I hoped like heck the Corvette had bucket seats. But then, visions of hugging and kissing tried like heck to crowd into my bean-box brain-container.

A couple of miles short of home, Dead Man's Curve loomed. A thought snuck in: *The plan, NESEP, college, marriage, house with a picket fence, four kids, poof. Gone. Speed up. Just drive into the tree and get it over with.*

Then Pop's voice sliced through all the crap piling up in Eddie's head. *"Boy. You drive into that tree you will go to hell and hurt your Mom something fierce. If you go to hell, I will go there too, and I will find you, and you will see why, when you needed a spanking, it was always your Mom who give it to you and not me."*

Eddie did not drive into the tree. At home he parked in the driveway, not beside it. He'd intended to leaving early the next morning for a daytime drive back to West Lafayette, but he went inside, threw his stuff together, returned to the Valiant, and headed back to college.

CHAPTER TWENTY

During the dead-of-night drive back, halfway through Illinois, Eddie's litany chant: *Keep your fribble frapping mind on driving, Watch the stupid speedometer, Check the stinking rearview mirror* morphed into *Watch the damn speedometer* and thereafter, damn became the universal modifier of choice.

The evening after he arrived back at Purdue he wrote to her: *I don't know what to say, to write, except I love you and always will. Always.*

On the backs of his envelopes addressed to her, he always wrote SWAK (Sealed With A Kiss). That night, he went to bed with the back of the enveloped pure and naked. The next morning, just before he mailed the letter, he SWAK-ed it.

The weekend after he arrived back at Purdue, one of his roommates invited Eddie on a double date. The roommate was going with a girl from Indiana University, and she was driving up for a concert at Purdue with a girlfriend. "You're not scared of a blind date, are you, Eddie?" Roommate asked.

Date other people, The Squeeze said.

Roommate drove. It turned out Eddie's date was very good looking. The blonde pegged the attractiveness meter at the knockout end of the scale. But, she was as cold as that ice cube that had dropped into his chest when The Squeeze said, "Date other people." Roommate's girlfriend got in the front seat, and she slid against him, just like The Squeeze did when with Eddie. Or at least, she used to. Eddie's date pressed herself tight against her side of the car. At the concert, Blonde sat next to Eddie, but they both took care to avoid touching. At intermission, he bought her a Coke. She said, "Thank you." Those seemed like the only two unforced words exchanged between them.

At the end of the concert, Roommate's date suggested they drop Eddie off first. Which they did.

After he got out of the car in front of the house with four NESEPers renting the upstairs, Eddie stood on the sidewalk and watched the blue Chevy pull away with Miss Iceberg now moved to the center of the rear seat.

He'd bought a concert ticket and a Coke for Miss Cold-Everything-Not-Just-A-Stinking-Cold-Stinking Shoulder. *Biggest waste of money there ever was.* But then, did he even need to save money for an engagement ring anymore? He didn't know—and there was no answer in the taillights speeding away from him. He turned and walked to the outside wooden steps leading up to the apartment.

The other two guys were in the living room watching TV.

"How was the date?" one asked.

Eddie continued on to his room.

"That good, huh?" caught him in the hallway outside his bedroom.

TBGH

Eddie thought about writing a letter, but he did not want to tell The Squeeze about his date. He sure did not want her to write to him about her dates. He hated thinking about that, about her close to someone else driving to—Dear, God. A drive-in movie!

As he sat in a puddle of light from his desk lamp in his dark room, with a deaf, dumb, and not happy ballpoint in his hand, he remembered being in high school.

SBT

With a teacher's help, he'd applied for a ROTC scholarship and received a letter from the Navy informing him he was selected as a fourth alternate. If four higher ranked alternates dropped out, Eddie Walsh would get a scholarship.

His high school teacher told him, "Alternate is good. After the selection process, a good number of the selectees decline the appointment for any number of reasons. Maybe they received an offer from another service they preferred. Maybe they enrolled at another college where their girlfriend was going to school. Hang in there. Chances are you'll get an appointment."

Pop said, "They just ain't got guts enough to tell you, 'You flunked.'"

The next Saturday, Pop shanghaied Eddie into the Navy.

SBT Rejoins Main Trail

Now Pop's voice was telling him, "Date other people just means she ain't got the guts to tell you it's over."

Near the end of his second semester at Purdue, Eddie checked a Steinbeck book out of the library. He read *Of Mice and Men* and resolved to read all his novels. The afternoon before his double date, he'd checked out *The Grapes of Wrath*. Now, after having dated another girl, he laid aside the useless pen and picked up *Grapes*.

The story sucked him in, and he read until 02:30. Then, worn out in body, mind, and soul, he climbed onto his bed with his clothes on—he did remove his shoes—and slept.

And woke wondering why the ship wasn't rocking and rolling. He squinted. The sun had slithered fingers of light through the venetian blinds.

Oh! Purdue. NESEP. Date other people.

Inside his head, a voice sniggered: *If you ever wondered what's worse than waking up seasick, now you know.*

St. Michael the Archangel, defend me in battle against the damned devil.

Eddie swung his feet over the side of the bed, sucked in a big breath, and huffed it out. Then he sat there thinking about his One and Only Squeeze, on a date with another person, and going to a drive-in movie.

Then he remembered one of her rules. She would only go to a drive-in with Eddie if it were a double date. He felt the corners of the mouth of his soul tweak up into a tiny smile, but then he felt the smile turn upside down. Maybe that rule did not apply if she were dating a doctor.

Sh—

Shoot!

Git up!

He got up. All his roommates were still asleep. He completed his business in the head and made a pot of coffee and breakfast. As he ate, he came up with a new plan. He knew the dining hall was hiring students to help prepare and serve meals. Eddie Walsh had no small amount of experience with that line of work. He'd get a job there, hopefully working breakfast, say from 05:00 to 07:00. With the money he made there, he could pay off the debt he owed Lennie.

The dining hall was happy to have him. Breakfast was the hardest to get students to sign up for. Monday was the first day of classes. Eddie would start work then. He reported to a woman, about five feet tall, not stout, but substantial, and If Chief ET would have been a woman, Eddie knew Chief ET would look just like his new boss. She certainly acted like he did.

Eddie liked the money he earned, and he liked all his courses that semester. His evening study time, though, he split between homework and reading his new best buds, Steinbeck and Hemingway. Course work did not keep thoughts of The Squeeze going to a drive-in on a date with a doctor out of his head as effectively as those two authors did.

The day after he landed the dining hall job was Saturday. Sometimes Eddie went to Mass on Saturday evening. That night he decided not to go. He was reading a book of Hemingway short stories. Instead of hearing the Word of The Lord, he read Ernie's words.

The next day, Sunday, over coffee by himself in the kitchen, he remembered last spring semester, sitting with guys in the dorm dining room as they discussed whether there was a God or not. One of them said, "There is not one shred of scientific proof He exists." "Right," from another. "Everybody who writes about **him** and capitalizes the word is just brain-washed stupid."

At the time he'd heard those guys spouting off their educated theorizing, he'd considered them to be **"brain-washed stupid."** Now he wondered. Then he decided he would not go to Sunday morning Mass, either. Instead, he picked up one of his textbooks. After two hours of that, he read Hemingway for two hours. That's how he spent the day. Two hours of textbooks followed by two of fiction.

Monday morning. Early wakeup. Drive across the Wabash River from Lafayette to West Lafayette for the job in the dorm dining room. Work there for two hours. His full day of classes began at 08:00.

Neither his courses nor his reading could banish the persistent image of The Squeeze and her drive-in date. Those two activities did, however, tamp down the level of anguish from contemplating the godawful vision. He reminded himself of the time when he'd told The Squeeze he would not be going to college and that she should find a doctor to marry. He only wanted what was best for her. Eddie's brain had banished the crap out of that recollection. Now, it was back, and it brought no comfort with it.

Through the first week of the fall semester, Eddie was some kind of sick. It wasn't seasickness, though, sort of like it. Not the flu, either, but sort of like it. Then, on Saturday, the mailman dropped three letters in the box for Eddie. From The Squeeze. He hurried upstairs to his bedroom and tore open the one with earliest postmark.

What the heck? It was a normal Squeeze letter. There was no hint of *Oh, Eddie, I'm dating other guys now.*

He read the letter a second time and was even surer. A time-tested and true love letter. Tear open the second. Devour it. Same with the third.

A spike of anger arced across the darkness in his head. *Date other people.* What could that possibly mean but serve as a prelude to HIT THE ROAD. Even though he'd never admitted to himself that she was casting him adrift, he'd spent the week trying to prepare himself for exactly that.

Now love letters. What the heck?

He opened his desk drawer and looked at it his stationery box for a moment.

You're dating doctors but you write to me like nothing has changed, when everything has. I mean, can I even address you as Dearest while I'm dating other girls? Do I have to change the salutation to just Dear?

Then he had another thought. He had dated Miss Iceberg, there'd be no quibble over use of a grammatical superlative if he wrote to her. *But why would I write to her?* He watched that thought recede in front of him like the taillights on the caboose of a train rolling away from him, and he was right back into his confused funk. Writing to The Squeeze in his present state had a 99.8% probability of making a screwed-up situation screwed-*uppider*. Calling her also seemed fraught with the same promise of an undesired outcome.

He closed the drawer on his stationery box and spent two hours doing homework.

Saturday evening, he again didn't feel like going to church. So, he didn't. The next morning was a no-work-in-the-dorm-dining-hall day. Student employees were not permitted to work seven days a week. Eddie slept in, rose at 0530, and zipped through the morning business. There was an 0800 service at the Catholic church near the campus in West Lafayette. He always attended Mass there. Sometimes Saturday evening. Most of the time the 0800 on Sunday. He thought about not going to Mass. He thought about going. He recalled finding answers in church. He thought about Sister Daniels.

He went to church, and participated in the prayers, the rituals, except for communion. Receiving the body and blood of Christ into his doubting soul did not seem right. But then he wondered. *Do I really doubt? Or am I just screwed up by this* Date other people *thing?*

After Mass and everyone left, he stayed. For forty-five minutes. No answers came to him.

He thought about one of the unwritten rules students had. If you go to a class being taught by a teacher's assistant, and if he was late, it was okay to leave after five minutes. For a full professor you waited fifteen minutes. But how long did you wait for God?

Long as it takes. If you had a lick a sense, you'd see that.
Yeah, yeah, Pop.

Back at the apartment, the guys had grilled hamburgers and prepared a few go withs.

"Wanna a burger?" Roommate One said.

"Yeah, thanks."

"Double digits," Roommate Two said.

"Double digits?" Roommate Three queried.

Two: "Yeah, since the start of this semester, Eddie has spoken nine words to us. Not counting the 'Hello,' and 'Goodnight,' he spoke to his blind date the night of the concert. 'Yeah, thanks' plus nine equals eleven. Double digits."

Three: "You counted Eddie's words?"

"I did, but I won't be able to anymore."

Three: "Cause you ran out of fingers with Eddie's 'Yeah,' right?"

One: "You're not joining in the snappy repartee, Eddie?"

Eddie picked up his plate from his place at the table. He'd already said thanks. He turned and carried lunch to his room. *Heck. Maybe it'll even taste good in there. It sure won't out here.*

As he ate the scrumptious burger, he finished the last tale in a book of Hemingway short stories. He planned to take it back to the library that afternoon, but he flipped back to the first story. *The Short Happy Life of Francis Macomber.* Francis was on a safari to Africa. We learn he is hen-pecked, dominated by his wife.

Is that what has happened to me? The Squeeze controls me and my life. Date other people. I should have said, No. I'm not dating other girls, but if you feel like you have to date other guys, well, it's your decision.

Out of the confused mess in his head, Eddie knew one thing. He could not write or talk to The Squeeze the way he was thinking. Fundamentally, he did not know how to disagree with her. And even more fundamentally, he did not want to know.

TBGH

Nobody has figured out how to stop a Monday from appearing when it wants to. *Git up* got Eddie up that day and the succeeding ones. And each day was pretty much the same as the one before.

Then, Thursday happened. September 13. The University declared it Sadie Hawkins Day for Impatient Sadies. The real day was two months hence, but impatient Sadies could ask men, males, boys to the evening dance. The only permissible excuse for refusing an invitation was being married to someone else.

Just before his Thursday morning Chemistry class began, Eddie was reading through the notes he'd taken during the last lecture, when a pink, greeting-card sized envelope plopped onto the page he was reading. He looked up at a brownette standing next to his desk. A bright cheerful face smiled down on him. At first, it felt like she'd dumped a big bucket of sunshine all over him. Then there was a hint of "Gotcha!" around the eyes. Then she turned and flounced to a desk three rows in front of him and one row to the left.

He didn't recognize her. Of course, the only ones in the class he did notice were fellow NESEP-ers.

He tore open the envelope. Inside, he found not an invitation to the Sadie Hawkins Dance for impatient Sadies, but a summons to the dance. Printed words instructed: Pick up your "Sadie" at, address handwritten in, "six p.m. Friday evening." A West Lafayette address was included, along with, "My name, in case you don't know, Eddie, is Angelina Hawkins. For real." She ended with: **6 p.m. SHARP.**

TBGH

Friday at 17:58, Eddie parked in the driveway and turned off the Valiant, muttered *Poop!,* left the car, and walked to the front door. With his finger poised over the bell button, the door jerked open.

Angelina wore a radiant smile and a dress with no neckline, rather, it had a chest line.

"Don't you look nice!" jerked his eyes upward.

He'd worn his sport coat and tie. So, yeah. Nice, well, nice as he could get.

She put her hand on his shoulder and nudged him aside so she could step out. And close the door behind her. And walk to the passenger side of the Valiant. And wait there.

It was like Eddie had to wake up. He hurried to open the door for her. She sat and looked up at him with—the guys on the ship used the term, but he'd had no idea of what they might look like—come hither eyes.

Eddie Walsh, what the crap are you doing here?

Date other people. Hit-the-road prelude. He closed the door on Miss Hawkins, and stood there a moment, thinking back to junior year in high school, before the Sister MM's F grade, before Cupid's gizzard arrow. What he'd have given for a *come hither* look back then. But that was a big **then** ago.

He took a step toward the rear of the car. *Keep going, Eddie. Walk home. Let her have the car. The Squeeze is going to leave you. The Valiant doesn't mean a stinking thing right now.* He walked behind the trunk, but instead of continuing down the sidewalk, he turned and got into the driver's seat. She slid over and tucked her arm under his and squeezed his to her.

CHAPTER TWENTY ONE

Finally, at 23:15, the longest date in the history of the universe was coming to a close. The Valiant was carting Impatient Sadie Angelina back to her house.

Eddie was thinking about what he would say to her. She'd bought him dinner. So, *thanks for dinner*. He was **not** going to say he had a good time. So, just *Good night, Angelina*. And oh yeah, the other three words. And he'd leave her on the front porch and drive away.

She was already sitting close to him. Then, she pressed herself tighter to his side.

Judas priest! Thank God, the trip was almost over.

The Valiant turned onto her street and, six houses later, pulled into her drive. He put it in Park and did not turn off the ignition. No, sirree. Say his three, no, six, words, walk her to the door, and get the heck out of there. And end the longest date in the history of the universe.

He turned toward her, and said, "Thanks … *mmmmph*.

She'd laid a vacuum-cleaner lip lock on him.

GAAKKKK! Eddie's mind puked! A tongue was in his mouth, wiggling around!!!!!

He shoved her back. Their mouths came apart with a little *Pop!* "I … I … I… have to go." And he was out his side, around the front of the car and pulled open the shotgun seat door. She bolted out of the seat, pushed past him, and snarled, "Queer!" and she was up the sidewalk and into the house.

The longest date in history had the ugliest possible ending!

He stood there a moment, as *Glad it's over* and *Sorry it ended so bad*, wrestled inside his bean box. Then, *what if she comes back out?*

Slam the door. Around to his side and in and punch "R" and back out and hit "D" and breathe. As the Valiant took Eddie across the Wabash River bridge, Pop's voice growled: *Ever boy got to have a worst date. Good thing is, he only got to have one a those.*

Pop with a sense of humor, or Pop giving him wisdom about girls! Which of those two thoughts was weirdest? No answer. Apparently, a boy could have two weirdest thoughts about his father at the same time.

The Valiant parked in the open slot on the concrete slab between the garage and his current residence, and he sat holding the wheel, trying to slow the world down. It seemed like it had gotten to spinning so fast it was about to fling him into space.

He thought about seat belts. The Valiant didn't have them—yet, preview of a coming attraction, he will get them soon—and he was sure glad he didn't have to unbuckle a belt to escape from Tongue-kisser.

Anyway, the longest, the ugliest-ended date in the history yada, yada, was over. Or so he thought. Inside, in bed, sleep took a while but finally came.

Then, up at 04:00 to make 05:00 to 07:00 in the dorm dining hall. He half expected the guys on his shift to ask him if he was queer. They didn't, but there was a lingering sense of unease over having the term flung at him. That morning, pots and pans needed scrubbing, so, he flung himself at that task.

07:45. He entered the kitchen area from the outside-the-house steps. Only Roommate One was at the table sipping coffee and reading the funnies. He looked up. "Cha Cha says to call her as soon as you get back. You're back. So, call her."

Charlsie Chambers, Cha Cha, wife of Petty Officer First Class Hank Chambers, who'd just been selected for chief petty officer. Once a month, the Chambers hosted a gathering of NESEP-ers at their house on a Saturday evening. Eddie had been to a couple of their gatherings.

Once, during freshman year, when The Squeeze had come to West Lafayette for a Purdue football game. Cha Cha and The Squeeze had hit it off. They wrote monthly letters to each other.

He dialed. It rang. She answered.

"Good morning, Cha Cha. It's Eddie Walsh."

"Come over for breakfast. Come over now."

"I ate in the dorm dining hall."

"Then come over and fix me breakfast. It takes fifteen minutes to get to our house. Don't let it take sixteen."

He figured it was fifteen minutes and fifty-five seconds when she answered his knock and let him in and led him to the kitchen. "An omelet, please. Cheddar Cheese. Cherry tomatoes, halved. Sliced mushrooms. And bacon. You want a coffee?"

Cha Cha had everything laid out on the counter between the sink and the stove. "Black, please."

He set bacon to frying in a skillet. She brought him a steaming mug. He felt the sides. It would have to cool a couple of degrees Celsius.

Using a cutting board, he halved and sliced the veggies she'd ordered and dumped them in another skillet to brown up a bit. When he laid the knife down, Cha Cha started talking. Pretty soon, he just stood and stared with his mouth hanging open. She moved him away from the stove and took over the cooking.

When the eggs were done, she hollered, "Hank!"

Selected but not yet promoted Chief Petty Officer Chambers entered the kitchen, said, "Mornin,'"and sat at the table.

Cha Cha brought plates for Hank and herself. They began eating without saying a prayer. Eddie said a silent one for them.

Hank swallowed, dabbed his lips with a paper napkin, took a sip of pale white coffee, and set the mug down. "Eddie, no matter how old a man gets, he will never know enough about how women think without needing help now and then. When I was in the same position you are, a friend of Cha Cha's explained the facts of life to me."

Then Cha Cha explained them to Eddie.

The Squeeze did not want to date other guys. She did not want him to date other girls, but, the two of them had been going steady for four years. It was high dad-burned time the two of them became engaged.

For a moment, Eddie thought he might fall off the chair, and he thought: *Well, why couldn't she just say that?* His mouth stayed shut. And the notion that it sort of, kind of, almost, halfway, just about made sense elbowed its way into his bean box.

"I have to leave," Eddie said. "I have a phone call to make. But I'll wash the dishes first."

"Call her now," Cha Cha said. "Use our phone."

"Use the one in our bedroom," Hank said.

"No. I ... I have to make two phone calls. I'll make them from the apartment.

"Eddie," Hank said. "Make your two phone calls now. Use the phone in our bedroom."

Hank sounded like a chief. Eddie almost said, "Aye, Chief." Almost. He went to make his calls.

The first was to the jewelry store in St. Charles. He asked the owner if his ring could be finished by next Friday afternoon. It could. Eddie asked what the final bill would be. He was pretty sure he could cover the cost with the money he'd earned working in the dining hall. "I'll pay the full amount Friday when I pick up the ring, okay?" It was okay.

Next, he called The Squeeze. Her roommate answered the phone, and then passed it over.

"Eddie," she said.

"Um, a ... do you have a date next Saturday?"

"No. No, I don't."

"Will you go out with me?"

It sounded to Eddie like she really would love to go out with him. And the day after Sadie Hawkin's Day for Impatient Sadies, the bits and pieces of Eddie's blown-apart world started falling into a reassembled coherent entity, where up and down, and right and wrong, and love all fit together. Harmoniously. Until Monday afternoon, just before Chemistry class kicked off.

As Eddie stood by his desk digging his book and notebook from his bag, a rough hand grabbed his shoulder and spun him around. A scowling, snarling big guy, a foot taller and a hundred pounds heavier loomed over him. Eddie didn't know him but knew he was called *Beef*.

"Queer!" Beef said and jabbed a hard index finger into Eddie's chest.

Eddie grabbed the finger and jerked it up.

Snap! It seemed like a little snap, but it sure sounded loud in the auditorium.

"Ow (Cuss Word)! Ow (Cuss Word)! Ow (Cuss Word)!" Beef knelt on a knee in front of Eddie, cradling his right hand in his left. The index finger was definitely broken.

Beef whimpered.

Eddie said, "Beef. Is this an instance of 'It takes one to know one?'"

That's when the professor walked in and wanted to know what was going on.

Two of Beef's buddies took him to the hospital in Lafayette, and when the class began twenty minutes late, Angelina Hawkin's desk was empty.

Eddie's mind did not pay attention in class. Rather, it roamed back to the second summer he worked for Heiny Horstwessel. Heiny had a younger brother who'd just left the Marine Corps after serving twenty years. He'd live on the farm until he found a job and a place of his own. The morning after Marine Brother showed up, Eddie showed up for work, not riding his new ten-speed but riding in the passenger seat of Pop's car.

Heiny and his brother left the breakfast table to see who was coming up the driveway. Eddie climbed out of the car. Marine Brother noted the fat lip and the black eye. "What happened to you?"

Eddie related details of his bike ride home the evening before. He was stopped at the top of Church Hill and beaten up by a big kid and another one his own size. His-size Kid just watched, laughed, and urged Big Kid to "Hit 'im agin!" In addition to getting his face redecorated, Eddie's new ten-speed had gotten the spokes kicked out of the front wheel and the rim of the rear bent. Eddie had to carry the bike a mile to home.

Emanthaller's Garage repaired Eddie's bike in a day. Eddie's shiner lasted a week. Through that week at work on the farm, Marine Brother spent a couple of hours each day teaching Eddie not how to defend himself but how to take the fight to the other guy. So, the following week, Eddie pedals home after work. And there, at the top of Church Hill again, he finds Big Kid and His-Size Kid blocking the road. They are standing in the middle of the road, arms akimbo, and His-Size Kid looking like a six-year-old mimicking a teenaged sibling.

Eddie braked, placed his ten-speed in the ditch, and waited. The two marched toward him. He waited until Big Kid reached for him. Eddie grabbed Big Kid's index finger and snapped it. He stepped around howling, cradling one hand in the other Big Kid, and caught His-Size kid on the jaw with a left jab.

His-Size kid fell onto his back in the ditch and started crying. Big Kid was pacing in the middle of the road with his cradled hand bobbing up and down going, "Ow, ow, ow. (Cuss word, cuss word, cuss word)." Eddie grabbed him by the arm, steered him to the ditch, and sat him down with his butt on the far side rim. "Wouldn't want you to get run over," Eddie said, and pulled his bike from the ditch and pushed it past his would-be assailants, watching them. When he passed by the two wounded, he looked over at the church steeple poking above the grade school building and the trees.

Thank You, God, for Heiny's brother, and I'll bring this to confession come Saturday. Then he rode home and had supper.

Sitting at his desk in the Chemistry class, Eddie decided he would not wait until Saturday to confess breaking Beef's finger. After confessing that afternoon to the priest in the rectory, Eddie went into the church to pray for Beef and for Angelina. He considered lighting candles for both of them, but candles cost a buck, and he couldn't afford to squander a penny if he was going to buy the engagement ring. And he was going to do that.

TBGH

Saturday night, after their date, Eddie parked the Valiant short of the elm tree, and he proposed, and she accepted and said, "Come in with me."

Inside, she left Eddie standing in the middle of the living room while she knocked softly on her parent's bedroom door and entered. A few seconds later, The Squeeze's mother rushed out and to Eddie and wrapped him in a big enthusiastic hug. Then she stepped back and smiled warmly at her prospective son-in-law. "I'm happy for all of us," she said, and, on the way back to the bedroom, she paused. Eddie thought she almost looked over her shoulder. He wondered if she was hoping that, somehow, he had turned into a doctor but then realized if she did turn and look, she'd have been disappointed.

The lock on the bedroom door clicked. The Squeeze came to him, held up her hand to look at her ring with the emerald cut diamond, and then she kissed him.

Driving home, Eddie recalled the kiss and the line from the hymn, "Oh, what transport of delight!" The words from a song of praise to God. He had used those words before to describe his feelings for the most beautiful woman on earth, and he was sure God did not mind his using them to cement in his bean box the breadth and depth and glory of his One and Only.

And thank You, God, we don't have to date other people anymore!

And then a new thought: *Her father hadn't come out of the bedroom.*

And another: *Oh, poop. I didn't ask for his daughter's hand in marriage!*

A picture formed in his bean box of The Squeeze's mother and father coming out of the bedroom together, both with a robe over gown and pajamas, and both wearing an elastic banded sleep bonnet, when he caught a real-world image. A roadside warning sign of a curve ahead.

Oh, poop! Dead Man's Curve. And I'm going sixty-five.

And, of course, there was Pop: *A boy oughta not wear his brakes out so fast.*

TBGH

The Squeeze and her mother wanted a wedding date. The engagement would not last four years like going steady had—except for the brief dating-other-people interlude.

The new plan: After the first of the new year, Eddie was eligible to take the exam for Petty Officer Second Class. The PO2 pay bump was significant. And enough, once you factored in the housing allowance that would cover the cost of living in Purdue Married Student Housing. Plus, The Squeeze would graduate from nurse's training at the beginning of the year, 1963. She already had the promise of a job in the hospital in St. Charles. She'd be making money, too. So, wedding date in August after summer school was finished.

The Squeeze countered, "What about before summer school starts?"

"Uh … June?"

"A June wedding!!!"

Her words punctuated by those exclamation points, expressed so clearly that she was being transported by delight. And Eddie didn't realize it just then, but it would be the last time he was asked for an input on how the wedding plans would evolve.

That did not matter. What mattered was he loved The Squeeze, and she loved him. Back in the summer of 1958, that was such a … sufficient feeling, like if there was more to being in love with her, it wouldn't fit in his heart anyway. Then she put his high school ring on her finger, and holey moley! Just like that, his love for her got bigger. And he was pretty sure her love for him grew, too. And he was pretty sure he wasn't imagining it or engaging in wishful thinking. And he was pretty sure that state of bliss could go on and on and on. Which ended when his casual drift through the glowy fog of going-steady bliss smashed him face first into a granite, date-other-people wall.

Now, though, they were engaged, and this brought with it a love magnifier that radiated enough heat to warm a Lascaux cave in the dead of winter even though you were out of firewood. His love for his One and Only filled his soul from earth to heaven.

The hieroglyphs in the Lascaux cave in France. Eddie's sociology professor had talked about those paintings and how they dated to almost twenty thousand years ago. This indicated, according to the prof, how long humans have been clawing their way out of the animal kingdom and into one of their own manufacture: the human condition. Where the law of fang and claw and eat or be eaten no longer ruled. At least not all the time.

The Bible creation story was so different from the professor's history-and-science-based version. Eddie had questioned his faith briefly during his freshman year. But that was behind him. And it would stay there.

The Squeeze would never have stayed with an atheistic Eddie Walsh.

CHAPTER TWENTY TWO

Eddie had Thanksgiving dinner with The Squeeze, her parents, and her grandparents. He knew enough to place his napkin on his lap, but he also had his handkerchief there. He used that to mop sweat from his brow. The six adults, well, more adult than he and The Squeeze, made him feel like a bug they were studying under a microscope.

Hick kid from the sticks, Eddie Walsh, would fit in with The Squeeze's city-slicker family just like he did with Chief ET's gang of technicians. After dinner, when he offered to wash the dishes, the grandpas sat back like they'd been slapped.

When he'd had The Squeeze to dinner at his house, after they'd started going steady, she'd helped Mom with the dishes. Washing dishes was something Eddie knew a lot about. So, what was so strange about him putting that knowledge to use?

The Squeeze and the grandmothers started clearing the table. Her mother brought out coffee cups for the men. Teresa poured. She came to Eddie last. "None for me." Eddie was already perspiring, and even the thought of the hot liquid opened his pores another notch.

Her mother placed a whiskey bottle and four shot glasses in front of her husband. He poured and passed jiggers to the grandfathers. When he reached for the third, Eddie said, "None for me, Sir. Thank you."

Junior year of high school, Eddie worked in the grocery store in town. On Christmas Eve, the store would close early, but that afternoon,

WHAT AM I?

the owner brought a whiskey bottle back into the storeroom with its stacks of canned and bottled goods. He offered the stock boys a shot of whiskey. Eddie thought it tasted like drinking gasoline. He'd once had a beer and thought the stuff tasted awful, not like Coke or 7-UP. The whiskey was worse. The owner then poured the stockboys glasses of eggnog "with a little snort," he said. A bit later, Eddie wound up bagging groceries at a checkout stand and placed a gallon of milk on top of a bunch of bananas. The lady screeched for the owner. The owner sent Eddie home.

Eddie remembered how stupid the whiskey made him. From the front of the store, he crossed Main Street to get to the side-walked side of, well, the main thoroughfare through town, without getting run over. He did get honked at. On the walk, he stood there for a moment, trying to decide if he needed to go left or right. Left was the way to the house he'd lived in through sixth grade. *Oh, yeah. I'm in high school. The new house. To the right.*

Back in the Squeeze's family's dining room, Eddie knew what was coming. The women were in the kitchen, with the door shut on their chitter chatter. It felt exactly like being in the ET Shop on the ship with ETC blabbering away with the rest of the gang and ignoring Eddie. The three men talked about the last baseball season and the Cardinals, and they didn't even look at Eddie or invite him into their jibber jabber.

The three men sipped whiskey, returned half-full shot glasses to the table, and raised coffee cups to their lips like some synchronized whiskey-sipping-coffee-drinking team at the Olympics. Eddie sucked in a lungful and let it out as three cups settled onto three saucers with a single *clink*. Then it was like three ET Chiefs synchronized stares swung to Eddie, and the nails in their eyeballs entered his, passed through his body, and fastened his glutes to his chair.

"You're in the Navy," Gray-haired Grandpa (He was married to Gray-haired Grandma) said, delivered as an absolute statement of fact.

The inflections in his voice held, *I double-dare you to challenge my assertion.* There most certainly was no inflected interrogative in what he'd said.

"You going to answer my question?"

"Sir, I didn't hear a question mark in what you said. It sounded like a statement. It's true, so what's to answer?"

"You hear question marks … and other punctation?" from White-haired Grandpa (He was married to White-haired Grandma).

"Sir, in our spoken language, inflection and tone of voice convey punctuation." Word for word from his prof in the hated Speech class during his first year at Purdue.

"Weisenheimer! A smart-alecky college kid with an ounce of education, and he thinks it's worth a ton!" from GH Grandpa.

"You're studying Electrical Engineering, right?" said WH Grandpa. "But when you talked about hearing punctuation, that sounded like a combination of English and Speech."

There hadn't been a question mark closing out that string of words, either. It was clear, though, it was Eddie's turn to talk.

"That's correct, Sir. Both the Navy and Purdue think it's important to graduate well-rounded students who are not narrow-minded technical whizzes with no good ability to communicate. Speech and English are required courses. And we get to choose from a set of electives, as well. For instance, I am taking a Sociology class this semester. I have learned a number of things about how we function together in society. And I learned a couple of things about how our minds work. One simple-minded thing involves understanding how you might remember a string of numbers. It turns out, if you break the string down into groups of three digits, it is easier to remember the entire string."

GH Grandpa leaned toward me. "Seven six one, three five four, nine two eleven."

I regurgitated his string of numbers.

"Did he get it right?" WH GP said.

"Aaaahhh—"

"Ach! You forgot the numbers!" WH GP said.

"He got it right," The Squeeze's father said. He was the vice president of one of the banks in town. "Nice trick. Breaking up a long string of numbers into boxes holding three each."

Eddie wondered if the ice was beginning to thaw, if he was beginning to fit in, if they were letting him in. His pores recognized the end of the after-dinner interrogation, and from that point on, the three launched comfortably intoned questions at him. One of them was about KP duty in the military, and he told them about his experience with it.

He'd gotten so comfortable with the conversation in the dining room, he almost blurted out his work in the dining hall of the dorm back at school. That job enabled him to pay the jeweler for the Squeeze's engagement ring. But he had just enough sense to not go there. He could see the three of them giving him a bad cop, bad cop, bad cop, complete financial circumstances audit.

The next day, The Squeeze told him the GPs were playing good cop/bad cop and that they'd drawn straws to see who got to be Baddie. "They also said to me, 'At least I didn't bring a box-of-rocks-for-brains dummy to dinner.'"

Eddie knew that did not mean he fit into the Squeeze's family. The important thing, though, was it did not mean he fit out of it.

Saturday evening, Eddie and The Squeeze took in a movie in St. Charles. While they were in the theater, it started snowing. When they left, it was not quite ankle-deep but still coming down. Eddie offered to carry The Squeeze to the car.

"No, Silly. You'll slip and fall, and we'll both get hurt."

"I wouldn't want you to get hurt. Not bad, anyway. But if we were in the hospital, we'd be in the same room. Separate beds, I mean—"

"The way it would work is you'd be in a room with another man, and I'd be with another woman."

"Oh."

Eddie opened the door for her. She sat on the passenger seat, and he said, "Scoot over and start the engine, please." She did, and he scraped snow off the windshield, the hood, and the windows with his hands, and thanked God he had leather gloves. As he scraped and after thanking Him, Eddie thought about what The Squeeze had said about being in the hospital. He'd be with another **man.** She'd be with another **woman.** Through their engagement, through their promise to marry, they'd departed childhood. She was in the car. He was outside working to make the car safe to drive her home. He was taking care of her, of his woman.

When he finished his snow job, he opened his door, sat behind the wheel, kicked his heels together to dislodge as much white stuff as he could, then swung his legs inside and closed the door. She slid next to him and kissed him.

"Your nose is cold."

"Was there an icicle hanging from it?"

"Just a tiny one." She giggled.

Ratsnot! Outside the car, I was a man. Then I get inside with her, and I become a boy again. Just like that.

He sucked in a breath, huffed it out, checked for traffic behind them, pulled into the street, and carefully and slowly drove his woman—and most definitely not girl—home. There they found her father had scooped the sidewalk to the house.

The cleared walk said to Eddie: *Boy, I'm taking care of her.*

Driving out of the city, his was the only car making tracks in the snow covering the streets with, he figured, not quite six inches. On the highway, a lone trailer truck motored slowly east, about like Eddie did in the other direction. The heavy fall of flakes muted the truck's headlights, as it limited his visibility. Like driving in fog almost. The two vehicles were on the four-lane section of what was becoming Interstate Highway 70. Work had started on the interstate project when Eddie was in seventh grade. A number of obstacles had gotten in the way of completing the building of the four-lane. One Eddie remembered. While the new, wider roadway was being graded about seven miles to the west of where he was presently, the remains of an ancient Native American village was unearthed. That stopped construction for months while the site was explored by archeologists.

Keep yer mind on yer drivin'!

Yeah, Pop, yeah.

But his mind wanted to think about being engaged. Which he now was, at long last. A thing he'd wanted, yearned for, for a long time. It was here now, but the elation he expected to feel was like a balloon that would burst with even a small breath of air breathed into it.

The good cop/bad cop grandpas. He'd thought their message was: *Hick town farm boy, you're just not good enough for our granddaughter.*

He'd gotten that resolved by considering it to be no more than the technicians in his—the chief's—shop on the ship subjecting him to new-guy treatment.

That night, he'd had the thought about taking care of his One and Only Squeeze, only to get her home and find that sidewalk from the drive to the house scooped clean with its message: *You don't know anything about taking care of—*

Oh (cuss word goes here)!

Eddie had come up to Dead Man's Curve, where the four-lane snaked back into two-lane. His speed had crept up to forty. He took his foot off the gas, and the front end started sliding to the left of straight ahead while the car skidded to the right.

Steer into a skid.

He turned the steering wheel to the right, and the car bumped as it slipped off the edge of the road. The warning sign "Sharp curve ahead," the Valiant headed for the sign, clipped it, and came to a stop.

Another cuss word came real close to going here.

Eddie left the motor running, checked the review, saw no lights behind him, stepped out of the car, and got snow in his shoes. It didn't matter. The rear of the Valiant had hit the signpost and snapped it off. The sign lay sunk into the snow. It'd be buried soon.

The Valiant had a dent in the chassis just above the rear wheel. A cuss word came even closer to going here. He noticed the dent didn't reach the tire and managed a "Thank You, God," for that. The thank You didn't hang around long.

The Valiant was more their car than it was Eddie's. And it was ... dinged, damaged, disfigured, despoiled. That automobile was such an important part of his plan for their future. It sure seemed like the devil had to impose relentless reminders that plans were so very easy to blow apart. He stood in the snow, looking at that dad-burned dent until he noticed his feet were getting wet and very cold. He said the St. Michael prayer ... "Cast into hell, satan———he would not give him/it a capital S—and all the evil spirits, who prowl about the world seeking the ruin of **my soul.**

Eddie shivered, said, "Amen," and drove home, his concentration on driving safely fiercely focused.

In the bed he'd shared with Lennie, sleep hovered above the bed but seemed as reluctant as all get out to come down and give him some restorative rest. His dream, his plan to realize that dream, Marriage to the Squeeze, had come awfully close to being smashed on Dead Man's curve. The Valiant was a critical part of the plan. They were engaged, sure, but their letters and phone calls had been okay in the past. Now they needed to see each other, to be with each other, at least once a month. And the Valiant had almost been smashed, and with it, the whole blinking dream.

Then he remembered his mind had been engaged in mulling over their engagement, over the good cop grandpa and the bad cop one, about fitting into The Squeeze's family. He should have been totally focused on driving. Like he had been after he smacked the sign.

He thought about how The Squeeze would have handled the situation. She'd have said, "Almighty Father, I almost crashed the car. Thank You for the **almost**."

TBGH

The smell of Sunday morning bacon woke Eddie. He opened his eyes and squinted. Bright sunlight streamed through the partially open blinds. 06:30 by the clock on the wall. Mom, Pop, his two younger brothers, and sister would all attend 08:00 Mass. He would go with them … He'd told The Squeeze he would pick her up at 09:30 for 10:00 Mass in her church, where they would be married.

"But, I'll call you in the morning after I check on road conditions and the weather," he'd also told her.

"Don't call too early," she'd replied. "After eight'll be okay."

Eddie yawned prodigiously, got out of bed, got dressed, and descended the stairs. The bathroom door at the end of the hallway was closed. When Pop completed the in-house bathroom, he kept the outhouse in order.

Outhouse it is. It's what I deserve for sleeping in.

During Walsh family breakfasts, nobody had much to say—until the arrival of Eddie's sister.

She said, "Good morning, Eddie." Bright, cheerful words.

"Whadjuh do to your car?" Not bright. Not cheerful.

"I, uh, I, uh—"

Pop glared a *you're keeping me from my breakfast* stare at him.

"I got into a skid going around Dead Man's Curve and clipped a road sign."

"You hurt the sign?"

"Yeah, Pop. I snapped the sign post off."

"Call 'em."

"Who?"

"The Highway Patrol."

Eddie nodded and left the house, as much to escape Pop's bad cop performance as for the other reason.

Alongside the drive, Pop had laid down a stretch of sidewalk leading to the garage. That strip of concrete, as well as the steps leading up to the side door of the house, had been scooped clean. Pop had done the scooping. Of that Eddie was sure. He'd done it before anyone else had awakened.

Eddie squinted at the light from the big egg-yolk sun reflected off the snow covering the empty lot next to the Walsh's yard. To his left, Main Street, which was also part of the state highway system had been plowed and salted and it was clear of snow. The temperature was mild, surprising him. Mild temperatures with snow on the ground? It made as much sense as imagining Pop pulling a good cop routine.

In the outhouse, he recalled: "Call em."

Dear, Lord. He wondered, for just a moment, about the inappropriateness of his choice of prayer site then, continued. *What'll happen when I call the Highway Patrol? Will they fine me? Take away my driver's license? Please, God.*

He rendered those last two words in his thoughts with very modest punctuation.

When he made the call, the lady on the phone wanted to know if anyone had been hurt.

"No, Ma'am."

"Good. And thanks. We had a number of signs knocked over last night. Yours was the only call we received. Glad no one was hurt."

Thank, You, and, uh, next time, I'll wait till I get to church to pray.

He heard Sister Daniel's voice say*: Never wait to pray.*

Later, kneeling beside The Squeeze in St. Peter Church, where they would be married—*Please, Lord*—in June, the world seemed to steady, for Eddie instead of wobbling like crazy. Attending Mass with his intended set the world aright.

The warm temperatures melted the snow and cleared the roads. He'd planned to leave for Purdue after lunch. Now, he would not have to go early. Clear roads and overnight temps above freezing meant departure at the normal time: 220:0. After watching "Bonanza" on TV with The Squeeze beside him.

It was 22:45 when he picked up the last of the three Purdue students who'd ridden home with him for the Thanksgiving break. As Eddie aimed the Valiant east, all his passengers snuggled into a corner. One said, "Good night, Eddie."

As the Valiant crossed the Mississippi, Eddie's eyelids grew heavy. He hoped one of the dozing riders would snore. None did. He cracked open the driver-side window.

"Hey!" From Right Rear Corner. "Close the window."

"I need it open."

Mumbled complaints issued from three corners. Then they pulled their jackets up over their shoulders. Shortly, silence ensued.

When Eddie turned northeast to head for Springfield, Illinois, his eyelids again wanted desperately to slam shut. He opened the window farther.

Complaints and one cuss word fired from the corners.

"Pull the damned car over," Right Rear Corner snapped. "I'll drive."

By the time RRC got the car back onto the highway, Eddie was asleep in the right rear corner. The riders took turns driving. Eddie slept through the stops for that purpose, but when they stopped in West Lafayette to buy gas, he woke. Normally, his riders bought the gas for the trip home and the ride back again. This time, Eddie bought the gas.

Made your riders drive. Didn't live up to your end of the bargain, Pop in his head said.

CHAPTER TWENTY THREE

I enjoyed freshman year of college and pretty much loathed, despised, and hated first semester of sophomore year. The course load was heavy and degree of difficulty in math and electrical engineering classes had ratcheted up a notch. Plus, working in the dining hall at the dorm on campus ate into available hours for things like sleep. His frequent phone calls to plan aspects of the wedding ate more time. Rather, the calls were to hear how The Squeeze's mother was planning their wedding. Our phone calls had become sort of like the difference between being overjoyed and joyed. But we were talking about our wedding!

Another entry on the good side of the ledger, I was putting a little into Lennie's bank account to repay him for the loan.

All of it pushed me a lot harder than Heiny Horstwessel, or even Chief ET, had pushed me.

Christmas break appeared. I thanked Baby Jesus for being born every year, but especially that year. I needed a break. My usual riders were with me. One guy rode the shotgun seat. We always picked up the girl, the young lady, last. As we pulled away from her sorority house, I yawned, even though I'd gotten two extra hours of sleep the night before.

"You're not going to drive with the window open again, are you?" Shotgun seat wanted to know. It was a bright, clear day but twenty-five degrees out.

"No. I think I got too much sleep last night."

"I'll drive if you want me to."

Both the back seaters also offered to take the wheel.

"Just don't open the (CWGH) window!" Guy Behind Me said.

"I'm driving."

I drove. Assiduously. Since I clipped the signpost, I paid attention to driving like my life depended on it. Even more assiduously than that. I drove as if the Squeeze's life depended on me driving safely.

We departed West Lafayette around 08:30 on a Friday. A lot of chatter went on between my three gas buyers (they bought the gas as the price for a ride home) for the first hour or so. Then they ran out of words. It got quiet inside. It got a little easier to concentrate on driving, but not too much easier. Driving assiduously was important as all get out.

We hit the town of Rantoul, Illinois, and I slowed to the through-town speed limit of thirty.

When the Valiant slowed, Shotgun Seat sat up. "Where are we?"

"Rantoul."

"Poop! Not even halfway! I was hoping I'd slept all the way to St. Louis."

"Go back to sleep, then."

"Sleep doesn't happen when you want it to … **especially** when you want it to. Stop the car. I want to get a book out of my bag in the trunk."

"I'll stop on the other side of town."

Shotgun Seat emitted mumbles with the only distinguishable word, "Eddie." The mumble and usage did not sound complimentary.

The road we followed was a four-lane. A car in front of me was going twenty-five. I checked the rear view and passed Mr. Slow Pokey Pants. I considered getting back into the right lane, but we were coming up to an intersection, so I kept my attention focused forward. The stoplight was green. Ahead, coming from the other direction, a cement mixer truck occupied its left lane. I wondered if it intended to make a left turn.

However, Cement Mixer Truck did not have its turn signal blinking. Just before I entered the intersection, I thought: *He's going too fast to turn.* So, I proceeded.

The nose of Valiant entered the intersection, and suddenly, the windshield was filled with the image of the biggest cement mixer truck in the universe. I jammed on the brakes. But a half second later, the left corner of the truck's bumper clipped the Valiant. The Valiant stopped dead in its tracks. I flew forward and hit my head on the top of the windshield; then, I flopped back onto my seat. My right hand felt my forehead and came back with bloody fingers. Shotgun Seat looked okay. He still had his hands on the dashboard as if he was afraid to let go of it. To his right, I saw Cement Mixer Truck parked on the side of the street he'd turned into. The girl in the right rear seat held her hands over her face. Guy Behind Me cussed, but he looked like he was okay. The hood of the Valiant had sprung open.

I got out of the car and walked behind it. The Valiant had laid two-feet-long rear tire skid marks on the street. Suddenly, I felt dizzy and put my hand on the trunk of the car to keep from keeling over.

A police car, lights flashing, stopped behind the Valiant. An officer bolted out of his vehicle, grabbed me by the arm, and told me to sit on the driver's seat of my car. I did, and he leaned over and asked if anyone else was hurt.

"Girl's got a broken nose," Guy Behind Me said.

Police Man looked across the seat at her. I turned and looked, too.

She had her hands over her face. Her shoulders shook as if she were crying, but she made no crying sounds.

A siren approached from the opposite direction, turned in front of the Valiant just like Ginormous Cement Mixer truck had done, only it didn't hit my ... **our** car. The siren stopped, and it was like the blaring left planet earth and took all other sound with it. Quiet ruled the earth—at least it ruled that intersection in Rantoul, Illinois. For a tick and a tock.

The sound of cars passing in the opposite direction returned, and a crow cawed as medics boiled out of the front doors of the ambulance and hustled to the right side of the Valiant. They asked Shotgun Rider if he was okay.

"Yeah. I saw the truck cut in front of us, and I just had time to get my hands on the dash to brace myself. Girl in back's got a busted nose."

"Can you stand?"

Shotgun Rider said he could, and with a medic on each arm, he did.

Then Ambulance Driver flopped the passenger seat forward, leaned in, and lowered the girl's hands. Blood trickled from the bent proboscis and over the girl's pressed-together lips. Ambulance Driver backed out of the car, hustled to the rear of the ambulance, and returned with what looked like a toolbox. He took a pad of gauze from inside, told the girl to hold that over her face, and helped her out of the back seat. With a medic supporting each arm, they led her to the ambulance. Ambulance Driver climbed in the rear. Other Medic turned Busted Nose's back to the rear bumper, and the two lifted Busted Nose into the ambulance and onto a stretcher.

Other Medic then came to me and handed me a pad of gauze.

Police Man said, "If it's okay with you, I'd like the driver to ride with me. I need to talk to him, and I'll be right behind you on the way to the hospital. I'll bring the other two guys as well."

Once we were loaded up, the ambulance turned on its siren and headed east, the way we'd been headed. Police Man tucked his car close behind the ambulance.

"Tell me what happened." He cut a quick glance at me.

A wave of panic hit me. *Had I run a red light? But, wait. The guy was coming from the opposite direction. He couldn't enter the intersection if the light had been red. But wait. What if he had a green arrow? My light would have been red. Oh, Dear God in heaven. It was my fault!*

From the back seat, Shotgun Rider spoke up. "We were approaching that intersection in the right lane but came up behind this car going about twenty in the thirty zone. Eddie shifted to the left lane to pass her. At the intersection. Our light was green."

Thank You, Father, God, Lord of heaven and highways!

I took over, "I saw the cement mixer truck coming down the opposite side of the street. He was in his left lane. Nobody was in his right lane. I wondered if he intended to make a left turn at our intersection, but he did not have his blinker on. And I thought he was going too fast to turn. If he did turn, I thought that big truck would flip over. Just as we got the nose of our car into the intersection—and the light was still green for us—the truck whips a sudden left turn right in front of us. I jammed on the brakes, but only a split-in-half second before that truck clipped us. He keeps on going like we were no more than a grasshopper splattered on his windshield. We went from thirty miles an hour to a dead stop. Just like that."

It was quiet for a moment, then Police Man said, "Eddie, was it?"

"Yes, sir."

"Anything else? To add or to change?"

"No, sir. I saw that truck in the left lane. He didn't have his turn signal on. One minute the way was clear, and then this mountain of a truck was coming right at us. I had time to get my foot on the brake, and we hit."

Police Man nodded. "When we get to the hospital, I'm going to need written statements from you two in back."

"I was asleep," Guy Formerly Behind Me said.

"Then you write that and sign it."

At the entrance to the ER, Police Man parked next to the ambulance. Two people in scrubs opened the rear doors of the ambulance and pulled out the wheels-folded-under stretcher. The wheels snapped down and into place. The two Scrubs wheeled … I couldn't remember her name, the girl away.

Two additional scrubs waited with a wheelchair. For me. One of them helped me out of the car. It was easier to let him than to argue I didn't need help getting to the wheelchair, which I didn't think I needed either. Oh well.

They wheeled me inside and into a curtain-defined cubicle. They helped me up onto a bed. They wouldn't let me take my shoes off.

One of the Scrubs left, while the other removed the gauze pad from my forehead, cleaned the wounds—two gashes, one above the other—and taped a fresh bandage over my wounds. While he worked, he fired questions about headaches, blurry vision, and dizziness. When he finished bandaging, he finished interrogating as well.

"Yours isn't the only accident we are dealing with right now. Someone will be with you … as soon as possible."

He left through the curtain door.

I lay there, and it was funny. It was sort of like when Gutter Mouth came onto the Mess Deck and told me I'd made third class and was selected for NESEP. It was like he plopped that glorious news in front of my mind, but my mind was afraid to let it in. Was it some kind of newbie trick the ET gang was pulling on me? Was it some kind of cruel trick ET Chief had orchestrated? Only in this case, the news was crystal clear, unequivocal, and there was no way to argue it away.

The Valiant was wrecked. The front dented way in, the hood sprung open, and green car blood puddled under the front bumper. Well, alright, radiator fluid. But the car was wrecked, no question about that. And the car had been the centerpiece, a key part of the plan to marry The Squeeze. Wrecked car = wrecked plan = the path to marrying The Squeeze, wrecked. But I lay there on that hospital bed covered by a white sheet with my shoes on, and I didn't feel a thing. I didn't even feel empty. From the back of my mind, a memory crawled to the front. It concerned the difference between being joyed and overjoyed.

Hmmm. I really did think: *Hmmm. There's a difference between whelmed and overwhelmed, too.*

The Squeeze knew all blessings came from God. When she received one, she was overjoyed, but she gave the "Over" to Him, and was happy to be joyed.

Even a goober and slow learner like me understood I couldn't just give the "Over" from whelmed to Him. I had to ask Him to cast that "Over" into hell and to help me handle being whelmed.

If I'd have had stationery and a pen, a letter would have been forthcoming forthwith. But now, I'd have to wait and tell her. With spoken words.

Peace, quiet, and calm enveloped me. Whelmed I could handle. With His help, of course.

A young woman walked through the curtain at the foot of the bed. She was wearing casual clothes, so I didn't think she was a nurse or hospital admin person. She also had a honking big nose. Like Pop's potato nose. It was akin to an Idaho baking potato, not those small round red ones he grew in the garden.

"Are you hurt bad, Eddie?"

Oh! Sarah. Broken nose Sarah from the back seat. Like Sarah Sissy Sanford from high school.

"I don't think so. I'll need a couple of stitches. How about you? And the nose?"

"It's hideous! And they told me it would take time for the swelling to go down. Then I'll have to see a doctor either at home or at Purdue to get a proper brace fitted. Maybe by the start of junior year, I'll look normal again."

"Sorry, Sarah."

"Wasn't your fault. I talked to the guys. They found out the driver of the truck is being charged with careless and reckless driving. He was talking on the radio to his dispatcher and didn't even see us. Oh, and the guys, they gave statements to the police and are on the way to the bus terminal to catch a ride home."

She started raising a hand to her nose, stopped, and said, "I'm going to place a collect call to my parents. Would you like me to call your parents collect for you?"

I scooched my wallet from my hip pocket, removing the twenty and leaving a ten, a five, and some ones. I handed her the twenty. "Would you please see if you can get a couple of rolls of quarters from the gift shop, maybe, and call your folks and mine. Tell mine I'll call them after I get my stitches."

She nodded and left with the twenty in her hand. The curtain closed without a sound. Which was appropriate because that earlier peace, calm, and quiet still filled the cubic feet of my curtained chamber.

I got my stitches. The hospital decided to keep me overnight because I'd banged my head. They also decided to keep Sarah as well. Her doctor thought the swelling might go down enough to fit a temporary brace to her nose.

Sarah had only used seven dollars-worth of quarters, so I went to a pay phone, in a wheelchair propelled by an orderly. I called The Squeeze at her nursing school dorm room. She was concerned, but when I explained what had happened and my minor injury, she said, "Thank You, Lord." And then she said, "We'll get through this. Together."

Considering the circumstances, we had a darned fine phone call.

I called my insurance company and had just enough quarters remaining to call Mom. After Sarah's call, Mom had arranged for one of my St. Charles cousins to drive her up the next day to get me and bring me home. I asked if Sarah could ride with us, too. No problem, she said.

But Sarah's parents were driving up, too. They were not entrusting her to any relatives of that (CWGH) accident-prone Eddie Walsh.

TBGH

Thirteen stitches darned up the gashes in my forehead like I'd seen Mom darn socks.

> Note: Sailors don't darn socks with holes in them. They (CWGH)-ed them.

The next morning, the hospital discharged Sarah and me at 09:00. The brace taped to her nose made her look like a hockey goalie, sort of. Her parents were there, in the waiting room. They scowled at me, swarmed to either side of her wheelchair, and escorted her through the exit. Mom and Dad both gushed words like a pair of mynah birds who'd just shared a whole bottle of blabber-mouth pills.

My chair pusher said, "I'm supposed to stay with you until I can put you in a car, but we have a lot of auto-accident victims being discharged this morning, so I'm releasing you here. Like on your own recognizance or something."

Before they headed home, my two male riders on the trip home had visited the collision repair facility and retrieved our belongings for us. I had a book in my suitcase. The book helped me wait a lot more than whatever amount of self-recognizance I possessed.

I'd sat facing the door, and every time the door opened to permit someone to enter under the exit sign, I put a finger on my page to mark my spot and looked up to see if it was Mom, and my cousin. When it wasn't, my eyes picked up my bookmark, erstwhile known as booger finger, and picked up the storyline again. After a while, I heard the door open and placed Mr. Bookmark Finger on the page.

"Eddie!" It was Mom who'd screeched.

I stood up.

"Don't stand," she said.

Before I could sit down again, she folded me into a major hug.

Number Three Hug.

My cousin's greeting was considerably more restrained, and then he went to bring the car to the entryway/exit.

I sat in the shotgun seat as my cousin drove us to the collision repair outfit working on the Valiant. There, the job, they said, would take three weeks. I got a card with their phone number, and we headed for home. This time I rode in back. And as soon as Mom stopped asking me questions, I fell asleep and slept the whole way.

The first thing I did after my cousin dropped us off at Pop's and Mom's house was to call Emanthaller's garage. Sometimes they had cars to rent. They did then, and I rented one. My insurance company told me I could rent a car and file a claim with them and be reimbursed. Of course, I'd have to pay for it and getting repaid would take some time. Well, I didn't want to borrow Pop's car. So repaying Lennie would have to wait. For the claim to be filed. For the payment to come.

CHAPTER TWENTY FOUR

I remembered how freaked I'd been when I dinged the rear fender, but this time, after totally wrecking the car by driving into a steel mountain at the relative speed of sixty MPH, I was calm, cool, and collected?

Uh. Don't get me wrong here, God. Please. I am not asking to feel more grief just now.

I remember thinking that **to** God, despite all the contemplation I'd done about overjoyed and joyed, about overwhelmed and whelmed. And having talked myself into letting God help if He wanted to. I wasn't quite smart enough, being a slow learner and all, to see that lesson, trusting completely, unequivocally, in the Lord would be a lifelong quest.

Note: I admit, I'm still working on it.

That evening, when I picked The Squeeze up from her nurse's training dorm, and I saw and heard how concerned she was for me, and saw and heard how much she loved me, well, seeing her that evening, it was like I had just been created from one of her ribs and was joining her in Paradise.

At Mass on Sunday, in her church, sitting, kneeling, standing, and praying beside her, there was such togetherness in our being together, of the what-God-has-joined-together kind. The Squeeze sang. She had a nice voice. Mine was, at best, 66 and 2/3% praying.

The Good Cop and Bad Cop grandpas questioned me about the

wreck. Once they were sure Cement Mixer Truck Driver had been talking on his radio and hadn't even seen me, they let up.

"Your car get totaled?" Good Cop asked.

"It's being repaired in the town where the accident happened. Should be ready in two or three weeks."

"Darned good thing you didn't have one'a them flimsy import, tin-can, pieces of junk," Bad Cop put in.

I didn't know anything about imports. Maybe I should check them out. Then, I had another thought. Maybe I knew everything about them I needed to know.

The Squeeze came to dinner at my house one night. Lennie called from Boot Camp. He'd gone to the Great Lakes Recruit Training Center. It was cold up there in the winter.

"Did you request San Diego?" I asked.

"They told me everybody wants to go there in the winter. Your name starts with a "W.""

It was nice talking to Seaman Recruit Lennie near-the-end-of-the-alphabet Walsh. About Navy stuff.

Christmas leave, like most things gilded with glory, flashed past so fast I couldn't count the days, only the weeks. One. Two.

The ride back to school, despite my proclamation that I'd ridden my last bus, was via Greyhound. Emanthaller only rented locally. Besides, the bus enabled me to get a letter written and to study. Semester final exams were bearing down on us. I was worried about them. I knew my grades were not going to be pretty.

They almost didn't qualify for ugly. One D and the rest Cs.

Chief Chambers invited me to his house for lunch on Saturday after the semester ended. I stood next to him by the grill as he did venison burghers. He'd gotten a deer during the fall hunting season.

Chief had a beer. I had one, too. We sipped. We lowered our bottles. He said, "Eddie, it's time you got your duck in row."

"**Ducks** in a row. Plural. That's the saying."

"The Navy, Petty Officer Walsh, knows full well that telling you to get two quackers in a row would be expecting too much from you. Listen up."

He flipped a burgher and looked at me to see if I was paying attention. I was.

"The job in the dorm dining hall is too much for you. It eats too many of your hours each day. Your grades dropped from A's to C's. And the D, one whisker above an F. You need to quit that extra job."

He flipped a burgher and looked at me to see if I was paying attention. I was.

"After Prep School, you bought a car. Last semester, Cha Cha called you and told you it was time you asked Your Steady to marry you. Then you got the job in the dorm dining room. Eddie, buy a cheaper ring. Whatever you need to do to keep from flunking out of school."

That semester, two NESEP-ers **had** flunked out. The two of them had bought a trailer, and it was reputed to be **the** party-place to go, not only on weekends, but during the week as well. They were headed back to sea duty.

It was always nice to visit the chief and Cha Cha. Even if it was to get my butt kicked.

At the start of second semester, I was notified that the Valiant was repaired and ready to be reclaimed. Another NESEP-er drove me to Rantoul to pick up the car. The repair shop had installed seat belts for me.

Just after the start of sophomore year second semester, I made second class petty officer. That pay raise put me in territory where, as best I could figure expenses, and seeing how other NESEP married couples operated, I was pretty sure The Squeeze and I would be okay financially. Once we got married. There was, however, a tuxedo to rent, and there was to be a rehearsal dinner before the wedding. I wasn't sure if Pop'd make me pay for that. **That** would have been a pain in the wallet. But Pop said he'd pay.

Which was a relief because I had other things to buy. Like pajamas. I presume Mom put me into some kind PJs when I was little. I don't remember, though. Neither Lennie nor I wore PJs in the parts of our lives I remember. My two younger brothers wore PJs to bed. Nobody said so, but I think it was because my sister entered the family and changed the formula for calculating the necessity for PJs.

And I needed new shoes. The Squeeze's mother said my shoes weren't shiny enough to go with a tux.

As the wedding drew closer, I felt like I was in a railroad car shoveling scoopfuls of money out the door as the train sped down the track. But I got new shoes, took care of other expenses, and had a buck or two left over. Phew.

The semester grades came out. Mine were all As.

Then, it was time to get married.

The day that had been so unreachably far into the future had finally arrived. And the Mass, the service at the church, the rain of rice, lunch for the wedding party, and the reception that evening, those things ripped by so fast as if to make up for how slow it had been getting there.

When The Squeeze's mother said we could leave the reception, we left. It was quiet in the Valiant. We went to Good Cop Grandpa's house to change clothes. The quiet in the Valiant was the kind it would take bravery to break.

When the repair shop in Rantoul, Illinois, installed the seat belts, they were only going to put in two sets in front, the driver's and shotgun rider's. I asked them to put in a third in between the other two. So she could, you know, sit next to me.

Leaving the reception, though, she stayed on her side of the car. I'd expected her to sit by me. During the reception, it was like I danced with everyone but my wife. Now, I wanted her close. And it was like the quiet between us solidified, so we could only be a car width apart. Asking, "Is something wrong?" That'd be the wrong thing to say.

"Did someone say something to you at the reception?" The same.

"Did I do something? Or say something? Or fail to do something?" Wrong, wrong, and wrong again.

Sometimes, a person has a thing that can only be worked out by the person him/herself. With God's help. I can't claim to have had enough sense to keep my mouth shut on my own. I think my guardian angel clamped a hand so hard over my face, I'm surprised I didn't wind up looking like an albino prune.

We arrived at Grandpa Good Cop's house, changed clothes, and drove, again without speaking, to a motel I'd reserved on the other side of the Missouri River from St. Charles. I'd told The Squeeze, a couple of days before the wedding, I thought we should have a river between Mr. and Mrs. Eddie Walsh and their old homes. She'd agreed.

At the motel, I checked in, carried the suitcases into the room, and turned to find The Squeeze waiting outside the open door.

Oh!

I carried her over the threshold.

TBGH

The next morning, I woke at my normal time, 05:00. It took me a moment to remember where I was and who was there with me. Then, I remembered, and: *Wake her with a kiss?*

She slept on her side, with her back to me. Grabbing her shoulder and rolling her toward me would awaken her rudely. *Not a good idea.*

Get out of bed, walk around to her side, kneel beside her, and—That would wake her, but, out of a deep sleep, to find a man next to the bed laying a lip-lock on her—*What if she was a mouth breather?*

Boy!—Pop's voice—*Even if you got a two-holer outhouse, you let her use it alone whenever she wants to.*

I thought of all those times at the end of a date when I'd stood on her front porch wanting, with every fiber of my being, to not have to leave her, to spend all night with her, only to drive home filled with want and need and ache for her. And never be able to see beyond those needs.

I felt my chin. Need a shave. Again. I cupped my hand over my mouth and nose and exhaled. *Phew!* My budget for shaving cream and razor blades, toothpaste … and deodorant had just doubled.

I, Eddie W., the slow learner, had figured that out in … three minutes. At 0503, I slipped out of bed and into the bathroom and completed my business. It felt funny, though. In a way, it was a heck of a lot easier figuring out how to share facilities for private purposes with four dozen men than with one woman.

We did work things out that morning. I felt like a clumsy klutz doing so. She seemed to think it was the most natural thing and thanked me for not leaving the bathroom in a total mess.

We dressed and attended ten o'clock Mass at the Cathedral in St. Louis. We walked down the aisle with her hand on my arm, as if we'd been together **this way** forever, but, at the same time, **this way** brand new.

After Mass, we returned to the motel and went directly to the restaurant. Check-out time was 11:00, but I paid for an extra day, so The Squeeze wouldn't be rushed. At the reception the day before, we had received a number of cash gifts. Otherwise, I'd have been a little freaked over spending the extra money.

The day before, neither of us had eaten much. I can't remember if I ate breakfast or not. Lunch after the wedding, we were too busy posing for pictures to grab even a bite, and, at the reception, we both spent the whole evening dancing with friends and strangers alike, but mostly aplenty. At the dinner, I think we both got a bite before congratulators started lining up in front of where we sat.

In the restaurant, we were escorted to a table by a young man who pulled out a chair for her, placed a menu in front of her, and one across the table from her. But I sat where only a corner of the table was between us, not the whole table. This being together in a way that was like, now, nothing is forbidden, when before, almost everything was. It was very close to too-good-to-be-true, and I felt like if I didn't hold onto it as tight as I could, it would get away from me.

Seat The Customer Man left. Mr. Waiter approached and asked what we'd like to drink. I almost, almost blurted, "Coffee. Black." But my guardian angel clamped a hand over my mouth for a second, and I said, "Dear?"

"Orange juice, please."

I ordered black coffee with a please tacked on. If she hadn't been beside me, I'd have acted like I was on the Mess Deck of my destroyer. There, there had been no time for pleases and thank yous. Or maybe we just looked on mess cooks as the most junior form of sailor, fit only for the most menial jobs, and we didn't respect them. The only sailor who ever respected Mess Cook Eddie Walsh was Chief Cook.

Twenty-seven hours into the being married deal, it felt mighty strange. I considered it just like how Pop had taught me to swim. He'd tossed me into Crazy Woman Creek and said, "Swim." The night before, after the reception, we'd changed clothes … in the same room! And it had been okay to do so. Twenty-three hours prior, it would not have been okay to do so. The Squeeze's mother would have put me in front of a firing squad.

But one thing had not changed. The thoughts I'd had about respecting our waiter came from her, being near her. She'd been like a moral compass to me since we started going steady. She had a needle that pointed to good and sinless truth.

"What's going on in that bean-box-brain-container of yours, Mr. Eddie Walsh?"

The way she looked at me with her left eyebrow cocked up into the middle of her forehead—I had tried to teach my left eyebrow how to rise up like hers did without dragging Mr. Rightie along with it, but I never could learn her trick—I knew she thought I'd been thinking about last night. Before we went to sleep.

I intended to huff indignantly. Before I could do that, I blushed furiously, and my upper lip grew a sweat moustache.

Her hand found mine on my lap under the table. She squeezed it and said, "Husband."

My hand squeezed hers back. "Wife. *Earth Angel* Wife."

"Ahem," the waiter said and served us.

We ate, returned to the room, brushed our teeth—her first—changed, loaded the car, and I paid the bill. We were burning through our money at a goodly clip.

A boy don't mind his wallet, he won't need one.

I decided not to give him a *Yeah, yeah, Pop.*

We set out for West Lafayette, Indiana, The Squeeze used the center-of-the-front-seat seat belts. Our honeymoon destination was the southern shore of Lake Michigan. Good Cop Grandpa and White Hair Grandma had honeymooned where we were going for ours. West Lafayette was on the way.

When we arrived at Purdue, I drove to Married Student Housing and parked in the lot facing two cracker-box structures, four apartments

WHAT AM I?

on the bottom, four on top. A sidewalk split the grass between the two boxes, with walkways leading to each apartment.

"I don't want to see this until after our honeymoon," she said.

"Sweetheart. We have to stop here overnight. It would be foolish to go to a motel when this is already paid for."

I was acutely aware of how fast we were blowing through money, still, even a goober like me could see I'd disappointed her. But somebody had to worry about shekels.

I unloaded her suitcase from the trunk, opened her door for her, and offered my hand.

She looked at it for a moment, then sucked in a breath—of resignation?—let it out and took my offered appendage.

I led her down the center sidewalk to the second apartment from the end and opened the door. To the right, a set of stairs led to the apartment above ours. I unlocked the door to our place and swung the door open. We looked into the open door of the bathroom. There stood the toilet, the lid and seat raised, like the commode was smiling and saying welcome to us.

Poop! I mean, Shucks!
*Dear Upstairs Neighbors, please do **NOT** flush! Please!!*

SBT

Dear Beloved Children,

Look at the story thus far and see in it how Eddie Walsh sees it. This narrative is not about Eddie as much as it is about His One and Only Squeeze. She is the story. I state unequivocally that is how your father sees it. For him, sometimes he feels like it is so much about her, he almost isn't in it at all. Your father has tried to explain a feeling that sometimes taking what is a first person narrative and rendering parts of it in third person feels right somehow. And this is one of those times.

Eddie wants to tell you about two incidents reported in the last chapters. One was when your mother had tears in her eyes after we left the wedding reception. The second was in her desire to **not** spend a night in our apartment at Purdue until after the honeymoon.

The first thing, the tears. Eddie observed those and wondered if she regretted marrying him, but he also saw whatever sorrowed her was for her to sort out. He sensed that if he tried to get her to talk about it, he would make it worse.

Some decades after the two incidents, Eddie read a book about prehistoric people residing in North American. A prehistoric graveyard had been discovered in Mexico. The skeletal remains of the interred females were all of lesser stature than the males buried there with them, and many of the bones of the females had suffered fractures. The book surmised that Oog had wanted to play hanky panky with Oona behind the gooseberry bush, and she didn't want to. Bam, Oog smacks Oona over the head with his Louisville slugger and drags her behind the bush.

After Eddie read that book, it resurrected memories of the two incidents listed above, and he saw that in marrying him, His One and Only had given up her name, and given up a thing she wanted with all her heart and soul, and that was to be a nurse. She wanted to, lived to help people, and in marrying, she willingly gave up both her name and that life.

Eddie, on the other hand, gave up nothing. He acquired what he wanted as much as air to breathe.

For Eddie, gratification no longer had to be deferred. Gratification was there, and it was then.

For her, what would have been gratification was not continuing in a deferred state. It was derailed, and large cranes had to come and set her locomotive on a new set of tracks leading in an entirely different direction.

Decades It took Eddie to get it. Once again, Eddie establishes his credentials as a slow learner.

End of SBT

CHAPTER TWENTY FIVE

There was only time for a one-week honeymoon. Summer classes were cranking up. Another reason to hate those summer half-semesters with twice the work to get done in half the time.

Eddie parked the car in the lot in Married Students Housing at 1300 on a Friday.

"Leave the luggage, Eddie," The Squeeze said.

SBT

AOC (All Our Children), I know we just got off one of these, but this is necessary. Sort of. Eddie Walsh, after two days of honeymoon, learned that when his One and Only said something in a certain way, it was very wise for him to do what she said. "Leave the luggage," was one of those.

End of SBT

"Yes, Dear."

I hustled around the car and opened her door for her. We walked hand-in-hand down the sidewalk between the two rectangular box apartment buildings to the door of our … home.

I opened the door. The one to the bathroom was closed. She had closed it before we left the place to start our honeymoon. I stood aside to let her enter first. She stared at me.

Oh!

I scooped her up into my arms and carried her—very, very, very carefully so as not to bang her head on the doorjamb—across the threshold. Once inside, she pushed the door closed behind us, and as I stood there with the living room/kitchen to our left and the bedroom to the right and the closed door to the toilet in front of us, she kissed me. That kiss sealed the deal. As much as our wedding Mass and saying vows in front of God and everybody, and more than the honeymoon, that kiss made us Mr. and Mrs. Eddie Walsh. And not just "till death do us part," but forever and ever amen.

And carrying her across the threshold and her kiss made the place our home. Actually, of course, the place belonged to the university, but sometimes moments of life contain so much power that a word like "actually" can be rendered impotent and can even un-enter the word from my William Faulkner dictionary. Actually!

TBGH

Saturday night, we had get-ready-for-the-dadburned-summer-semester's-about-to-begin dinner at Chief and Cha Cha Chambers' house. The Squeeze spent most of the evening talking to two of the wives. They were nurses at St. Elizabeth Hospital in Lafayette. On Monday, the first day of stinking summer session class for PO2 Walsh, Mrs. Walsh would interview for a job as a surgery nurse.

Billie Billingsley also worked in surgery, and she had arranged for the interview.

I had met Billie, and her husband Bobby, at one of the Chambers' get togethers freshman year. Someone asked Billie if, once she discovered Bobby's last name, did it give her pause before continuing to date him.

"Hell no," Billie replied. "My last name was Zerjav. Look at how far up the alphabet I moved."

The other couple The Squeeze talked to—and so did tag-along Eddie—was Desmond and Alice Morris. Alice, also a nurse at St

Elizabeth, worked in Pediatrics. The Squeeze told her, "I would have preferred a job in Pedes, but Billie said the only opening was where she worked."

"Turns out," Alice said, "a lot of Purdue students are married to nurses. So, getting a job at the hospital is tough."

I said, "But there is a job in surgery?"

Alice nodded, and I had the feeling there was something I really needed to know, but she wasn't going to tell me.

TBGH

Sunday was pleasant. Mass with the Squeeze. I made omelets for us for brunch and wouldn't let Mrs. Walsh help with the dishes. For supper, I grilled hamburgers. That day, again, marriage seemed more sacramental in our Purdue Married Student Housing apartment than it had in church at our nuptial Mass. But I felt strongly that God was there with us, as powerfully in our house as He had been in His house.

Monday sucked. Mostly because the anticipation of an unpleasant task is more unpleasant than the actual unpleasantry. But, at 05:07, as I shaved, upstairs neighbor flushed his toilet. It felt like Monday had dumped on me. Sometimes, figuratively seems just as bad as actually. I sighed and finished my business.

The Squeeze didn't rise until six. I had cereal, juice, and toast ready for her. She was out the door at 07:00 to drive the Valiant to the hospital. I left right behind her and walked to my first class. And just like that, glorious Sunday appeared in the rearview mirror of life as the tiniest dot discernible. And summer school unloaded its daily dump truck loads of demands on us.

We settled into a routine, or maybe the routine was in charge and ordered us to follow it. Monday through Friday mornings were the same. Rise and get ready for work and school. The evenings ran according to whichever one of us arrived home first. I/she made supper.

Saturday mornings, I rose at the usual 0500, made a pot of coffee, and studied at the kitchen table. The Squeeze slept until 0700 and proceeded at a leisurely pace through her preps to meet the day. By mid-morning, she was ready to go shopping for groceries.

The first Saturday of summer school, we were invited to dinner at the Billingsleys'. They also lived in Married Student Housing. Desmond and Alice Morris were there as well as a couple we hadn't met before: Norb and Felicity Baumgartner. Felicity was also a nurse. Norb was pursuing a degree in business. The other three couples played bridge, and they invited us to join them on Saturday evenings for dinner and bridge.

The Squeeze had learned to play bridge in Nursing School. I had never fiddled with card games.

"We'll teach you," Bobby said.

They taught me enough to know how much I didn't know about the game. On Monday I bought a book. My course work made allowances for me to read that book twice. The second Saturday of summer school, I knew some stuff about the game. Also that summer, one of my classes was titled something like *Combinations, Permutations, and Probabilities.* Lessons from that class seemed directly aimed at helping me understand how best to win at Bridge.

The guys at Saturday night Bridge started laughing at me because I became, sort of, kind **of, almost obsessed. I even kept a notebook on the partners I played with including notes on** whether I won or lost with a particular partner.

Another thing about those weekend Bridge games, the players talked. Incessantly. It was as if the players brains were 90% occupied with speaking, while the other ten percent studied their hands, arranged the cards in suits, and decided which one to play without so much as an "um" or "er." I learned a lot about my fellow NESEP-ers, about life at PU, and about the hospital where The Squeeze worked.

As we drove home after one of those Saturday night card games, I related my observation about all the talking that went on, that the main purpose for getting together seemed to be talking, not playing cards.

She said, "Talking together. It's what friends do."

"Huh. It just occurred. I don't think Pop had any friends. He sure didn't talk much to anybody. I wonder if that's why he married Mom.

She could easily take care of 98% of all the talking required of their marriage."

"Is that why you married me, Eddie?"

"Of course not. I married you because—"

I had started putting my arm over her shoulders, when a voice inside my head reminded me that even in Purdue Family Housing I could encounter a cement mixer truck.

"I'll tell you when we get home."

"With words?" she said.

Sometimes, with her so close beside me driving, it was very difficult to keep my mind on cement mixer trucks.

TBGH

Three things happened during that summer session.

One: I stopped hating the pace of the classes. Married to The Squeeze and the routine we settled into, work, study, Bridge on Saturday, and church on Sunday, it just seemed like such a complete life. What more could either of us want?

Two: A baby. The Squeeze wanted to be pregnant. But she wasn't. Shortly after our honeymoon, I came home to find her sitting on the couch in the living-room-dining-room-kitchen and crying her heart out. I asked her what was wrong. She told me she wasn't pregnant. I was a bit gobsmacked. I mean, four kids were part of the dream. But I had not been so impatient for them to enter the scene. I thought it would be good to have some time with just The Squeeze and me adjusting to finally being together after such a very long time going steady. The Squeeze and being together with her forever and ever amen meant the world to me. Meant air to breathe, but apparently, I didn't mean that much to her.

Eddie Walsh had his feelings hurt.

It turned out that two of the three couples we played bridge with also had trouble conceiving. My thinking turned to: *What's wrong with the guys?*, which quickly morphed into: *What's wrong with me?*

Three: The Squeeze brought home her first paycheck from the

hospital, and we had a discussion about money. And she found out how much money I owed Lenny. She got mad. Her father was a banker. Apparently, she thought it was normal for people to owe her family money, but it was worse than abnormal for her to owe money to other people.

Eddie Walsh felt terrible for making her mad … and for disappointing her in that other way, too.

This was one of those "for worse" times on the other side of the marriage ledger, but I never stopped being grateful for the mind-blowing wonder of the "for betters."

We moved on.

I knocked down all A grades in summer school. The Squeeze was proud of me. We also finished paying off Lenny. The Squeeze, I think, liked Eddie the solvent a lot more than Eddie the debtor.

This next part, I **think** I have it sort of close to, halfway, almost right. I started a subscription to a writer's magazine during sophomore year. I had always loved books and was always reading novels and history along with class work. I wondered if I could write stories, so I subscribed.

The Squeeze picked up the latest *Writers* to hit the mailbox and paged through it. She found an ad for a writer's correspondence course. The course would cost her monthly paycheck, but she asked me if I'd like to sign up for program. I think she maybe, possibly, kind of regretted reacting so strongly to the Lenny-debt.

At any rate, I took the correspondence course and carried those materials around with us through all our moves in the Navy, through my time working in aerospace, until 2008, when on January second, I started writing my first novel.

So, this is another instance where the path my life was to follow was determined directly by my One and Only Squeeze.

And thank You God, for the greatest possible blessing a person could experience on earth.

TBGH

Going home after summer school, and during the Christmas and spring breaks was challenging. Both our families tugged at us, suggesting we were spending more than half our time with the other family. We also visited high school friends. Married-with-children friends. That tugged at both of us. I looked at the husbands and wondered if they were, you know, manly, and I wasn't.

Those trips home, in a way, seemed like we had one foot in what used to be and one in whatever will be, like we weren't at all connected to right here, right now. Maybe it was just me. My One and Only wanted and needed those trips home. Her father had never told her she'd "Fed long enough at the family trough." Or the banker talk equivalent.

Back at school, the challenge embodied in my junior-level classes ramped up. That kept my nose to the grindstone—figuratively because my nose never got smaller. For my writer's correspondence course, I wrote a story about a woman who wanted to become pregnant for a long time, and finally did. I never showed that story to The Squeeze. I think she thought writing might be something I'd grow out of, you know, if I ever grew up.

We did attend football and basketball games. Bob Griese was quarterback, and the football Boilermakers did really well. The Squeeze's parents drove to Lafayette and attended a football game.

Junior year and the summer passed with regular Friday and, or, Saturday Bridge games. Three childless couples and one with a boy and a girl. The Squeeze and I never talked about how it made us feel playing cards with those couples, all of whom wanted children but only one produced offspring. The important thing is we became lifelong friends with our bridge mates. And with Chief and Cha Cha, as well, even though they didn't play Bridge.

Just before fall semester of senior year kicked off, I checked out a book of Hemingway short stories. I'd read the stories before, but I didn't want a novel laying around demanding to be read after school started. A short story every other day or so, that I could handle along with the demands of my engineering classes.

The Squeeze had to work one Sunday. We'd attended Saturday evening Mass. That Sunday morning, I studied for a couple of hours after breakfast, then I gave myself a Hemingway break, and read a story. From the reading, I came away with the feeling that manly men drank.

Now it turned out that one of our card players, Norb Baumgartner, knew how to make wine. So, during junior year, we went together and bought a barrel from a root beer stand in Lafayette, cleaned the barrel, and loaded the barrel with smashed grapes and sugar water. Each family wound up with a dozen bottles of wine.

Back to that Sunday with the Squeeze working, I decided to have a glass of wine with lunch. Which I did. It didn't make me feel any manlier. So, I had another glass while I read another short story. In this one, I developed the notion that drinking whiskey was way manlier than that sweet wine we made in a root beer barrel in Norb's closet in Purdue Married Student Housing.

That's what led me to drinking. Not feeling like a man because I could not give your mother what she so obviously longed for, a child.

Funny, but perhaps a couple of decades later, I gave a young man the following advice: Just don't start drinking.

Another funny. Pop left me with a plethora of his pithy sayings, but nary a word about drinking. Something like, *Drinking, biggest waste of money there is, even if somebody else is buying.* But I don't blame him. I'm sure I would not have had sense enough to listen that advice.

Whether wine or whiskey ever made me feel manly, I don't remember. But I can say with a great deal of surety, booze had nothing to do with your mother becoming pregnant.

Junior year passed without the promise of motherhood, or fatherhood. The most noteworthy event during that year was the Kennedy assassination. I have this very clear memory, after hearing about the shooting in one of my classes, and later, walking toward Married Student Housing and crossing this grassy field, and feeling like the world still looked the same but that everything had changed.

During senior year, My One and Only's doctor ran some tests. She had a thyroid deficiency. There was a treatment for it. We were hopeful. I did not feel manly, however, I was afraid. Mom had lost three babies before she had me.

The Squeeze continued to work at the hospital. With two paychecks coming in, we were laying some aside each month having paid off Lenny months ago. We entered May with no baby on the way and graduation looming in June.

On the first or second Friday night in May, a number of us NESEP-ers went to dinner at this smorgasbord restaurant near the university. When we ate at that place, it was always a pig out for the guys, while the ladies talked and had a bite or two of dinner. We had a grand time to boot. Graduation and no more classes, no more books, no more teacher's dirty looks were drawing near. Of the seventy-five NESEP-ers who became college freshmen four years ago, sixty plus of us would finish the program, and I think all of us were anxious to get back to the real world.

After dinner, we drove back to our apartment. The Squeeze sat close to me, and we talked about the evening, how fun it had been, and how we'd miss our friends once we got scattered across the Navy, after we received our commissions, after we completed OCS (Officer Candidate School).

We got back to the apartment, and the most wonderful thing happened. The Squeeze marched smartly to the kitchen sink and puked.

The flu?

I hurried to her and put my arms around her shoulders.

She had upchucked her entire dinner. I knew some stuff about vomit.

She turned on a trickle of tap water, wiped her mouth, turned, hugged me, and said, "I think I'm pregnant!"

CHAPTER TWENTY SIX

She was.
   Pregnant.
"We should kneel down and thank God," I said over her shoulder.
"I want to brush my teeth first."
She did; then, I took her to the bedroom and had her lie down. I knelt beside her, and we thanked Him.

There was one other thing needed doing that night. The kitchen sink had no garbage grinder beneath it. Not to worry. Eddie Walsh knew some stuff about vomit.

The next day after morning morning-sickness, we called her parents and mine. After midday morning sickness, we notified Chief and Cha Cha. Everyone was happy for us, and I had that feeling I had had after the JFK assassination. The world looked the same, but everything had changed.

And during that next week, we got one unpleasant surprise. I was going to have to pay for a full set of officer uniforms. It sure seemed like the Navy went out its way to keep you from feeling like you were comfortable with your financial situation.

Morning sickness gradually receded. I finished the semester with all A grades.

The Squeeze's parents and mine drove to Purdue for my graduation.

Hosting our parents in our little apartment felt strange, backward from how things should be. But The Squeeze handled it smoothly.

Following graduation, the Navy divided our NESEP class in half. The first half of the alphabet departed immediately for OCS. Those of us in the last half, stayed at Purdue for another month. The OINC of the ROTC unit laid a bit of busy work on us. Mostly though, we goofed off, played basketball in the gym, or softball. It was the only thumb twiddling time the Navy ever allowed me—well, there was the time after I made NESEP and PO3 and got off mess cooking.

Then, it was time for us to move to Newport, Rhode Island, and report to OCS. We didn't have a lot of things for the packers to do. A couple of boxes of dishes, another couple of bedding and towels, some clothes, and we had The Squeeze's cedar chest. The Valiant handled the rest of it easily.

At Newport, we were lucky. Chief and Cha Cha had rented the bottom floor of a large old two story, and they had plenty of room for us. They had three bedrooms and only used one for themselves and one for their children. They offered us the other one and a split the rent deal.

After The Squeeze moved in, I checked in to OCS. I would live in barracks and get home on weekends for the next four months.

The Squeeze had just begun to show her baby bump, and she and Cha Cha shopped for maternity clothes. I'm sure Cha Cha was a help, whereas I, I am sure, would have been invited me to stick to things I really know something about—like puke.

Checking in to OCS was sort of like checking into Boot Camp for grownups. Boot Camp was definitely for kids. In our herd, we had chiefs, first, second, and third class petty officers, with a great majority of those NESEP-ers.

The first day started with medical checkups and getting shots for those who needed them. After lunch, we were separated into companies of about sixty guys, assigned to a barracks, and gathering up uniforms and bedding. After evening meal, we got our uniforms and bedding stowed. First thing the next morning, we had our rooms inspected.

The second thing the next morning, they assembled us in formation on a huge parking lot with no cars parked on it. A Navy lieutenant introduced himself as commander of Company Charlie. "Which you are assigned to." The LT (lieutenant) not quite shouted. There wasn't a lot of extraneous noise coming in off the bay or from behind us. A few seagulls squawked as they swooped and soared above the water. An airplane flew over.

"Listen up!" Now, the LT shouted. "I need one of you goobers to volunteer to be the student company commander."

I was in the back row and, being short, comfortably hidden from LT.

A profound silence settled over our formation. The seagulls ceased squawking. The plane had passed. It was so quiet watches were afraid to tick or tock. It really felt like time stood still.

In the stillness, I thought: *Eddie Walsh, to this point, you have been in the Navy for six years. Five of those have been in school. The other year, you scrubbed pots and pans and cleaned up compartments and heads.*

And it got a little funny because when I expected to hear Pop's voice in my heard, I heard the Squeeze's: "Eddie, this is a blessing and an opportunity from God."

After thinking *Crap!* I stuck up my hand and said, "I'll do it, Lieutenant."

In the row ahead of me, somebody snorted. Another snickered. Somebody said, "Dumb ass." A seagull squawked. Another plane flew over.

"Get up here," the LT said.

I got there and saluted and held it until he returned it.

He asked my name and whether I had ever marched a formation before.

"No, sir."

"It's not that hard. Pay attention."

I did, and thirty minutes later, I had Charlie Company doing things like flanking movements, and To The Rear marches. And Charlie Company marched like a precision drill team. Well, almost like one.

And the LT announced to the company that I was the student company commander. "Even if you were a chief petty officer before, when Walsh tells you to do something, You 'aye, sir,' him and do it.'"

That's how it happened, how I volunteered for something nobody else wanted to do.

How did it work out?

I'll tell you three things that happened during my time in OCS, and I think you'll see the answer.

One. One of the duties assigned to the Student Company Commander was to make rounds of **his** barracks in the evenings. He was to look for things like cadets using sheets, pillowcases, or towels to shine shoes or clean M-1s. A lot of cadets did that, and the bill for new linen was out of control at OCS. The order came down the line: "Student Company Commanders, get the linen situation under control in your barracks."

So, one night, maybe a week into my stint, after my round, I returned to the room I shared with another cadet. And found him cleaning his M-1 with a towel. I put him on report and instead of being allowed liberty from noon Saturday to 20:00 Sunday, he was confined to base. My roommate was mad at me and wanted a new roommate. "No," I said. "I want you where I can keep my eye on you." I will confess I worried for a while he might do something to me as I slept. But the lesson for me in this incident was that I was responsible for things being done the right way, and that responsibility trumped friendship and room-mate-hood.

Two. Another thing we did at OCS was to have competitions between the companies. Ball games of various types provided opportunity for determining the best company in the brigade. We also had timed runs of the obstacle course for five-man teams. One Friday, I could only get four for our O course, so I put myself on the list to run twice, first runner and last. That Friday, about halfway through OCS, the chow hall had served clam chowder to die for. I had seconds twice. At 16:00, we assembled at the O course, and at "Go," I hot footed it around and over the obstacles trying to save a bit for the second lap. On the second lap, I went all out and finished in good time, but did not finish in the top three times. After that second lap, I walked to the side of the field and barfed. About a gallon of clam chowder. OCS made a rule against one competitor running the obstacle course more than once during a competition. But, our team had scored a good time. If they'd made a rule against eating clam chowder on O course day, I'd have mutinied.

Three. At the start of the last month, leadership at OCS selected five students to be regimental officers. Student company officers reported to student regimental officers. I was selected to be the student assistant regimental commander. I was told placing my roommate on report, running the O course twice so my team would not have had to forfeit had favorably impressed the selection committee.

None of those things would have happened if I had not volunteered for something nobody else wanted to do. And I learned a heck of a lot from the experience I gained at OCS sticking a toe in the water of a ginormous lake entitled "Leadership."

And I had to volunteer to reap that priceless reward.

And I had to listen to your mother to realize the opportunity the question presented me.

The path this story has taken has surprised and blessed me every day, even if I added only a few words. Even the days I did not write a single word blessed me. Because I spent every spare second of the day thinking about what I would write when my butt made contact on my desk chair in front of my computer.

You know, I am sure, that I am going to type two words and we'll come to a place where this trail ends, So I keep typing words, that for some reason are hard as heck to see, even if I crank up the font.

Sorry. I got a Kleenex. That helped.

Anyway, we are going to get to those two words. Just a couple of additional things I have to throw in to complete this trek down the trail of life with copious side bunny trails.

One. Thanks, Number Five, for asking the questions, and especially for asking the volunteer thing.

Two. I hurried through the first two years of marriage, although I included what I thought was the important stuff. How much your mother wanted to have a baby right away, and that bothered me. She was so much more than **enough** for me, and I couldn't help but wonder if I meant very much at all to her. But, we both wanted to have a baby. I put in the manly business and drinking. During college is when I made that association, manliness and drinking. For the rest of my life, until the winter of 2021, I drank. Most of the time with moderation. But during that first year of COVID, drinking wine became important, then it became too important, and I stopped drinking.

The questions fired at me, by the service you subscribed to, Number Five, wanted to know some things about me. Answering these questions, and the main one, have at times been pure confession. And this journey has convinced me that "Confession is good for the soul," and leads me to say, "Amen."

Three. The volunteer question inspired me to ask myself a question of my own. And that is, "What am I?"

The answer to that one is I am all you, my children. I am you, my wife. I have bits and pieces of spiritual DNA rubbed off on me by thousands upon thousands of people I've encountered on the main trail that is the journey of life. Thinking about it now at 05:11 this morning, it is like the word "me" does have meaning for **me**. I am not me, but all of you.

But then I had another thought. Some of the things I included that were confession, those things came only from me. So there needs to be a me to cart those things around until I present the whole mess of what I am to St. Peter. All of it, the good, the bad, the ugly.

What am i? I am a lot of The Squeeze, some of all of you, and a bit of self-manufacture.

THE END

PS: Poop! Now, I have to go back to the beginning and edit all this. Writing is harder than work, and editing Is harder than writing.

PS2: When KN5 bought the subscription to the Two-Questions-a-Month (TQM) service, I really did not get into answering them. I was busy working on another book. Now, though, I am making a New Year's resolution, in September: I will go back and answer all the questions.

THE END
AND THIS TIME I REALLY MEAN IT

ACRONYMS

1MC	A Navy ship's general announcing system
Chief PNP	Chief Pop-Not-Pop
CIC	Combat Information Center
Div O	Division Officer
E1, E2	E1: First and lowest enlisted rank; E2, Second enlisted rank, etc.
ECM	Electronic Counter Measures
EWTLB	Eddie's Words To Live By
ET	Electronics Technician
ETC	Electronic Technician Chief Petty Officer
EWTLB	Eddie's Words To Live By
FNG	Fairly New Guy
GM	Gutter Mouth
GQ	General Quarters (Battle Stations)
HM1	Hospitalman First Class (an E-6)
HWF	Halfway Worth a Fart
KN5	Kid Number 5
KP	Kitchen Police
LT	Lieutenant
NESEP	Naval Enlisted Scientific Program
NROTC	Navy Reserve Officer Training Corps
OINC	Officer In Charge

OOD	Officer Of the Deck
PBS	Peanut Butter Sandwich
PO	Petty Officer
PO3	Petty Officer Third Class (E-4)
POD	Plan Of the Day
POOW	Petty Officer Of the Watch
PU	Purdue Univsity
ROTC	Reserve Officer Training Corps
SD	Skunk Drunk
Sister MM	Sister Mary Mark
SN	Seaman (E3)
SP	Shore Patrol
SS	Sister Superior
SWAK	Sealed With A Kiss
TBGH	Time Break Goes Here
WDS	Weekend Duty Section

CAST OF CHARACTERS

Eddie Walsh, Pop, Mom, Lennie
The One and Only Squeeze Capital T The
Heiny Horstwessel
Oliver Geld
Mr. C, high school teacher
Maurice Heffledinger
Sister Mary Mark
Guttermuthe, "Gutter Mouth"
Sister Daniel
Jimmie Joe Meinerschlagen
Mildred Hemsath
Sarah Sissy Sanford. Snake
Fatty
Ernie Emanthaller
Chief Hank Chambers, wife Charlsie, Cha Cha
Billie and Bobby Billingsley
Desmond and Alice Morris
Norb and Felicity Baumgartner
Sarah Hawkins

Milton Keynes UK
Ingram Content Group UK Ltd.
UKHW041327301124
451950UK00005B/35